Murder of Convenience

By

Linda Shenton Matchett

Murder of Convenience
By Linda Shenton Matchett

Cover Photo and Design: Wes Matchett

*Dedicated to the ordinary women
who served in extraordinary ways
during WWII*

Chapter One

Geneva Alexander stifled the impulse to roll her eyes as her mother complained about the latest difficulty in obtaining yet another rationed food item. Although the thought of a smear of butter on her roll made her salivate, Geneva poked at the last bite of potato in the congealing gravy on the heirloom Royal Doulton plate before lifting it to her mouth. Too heavy a meal for the humid, June night in Philadelphia.

"Stop fidgeting, Geneva. It's not ladylike." Father huffed a sigh then turned to his wife with a grim smile. "We must do our part, Oceana. Everyone is experiencing shortages. We can be expected to do no less."

Mother pouted. "But I don't have to like it."

He patted her arm. "No, you don't."

Geneva pushed away her empty plate. "Father, Bethlehem-Fairfield launched three more liberty ships today. That makes six this week. The yard has been producing the vessels at an unbelievable rate." Mother wouldn't care about the news, but it might serve to prevent further grumbling. "I wish I could have been there. Lorraine Perkins said it was terribly exciting."

"Tsk! What is wrong with Lorraine's parents, allowing her to loiter in a shipyard? It's not proper." Mother dabbed at her ruby-tinged lips with a linen napkin.

Geneva shook her head. How did her mother manage to eat an entire meal without smudging her lipstick? "She wasn't loitering, Mother. She works in the typing pool and used her lunch break to watch the first ship cast off. Lorraine said the president spoke for a bit and then a woman dressed in a fur cape and rather ornate hat broke a bottle on the bow. I would have loved to have seen the ten-thousand ton ship slide down the rails with a screech. Can you imagine the splash and the noise?"

"Lorraine's parents have plenty of money. People of our station don't mingle with laborers. Why on earth would they allow her to take a job, especially at a shipyard?" Mother shuddered then motioned for Bernice, the housekeeper, to begin clearing the dinner dishes. A young maid assisted with the task. "Rest assured, Geneva; you will never have to seek employment."

"She's doing her part for the war effort." Geneva folded her napkin and laid it on the Irish lace tablecloth. "I'd like to consider doing something as well. There are numerous opportunities. I just have to find the right one."

"Nonsense." Father set down his glass with a thunk and crossed his arms. "There are tasks you can do here such as rolling bandages."

"But the more important work is performed outside the home." Geneva spoke through gritted teeth.

"You can't see, Geneva. Who is going to hire you?" Despite her mother's soft voice, the words sliced through Geneva's heart.

Bernice gasped, then reddened. She ducked her head and continued to collect dinnerware.

Father frowned and raised his hand in a dismissive wave. "You may finish clearing later, Bernice."

The housekeeper and maid scuttled across the Persian rug into the kitchen, the swinging door flapping several times before it settled to a close.

"Are you telling me I have no value to the war effort with my diminished sight? Perhaps no value to anyone? I have extreme tunnel vision, but my eyesight isn't gone yet. The doctor said it could be years before I lose it entirely." Geneva swallowed the lump in her throat. "If you won't let me get a job, perhaps I'll seek volunteer work."

"Don't be disrespectful. You're oversensitive." His voice low, Father leaned toward Geneva. "Your mother did not mean you have no worth. Of course you have value, but you have limitations. And you must learn to live within them. It will be easier for you, if you do."

"I'm not willing to accept a sheltered, handicapped existence. There are plenty of blind people who lead productive lives, such as Helen Keller."

Mother reached across the table and covered Geneva's clenched fists with one hand. "We're simply trying to do what's best for you. Can't you understand? Miss Keller is not our responsibility. You are." She removed her hand, but the cloying scent of her lavender perfume clung to Geneva's skin.

Geneva dropped her fists into her lap, her fingernails digging into her palms. Maybe the physical pain would distract her from her parents' well-intentioned, yet unkind words.

Silence filled the room. It stretched on for several minutes before Father cleared his throat and took a deep draught from his glass of water. Mother's silver spoon clinked against the rim of her delicate teacup as she stirred milk into the presumably tepid liquid.

Her parents would never let her out on her own. She was trapped.

A distant knocked sounded on the front door. Muted voices filtered into the room from the foyer. A moment later, Bernice appeared in the doorway with a small, cream-colored envelope.

"Yes, Bernice?" Mother asked.

"This was just delivered by a messenger. It's for Miss Geneva."

"For me?" Geneva's voice came out as a squeak. "I'm not expecting anything."

Bernice entered the room and hesitated, the envelope held in the air like a truce flag.

Gesturing to the housekeeper, Mother held out her hand. "You may bring it to me."

It would be futile to remind Mother the letter wasn't addressed to her. Geneva clamped her lips closed.

Bernice laid the missive on the table near Mother, then backed out of the room, her footsteps fading toward the back of the house.

Mother slit the envelope with a manicured fingernail and withdrew an embossed card. After reading it, she sighed and passed it to Geneva. "It's an invitation to Evelyn Dangerfield's engagement party. How her parents can allow this wedding is beyond me. The young man has no credentials whatsoever. Still, I suppose we'll have to attend, even though I don't approve of her choice of groom."

"Perhaps he has some redeeming characteristics we're unaware of." Father shrugged. "There must be advantage in it for the Dangerfields for them to approve the match. Nick Dangerfield is no fool."

"Be that as it may, everyone will approve of our selection for Geneva." Mother tapped the empty envelope on the table in a staccato rhythm. "The timing of Evelyn's announcement is unfortunate. I had planned to disclose Geneva's engagement immediately following the Independence Day celebrations. We might need to consider waiting until the end of July."

Geneva bolted upright in the chair. "What? What engagement? To whom?" A chill swept over her body. "What are you talking about? I'm not engaged."

"Your father and I haven't completed the arrangements yet, but we've agreed to Thurgood Mayfield's request for your hand in marriage."

"You've agreed? What about me? I haven't agreed to anything, especially marriage to a man I barely know." Geneva shoved back her chair and stood. "When were you going to tell me about your plan to foist me off on him like an unwanted puppy?"

"It's for the best, sweetie." Mother smiled. "We wanted to surprise you."

"Surprise me? That's an understatement." Geneva folded her arms. She sounded like a parrot repeating her mother's words. Shaking her head, she sucked in a deep breath then exhaled. "I'm sure you mean well, Mother, but you and Father must cancel your arrangements. I will not marry Thurgood. Nothing you say will change my mind. That's final."

"What's final is you'll do what you're told. We won't always be around to take care of you." Father steepled his fingers. "Thurgood has the money and the connections to support you."

"I know little to nothing about this man, let alone love him."

"Love will come over time. Your father and I barely knew each other when our parents arranged our marriage." Mother patted her coiffed hair. "See how well that turned out? We adore each other now."

"An arranged marriage is fine for you, but I will not succumb to your schemes. Say what you will about my limitations and my need to be taken care of, but you're wrong. I don't need a husband, and I'll prove it to you." Geneva blinked back the tears threatening to spill. "I will find a job and somewhere else to live. I'll no longer be a burden to you."

Mother's lower lip trembled. "Oh, dear. You're not a burden."

"You will not seek employment." Father's face darkened. "I forbid it."

Geneva strode toward the doorway, praying she wouldn't stumble over an unseen obstacle. If she tripped, she'd prove her Mother and Father correct. She turned back to her parents. "I'm twenty-three years old, Father. You can't forbid me to do anything. I'll be out of the house by the end of the week."

"I hope you understand what you're doing, young lady. You won't get a penny from us. You'll be sorry when this little lark backfires, and you must return home." Father's voice followed her into the hall and up the stairs as she headed to her bedroom.

She choked back a sob. What had she done?

Chapter Two

Two days later, Geneva's voice filled the sanctuary as she finished her solo of "How Great Thou Art." Her right hand raised toward the ceiling, she smiled as she lifted her praise to God. She never tired of Stuart Hines's translation of the old Swedish hymn. The organ's notes blended with her soprano tones before fading away.

Seconds later, she hurried from the podium to the seat next to her parents. A frown wrinkled Mother's forehead, and she avoided Geneva's gaze. Geneva's shoulders slumped. What had she done to annoy her mother this time? Had she made a mistake while singing? Should she have selected a different piece?

Warmth suffused her face. Lost in the music, she had lifted her arm in worship. Mother would have something to say about that later.

Sighing, Geneva focused on the preacher as he stepped up to the pulpit. Pleasing Mother became more challenging with each passing day, especially since the argument about Thurgood. Perhaps Pastor Reid's sermon would contain a kernel of wisdom she could apply to this situation. She needed to claim her independence and thwart the engagement to Thurgood.

"Thank you, Miss Alexander, for that moving rendition of this morning's special music. You are truly gifted by God."

Geneva fidgeted in the pew. Mother's downcast chin went up, and she preened, obviously pleased by the attention.

"Please open your Bibles to the first chapter of Matthew. It's not December, but I wanted to talk to you about trusting God. The Christmas story is the perfect example." He grinned. "Follow along as I read verses eighteen through twenty-five. It's very exciting."

Geneva loved Pastor Reid's fresh approach to the scriptures. He made them come alive, and his sermons motivated her to dig into the Bible outside of church. As a result, her knowledge of God's Word increased, and her faith flourished.

"Now the birth of Jesus Christ was on this wise: When as his mother Mary was espoused to Joseph, before they came together, she was found with child of the Holy Ghost. Then Joseph her husband, being a just man, and not willing to make her a public example, was minded to put her away privily. But while he thought on these things, behold, the angel of the Lord appeared unto him in a dream, saying, Joseph, thou son of David, fear not to take unto thee Mary thy wife: for that which is conceived in her is of the Holy Ghost."

Looking over the congregation, Pastor Reid's face glowed. "Listen up. This is where it gets really good!"

Geneva stifled a giggle as he read. His joy was contagious.

"And she shall bring forth a son, and thou shalt call his name Jesus: for he shall save his people from their sins. Now all this was done, that it might be fulfilled which was spoken of the Lord by the prophet, saying, Behold, a virgin shall be with child, and shall bring forth a son, and they shall call his name Emmanuel, which being interpreted is, God with us. Then Joseph being raised from sleep did as the angel of the Lord had bidden him, and took unto him his wife: And knew her not till she had brought forth her firstborn son: and he called his name Jesus."

Pastor Reid took a deep breath. "Let's think for a bit about Joseph and Mary. Tradition would have us believe that Joseph was somewhat older than Mary. Probably already established in his trade as a carpenter. The Greek word for carpenter used here means someone who built furniture and household goods, a skilled woodworker. Mary was probably somewhere between thirteen and fifteen years old. A devout Jewish girl as indicated later by her response to the angel's announcement.

"Life is moving along normally for these two young people. They're engaged and planning a wedding. The women in the village are creating menus and making a special bridal outfit. The men are helping Joseph prepare a home for his new bride. Everyone is giddy in anticipation of the upcoming festivities."

Pastor Reid's gaze swept over the crowd. "Then Mary turns up with child *before the wedding.*"

A murmur swept over the congregation.

"I know, folks, we don't discuss pregnancy in polite society. But how do we learn about God's blessings if we don't talk about Mary's condition?" He shrugged. "Joseph was horrified, too. How could his fiancée do such a scandalous thing? How could she betray him like this? But, more than disgraceful, in this culture this was an act punishable by death." He lowered his voice to a whisper. "By law, he could have his beautiful, sweet Mary put to death."

Pastor Reid pointed to his Bible. "Fortunately for us, that's not the end of the story. Joseph apparently loves this girl, so he decides to put Mary away privately, where she can have her child in secret and not have to face the shame of unwed motherhood. Joseph is a good man. He goes to bed that night convinced he's made the right decision about the situation."

Folding his arms, Pastor Reid rubbed his jaw. "Haven't you done that? You face a tough circumstance, so you give it some thought and take the path of least resistance, the one that will seemingly take care of the issue. The only problem is, you forgot to discuss it with God. Oops!"

Chuckles rose from the sanctuary, and he waggled his eyebrows.

"So, God did what he does best. He met Joseph where he was. In bed. He visited him in a dream to remind Joseph everything was under control. That God himself was the one responsible for Mary's baby. It was okay to take her as his wife. The next morning Joseph awakens, remembers his dream, and *trusts the Lord*." Pastor Reid pumped his fist in the air. "Good for Joseph! What about you? Would you have believed the dream was from God? I'm not sure I would have been convinced. I might have thought my mind was playing tricks on me."

Geneva leaned back in the pew. God was telling her to trust him. Was she supposed to accept her parent's wishes and marry Thurgood? She shuddered. Perhaps God would come to her in a dream with a different answer.

"Do you have a situation that plagues you? Do you have an issue you are unsure how to resolve? Take it to God. Then trust him. He will help you. I guarantee it. Often in the most surprising manner!"

*

Geneva stood and stretched. The wooden pews did not lend themselves to comfort. She surveyed the congregation and spied her friends, Lorraine Perkins and Bridget MacLeod, two rows behind her. She waved, and Bridget slid from the pew and threaded her way through the crowd to Geneva.

"Are you okay?" Bridget drew Geneva into a quick hug. "You seem tired."

Lorraine joined them. "What did I miss?"

"Nothing yet, but Geneva's going to tell us why she appears weary this morning."

Geneva glanced over her shoulder. Her parents were several yards away chatting with a group of long-time friends. She turned back to the girls. "Let's go outside. I don't wish to be overheard."

"Sounds serious." Bridget cocked her head. "Should we find the other Musketeers?"

"Good idea. That way I don't have to share this but once."

Lorraine linked arms with Geneva. "Bridgie, I'll go with Geneva if you'll scare up the girls."

Bridget executed an exaggerated salute and slipped away.

Geneva sagged against her friend. "With any luck, the bench under the apple tree is vacant."

The two girls inched their way to the doorway behind the throng of people. Moments later, they stepped across the threshold into the sunshine. A warm breeze brushed Geneva's cheek and ran its fingers through her hair.

Lorraine pointed to the flowering fruit tree. "The girls must have ducked out the back door. They've already commandeered the bench."

"That's a relief. I didn't get much sleep."

Cleo Sorenson rushed toward them. "What's the skinny? Bridgie says you've got big news. It can't be good. You look awful."

Lorraine elbowed Cleo. "What a terrible thing to say. Give her some space. She'll tell us when she's ready."

"Sorry." Cleo hung her head. "I didn't mean to insult you, Geneva. You know my mouth runs away with my face sometimes."

"I'm not insulted, Cleo." Geneva barked a dry laugh. "I might not be able to see too well, but I'm sure I don't look my best. I've been wrestling with a terrible problem most of the night."

When Geneva was seated, Willie laid her hand on Geneva's forehead. "You do feel a bit warm. Perhaps you should see your doctor in the morning."

"Always the caretaker, aren't you?" Geneva sighed. "I don't have a fever, nor do I need to see my doctor. I tossed and turned till early this morning. And the inside of the church was like an oven."

"Nurturing people is what I do." Willie giggled. "I'm a nurse."

Cleo set her hands on her hips. "The suspense is killing me, and I have to dust three fields before sundown. What gives?"

Lorraine frowned. "It's Sunday. You have to work?"

"It rained the last two days. Crops don't care what day of the week it is." She glanced at her watch. "Time is wasting."

Geneva rubbed her forehead and blurted, "My parents are negotiating my engagement to Thurgood Mayfield."

"Thurgood!"

"Engagement!"

"Have you been holding out on us?"

A tear escaped and trickled down Geneva's cheek. She shook her head. "Mother and Father think I must be taken care of. They've decided he's the one to do it."

Cleo snorted a laugh. "Thurgood Mayfield has a house filled with staff. What experience does he have taking care of anyone?" She shuddered. "He's too smooth. Gives me the creeps."

"Have you met him?" Geneva stared at her friend.

"At the airfield. He took flying lessons for a while."

Willie patted Geneva's shoulder. "Maybe you should take some time and become acquainted with him. Perhaps he's not as bad as Cleo thinks."

"Maybe not, but I don't want to marry him, or anyone else at this stage in my life."

Lorraine nodded. "At least pray about it. We just sat through a sermon about taking our troubles to God. This is the perfect opportunity." She surveyed the group. "We should all pray for Geneva to get an answer."

Cleo crossed her arms. "Prayer is good, but I think Geneva needs to strike out on her own. Prove to her parents she can take care of herself, and do it soon, before they hog-tie her to that guy."

"I told them I would find a place of my own and be out of the house by the end of the week. They were not happy about that." Geneva swiped the wetness from her face. "Mother planned to make the announcement sometime after July fourth, but I told them to cancel the arrangements."

"Good for you!" A smug expression covered Cleo's face.

Lorraine tucked her pocketbook under her arm. "Maybe you should discuss this with Pastor Reid."

Geneva shook her head. "No, he may be in cahoots with my parents. I need to figure this out on my own."

"Willie!"

The girls turned toward the voice, and Willie said, "I've got to scoot. I promised Mom I'd help with dinner." She hurried toward the blonde woman waving from the sidewalk.

Lorraine smiled. "I need to run, too. I hate to leave you like this. Will you be okay?"

"I'll be fine, but I would appreciate you praying about this. It's a real quandary. The Bible says to obey our parents, but I simply don't want to marry Thurgood. I'm not convinced that's what God has in mind for me."

"You can count on me." She glanced at Bridget. "Ready?"

"Yes." Bridget adjusted the black beret perched on her chestnut-colored curls. "I'll be praying, too, Geneva. This is a tough one. Call me, okay?"

Geneva nodded, and the two girls crossed the grass to the parking lot.

Cleo dropped onto the bench and squeezed Geneva's arm. "I'm serious about you getting out on your own. We're all following our dreams and doing what we want. You should, too."

"Maybe my parents are right, Cleo, and I need to accept my limitations."

"That's ridiculous. You are one of the most capable women I know. You've organized fund raisers, collection drives, and taken a passel of Sunday School kids on a field trip." Cleo snapped her fingers. "And I've got just the ticket. My friend Ellie joined the USO. You could too. You're beautiful and sing like a canary. Exactly what they want."

Geneva trembled. Was this a solution to her problem? "What's the USO?"

"United Service Organization. They entertain the troops, here and overseas. They put on shows and have places where servicemen can go to write letters, dance, or just hang out. I'm not sure what all they do. But you're friendly and nice. You'd be perfect."

"Would they take me? Mother seems to think no one would want me with my diminishing eyesight."

Cleo shrugged. "Maybe the USO will agree with her. Maybe not, but you won't know until you talk to them. At least take the chance they'll say yes." She nudged Geneva. "Try it. You have nothing to lose." She jumped up from the bench. "Now, I've got to fly! I'll expect your call tomorrow night telling me you're the USO's latest catch!

Cleo bounded toward the parking lot, and Geneva chuckled before taking a deep breath. Her friend was right. She had to make the effort. She'd call the USO first thing in the morning.

Is this your answer, God?

Chapter Three

Geneva swallowed the bile in her throat and laid her fork in the center of her plate. If she took one more bite, she'd embarrass herself by losing her meal. However mortifying, being ill was a tempting alternative. Thurgood might actually stop talking.

She should have met him at home to discuss breaking their engagement. Forty-five minutes had passed, and he continued to talk. He'd even ordered for her. She laced her fingers in her lap and crossed her ankles to force her foot to stop tapping. Her face ached from smiling. The mole above his left eyebrow jumped and wiggled as he chewed.

"Geneva?"

Blinking, she cocked her head. "Yes?" Oops. He apparently expected an intelligent response to something he'd said.

"I asked if there was something amiss with your food. You've barely touched the steak." His forehead wrinkled. "I went to a lot of trouble to secure the beef. It's not easy to come by these days." He puffed out his chest. "Fortunately, I know people."

"The steak is fine. I'm afraid I'm not very hungry, Thurgood." She shifted in her chair. "It's a bit stuffy in here, don't you think?" Drat. She should have said something about canceling their engagement.

Thurgood's deep-set eyes swept the room. "I hadn't noticed." He lifted a hand toward the waiter.

Scurrying to their table and wearing an obsequious smile, the man dipped his head. "Yes, Mr. Mayfield, how may I serve you?"

"We're finished here. Please clear away this mess."

"Yes, sir." The waiter snapped his fingers at a teenaged boy in the corner of the room. The young man trotted to the table and removed their dishes before heading to the kitchen.

"Will there be anything else, sir?"

Thurgood pulled his billfold from the inside breast pocket of his charcoal suit. Withdrawing a sizeable stack of bills, he handed them to the server. "That should take care of tonight's charges. Tell Mr. Armstrong he did an acceptable job procuring our meat."

"Most assuredly, sir. Thank you."

Sliding the wallet back into his pocket, Thurgood rose and held out his hand. Geneva stood and placed her cold fingers into her fiancé's. Suppressing a shudder, she draped her purse strap over her shoulder and allowed him to lead her to the door. A lithe woman in a sapphire-blue, beaded evening gown handed Thurgood his hat. He donned the fedora as he and Geneva left the restaurant.

A carriage drawn by a pair of sleek cinnamon-colored horses waited at the curb. The driver was adorned in burgundy and gold livery. A second uniformed man guarded the open door. He jumped to attention as Geneva and Thurgood approached.

Geneva widened her eyes. "Is this for us? Where is the car?"

One of the horses stamped his hoof and shook his mane.

"The chauffer drove home after dropping us off. I thought a carriage ride would add some romance to our evening." Thurgood executed a deep bow. "Nothing is too good for you, my dear Geneva." He pointed to the coach. "After you."

Grasping the white-gloved hand of the attendant, Geneva climbed the steps into the vehicle, then dropped onto the polished leather bench. Thurgood clambered in and lowered himself beside her. She cringed when he scooted close enough for their hips to touch. He tucked her hand through the crook in his elbow and gave her a self-satisfied smile.

The attendant closed the door, and the vehicle lurched forward, the clip-clopping of the horses' hooves filtering into the carriage. Geneva peeked out the window. Gold and orange light beams mixed with purples and pinks in the sky as the sun dipped toward the horizon. The sweet scent of lilac floated on the warm breeze. She closed her eyes and took a deep breath.

It was a perfect night, except for the company.

They rode in silence for several minutes. Geneva laid her head against the back of the seat. Because she lacked peripheral vision, her neck soon ached from swiveling her head to see the magnificent mansions and their landscaped gardens along the route. She rubbed a hand across her face and stifled a yawn. Would the evening never end? She really should raise the issue of their engagement.

Thurgood cleared his throat. "Your parents indicated you are concerned over our union. I assure you marriage to me will be quite advantageous for you."

Geneva bolted upright, all weariness gone. Finally. The opportunity to address the situation. "I don't want to hurt your feelings, Thurgood, but I don't love you. I don't think I ever could."

"Who said anything about love?" He looked down his nose at her. "We don't need to love each other. In fact, it would make our lives easier if we did not."

She stared at him. "But love is the foundation of a strong marriage."

"Nonsense. Money is the foundation of any relationship. Without wealth, one has no power, and power is essential."

Geneva's mind spun. How could he be so clinical, so jaded?

He pushed his hat back on his head. "Is there someone else? Do you already have a young man? You needn't worry about that. I'm not expecting you to be faithful. I certainly have no plans of the sort. You may do as you wish in that area." He shrugged. "I promise to be discreet."

Her face warmed, and her chest tightened. She yanked her hand from his arm. "I'm not seeing anyone, but that's not the point. God calls us to fidelity with one another once joined in marriage. When two people marry, it should be because they have chosen to live together with God at the center of their relationship." She frowned. "Not because it makes a good business deal."

Thurgood chuckled. "You are naïve, aren't you, my dear? You and your God." He crossed his arms, a smirk spread on his tanned face. "You will do what you're told, and you will marry me. Your father and I have sealed the agreement. Put in the simplest of terms for you to understand, if you don't go through with it, life will become difficult for your family. I know things. Things your father would not wish to be made public." His eyes glinted. "Marry me, or I will ruin your father's reputation. The stain on you and your mother would be irrevocable."

Her skin crawled. He was a monster. No one had more integrity than her father. Thurgood must be lying. "What do you mean? Why would you do this?"

"I've already told you. Our arrangement is about money and power. After we marry, I become your guardian, and when your parents are gone, I inherit everything." He brushed a piece of lint from his pant leg. "Once that occurs, you're expendable."

Chapter Four

Two days after her dinner with Thurgood, Geneva sat in a taxi as it sped along Pratt Street in Baltimore. She clutched her pocketbook close and nibbled her lower lip. Her breath came in short gasps.

The grizzled cabbie glanced at her in the rearview mirror. "You okay, lady? You don't look so good."

She nodded and pinned a smile on her face. "Just a bit nervous. I took the train from Philly this morning. I'm on my way to an important interview with the USO."

His eyebrows shot up. "Like Bob Hope and Ann Miller? Are you famous?"

Grinning, Geneva shook her head. "I'm not a celebrity. I'm going to apply for a junior hostess position. They give out lots of donuts and coffee and do whatever necessary to keep up troop morale. Dance. Play cards. Listen to the men."

"Good for you. Those boys are a long way from home." He pointed to a trio of sailors sauntering down the sidewalk. "They act brave, but for the most part, it's all show. Deep down they're scared of what's to come, and many are just plain homesick."

The vehicle slowed and turned the corner onto Charles Street. Two blocks later the driver pulled to a stop in front of a low-slung, red-brick building where an American flag snapped in the stiff wind. Red and white geraniums lined the driveway. "This is your stop, miss."

The hummingbirds in her stomach launched themselves into flight. Geneva pressed her hand against her middle and took a deep breath. This interview offered her a chance for her own life. She dug into her change purse and handed the necessary coins across the seat to the cabbie. "Thank you."

He grinned. "You'll do fine."

She opened the door, and street noise filled the car. "Thanks again." With a curt nod to the driver, Geneva stepped out, smoothed her skirt and ran a hand over her hair. Tucking her pocketbook under her arm, she squared her shoulders and marched toward independence.

A thirty-something woman with raven-black hair sat behind the reception desk. "Welcome to the Baltimore USO. How may I help you today?"

"I'd like to help with the war effort, and my friend suggested I contact the USO." Geneva fiddled with the clasp on her purse.

"Wonderful!" The woman opened a drawer and withdrew several sheets of paper which she extended to Geneva. "The first step is to complete the application. Unless you're in a hurry, you can stay and fill it out at the table over there."

Geneva glanced to where the receptionist pointed. Two women who appeared to be her age sat together, heads bent over their work. She approached the table, and they looked up and shifted their chairs to make room for her.

The blonde lifted her hand. "I'm Penny, and this is my friend, Shirley."

"I'm Geneva." She sat down. "I found out about the USO a few days ago. I hope they'll accept me."

Shirley laughed. "Honey, if you can sit up and drink water, you're in."

Penny elbowed her friend. "It's not quite that easy, but the organization is anxious to fill their ranks. You must be invested in the cause, and not here to hunt for a husband."

"That's the last thing that interests me. In fact, I'm here to escape the man my parents have selected as my fiancé."

"Your parents have picked out your boyfriend?" Shirley grimaced. "And I thought my mom and dad were from the dark ages. What's wrong with him?"

"I don't love him." Geneva draped the strap of her pocketbook over the back of the chair. There was no need to share any more with strangers, no matter how nice they seemed.

Penny winked. "Is he cute? Could you learn to love him?"

"He's good looking enough, but that's not the point. I'm not ready to get married. I have plans."

Shirley stood. "Are you finished, Penny? We've nosed into Geneva's life enough, don't you think?"

Geneva bit her lip to keep from smiling. Shirley was apparently used to intervening on behalf of her friend.

Rising to her feet, Penny shrugged. She gathered her papers and followed Shirley to the reception desk. Geneva leaned close to the application and began to write. There was certainly a lot of paperwork involved in the process. All she wanted to do was support herself singing for the troops and handing out donuts. Why did the USO have to make things so complicated?

The sound of her pen scratching across the page filled her ears. Maybe it was as Penny said, and the USO was trying to weed out the husband-hunters. Thurgood's face came to mind. Could she fall in love with him? Tall and lean, he wore his sandy-colored hair overly long in the back. Intelligent and well-read, he could be charming and witty, conversing on any number of topics. Remembering his threat to ruin her family, she shuddered. He seemed to have a mean streak coupled with his intent to be unfaithful to her. She could never love someone like him.

Geneva shook her head to clear his image and peered at the paper in front of her. Was applying a lost cause? Would the organization be willing to take a woman with failing vision? She licked her dry lips. There was one way to find out.

Picking up her pocketbook and the completed application, Geneva made her way to the receptionist and held out the papers. "I'm finished. What's the next step?"

"You can wait—"

The sound of rapid footsteps echoed from down the hall. A woman dressed in a form-fitting, dark-green suit entered the foyer. Her silvery hair was swept into a victory roll.

The woman approached Geneva, her right arm outstretched. "Welcome!" She shook Geneva's hand, and a broad smile lit up her face. "I'm Mrs. Butler, and I've run out of applicants back there. I hoped to find more in the lobby, and here you are." Turning to the woman behind the desk, she plucked Geneva's application from her fingers. "I'll take care of this young lady, Miss Winchell."

"Yes, ma'am." The telephone rang, and the receptionist grabbed the receiver.

"This way, Miss…"

"Alexander. Miss Geneva Alexander."

"What a lovely name. Follow me, Miss Alexander. Let's get acquainted, so we can determine the best fit for you in our wonderful organization."

Geneva gulped and hurried after the woman who rushed from the room as if a train was going to leave without her.

Through hallways and in offices, periodic laughter punctuated the buzz of women's voices. Telephones rang, and the tapping of heels clattered on stairs. Mrs. Butler kept up a steady stream of narration as she pointed into rooms. Geneva's head swam with information, and she could taste the excitement of making a difference in the world.

"Here we are." Mrs. Butler entered a closet-sized room stuffed with a paper-strewn desk, tilting floor lamp, and two bookcases. She gestured to the ladder-back chair against the wall. "I hope you won't be too uncomfortable."

Geneva sat and took a deep breath.

Seating herself, Mrs. Butler laid Geneva's application on her desk. "The paperwork is a necessary evil, but I prefer to hear from the girls directly. Why don't you share a bit about yourself and why you're here?"

"There's not much to tell. I would like to support the war effort in a hands-on way. I don't have any work experience, but I have taught a third grade girls' Sunday school class and organized a couple of fundraisers for the Orphan's Fund. I've used a typewriter, but I'm not very fast." She hung her head. "I would have liked to attend college or entered the workforce, but my parents focused on preparing me for marriage."

Mrs. Butler made notes on the back of Geneva's application. "How do your parents feel about you joining the USO?"

Geneva rubbed her moist palms on her skirt. Would her adventure be over before it began? "They…uh…don't know I'm here. Will that be a problem?"

"Certainly not. You're of age, aren't you?"

"I'll be twenty-four at the beginning of August." *Where would she be on her birthday?*

"Can you sing? Read music? Do you play an instrument?" The pen in Mrs. Butler's hand hovered above the page. "We're here to raise morale, and entertainment is the best way to do that."

"I sing soprano in our church choir and perform solos on occasion. I've dabbled at the piano, but I have to learn each piece by ear." Geneva chewed on her lower lip. She needed to tell Mrs. Butler about her limited vision. How would the woman react?

"So, you don't read music. That might be a challenge."

Geneva gripped her pocketbook, and her heart raced. "I do read music, but I have difficulty seeing the notes."

Confusion crossed Mrs. Butler's face. "Do you need glasses? I don't understand."

"I suffer from Retinitis Pigmentosa. As a result, I have severe tunnel vision. According to the doctors, I will eventually lose my sight altogether." Geneva forced herself to meet Mrs. Butler's eyes. *Lord, if you care about me in the least, please don't let her turn me away. I need this opportunity.*

"How difficult for you." Mrs. Butler dropped the pen and laced her fingers together. She cleared her throat. "I'm sure you're a capable young woman, but your medical condition may create challenges in the execution of your responsibilities. I don't want to worry whether or not you will burn yourself carrying hot coffee, or fall off the stage because you can't see the edge."

"I have yet to scald myself at home, nor have I fallen down the stairs." Geneva leaned forward. "Please, Mrs. Butler, give me a chance to prove myself. I can do what is required."

The woman studied Geneva for a long moment. "Thirty days. I'll allow you a probationary period, but if I see any signs you might be a danger to yourself or the others, I'll have to let you go. Is that understood?"

"Yes, ma'am. You won't be sorry."

Mrs. Butler nodded. "You do seem to have a tenacity not often found in young girls. You've had to adjust to difficult circumstances." She stood and held out her hand. "Welcome to the USO, Miss Alexander. You may start on Monday. Be here at three p.m. sharp. We'll give you a brief orientation and determine your schedule at that time. Come ready to work."

Geneva jumped up from her chair and grasped the woman's hand. "Thank you, Mrs. Butler. You can't know how much this means to me."

Dipping her head, Mrs. Butler smiled. "I noticed you're from Philadelphia. If you don't wish to take the train every day, stop at the front desk. Miss Winchell can give you a list of boarding houses we recommend."

"You take care of everything, don't you?" Geneva stifled the urge to curtsy and hurried from the room. She threaded her way through the building and congratulated herself on finding the lobby after taking only one wrong turn. She couldn't stop smiling. *Thank you, God, for allowing me to join the USO. Thank you for the chance to serve others.*

Now, to notify Mother and Father.

She stopped at the reception desk and secured the list of available boarding houses. Turning, she gasped. Thurgood's sister, Florence, sat on a green, upholstered couch in the corner of the room. What was she doing in Baltimore? Had she followed Geneva?

Geneva's heart skittered. *Would Florence tell Thurgood she'd seen Geneva at the USO? Then her parents would find out and further arguments would ensue. They'd remind her that privileged young women didn't strike out on their own. Propriety demanded that she obey them, but her heart insisted she must prove to Mother and Father her ability to succeed.* She averted her face and hurried toward the door.

"Geneva? Is that you?" Florence's voice stopped her.

Turning, Geneva forced a smile. "Florence. How nice to see you."

Florence rose and tilted her head. "Are you joining the USO, too?"

"Is that why you're here?"

Grinning, Florence nodded. She glanced over her shoulder as if watching for someone, then snickered. "Yes, and no one in the family knows about it. I'm fed up with watching the world go by and not being allowed to help with the war effort in any meaningful way. My parents insist that employment is a lowly pursuit, not someone that our type of people do." She frowned. "How arrogant is that? Anyway I was tired of rolling bandages and being dragged to Women's Club meetings by

Mother. I saw an advertisement in the newspaper about the USO looking for girls, and here I am."

"Goodness, that's a huge step. You're very brave."

"It looks like you're being brave, too. You didn't answer my question. Are you here to join?"

Geneva clutched her purse to her chest. "Do you promise not to say anything to anyone? Even your best friend."

"Absolutely. No one knows where I am. I'm not about to change that by revealing that I saw you."

"Okay. Yes, I've been accepted to be a USO girl. I start Monday." She blew out a deep breath. "You probably don't know this, but my parents have arranged for me to marry your brother. I've joined up to avoid that."

"What? I didn't know you and Thurgood were seeing each other?"

"That's the thing. We're not dating. My parents are doing it to make sure I'm taken care of."

Florence shook her head. "That's crazy."

Geneva shrugged. "Of course it is, but I couldn't convince them to change their minds, so I told them I was leaving. They don't know where I am."

"Looks like it's time for a pinky promise. You keep my secret, and I'll keep yours."

With a chortle, Geneva held up her hand, little finger extended.

Chapter Five

A rainbow-hued blur of dresses, skirts, and blouses filled Geneva's closet. She fingered several items and sighed. Her parents claimed to have washed their hands of her, yet over the last two days, they had hovered like eagles preying the fields for dinner. They finally left an hour ago to visit friends, and she was able to pack. Cleo had arranged for the taxi, but it would be up to Geneva to board the correct train bound for Baltimore again.

"You want to your independence and all that comes with it. Regularly using the train system on your own is part of the deal." Geneva moved toward her reflection until her nose almost touched the glass. "You can do this. Don't be a coward. You can still see, and there will be plenty of people to ask for help. It's not weakness to seek assistance."

The grandfather clock downstairs chimed two o'clock, and she turned toward the sound. The taxi would arrive in a little over an hour. Talking to herself wouldn't get her clothes packed. The suitcase lay open on the floor beside her. Nestled in the bottom were her Bible, diary, and extra pair of oxfords. An interesting combination. She smirked. Or perhaps not. They all represented the practicalities in her life.

Staring at her clothes, she pursed her lips. Why was it so hard to decide what to take? What would Florence bring? She couldn't call her. Every family connected to their party line would hear their conversation.

"Geneva, if you can't decide what to wear, how are you going to learn to be on your own?" Mrs. Butler and the receptionist wore suits, but they worked in the office. Geneva would be on stage and in the canteen. A suit would be confining. Perhaps a few of her church dresses, and a couple of her casual, cotton skirts would be appropriate.

She scrubbed her hands over her face then yanked several articles of clothing from their hangers and dropped them into her luggage. Pulling out three white silk blouses, she tossed them on the pile. Marching to her dresser, she withdrew undergarments and two pair of stockings. Hard to believe they had survived this long into the war.

Dropping to her knees in front of the bag, she checked off the items against her mental list. Everything but pajamas. She rose and rummaged in the dresser. Her fingers met flannel, and she unearthed a pink floral nightgown. "That should be everything."

Footsteps hesitated outside her closed door. "Did you need something, Miss Alexander?"

"No, thank you, Bernice. You caught me talking to myself." Geneva cringed. The last thing she needed was the housekeeper or one of the other servants barging in.

"All right, miss. I'll be downstairs if you need me."

Geneva raked her fingers through her hair then knelt to finish packing. She folded each article of clothing and placed it into the suitcase. The heel of one of her oxfords peeked out from under a blouse. She ran her finger along the edge of the shoe then yanked the pair from the luggage and hurled them into the closet. Grinning, she crawled over to her collection of shoes and grabbed her black patent-leather, peep-toe heels. She waved them in triumph before tucking them into her bag. "Much better. Now I can entertain the troops in style."

She latched the valise and set it by the door. Moving to her lacquered jewelry box, she withdrew the filigree cross she received from Gram on her sixteenth birthday. She traced the edges of the delicate pendant before clasping it around her neck and then took a last look around the room.

A blue-and-white, log-cabin patterned quilt covered the walnut frame bed. How many nights had she snuggled under those covers scribbling in her diary, dreaming of what the future held? The ivory-colored walls decorated with oil paintings of the old masters were Mother's idea.

But the dresser was hers. Framed snapshots of Lorraine, Naomi, Bridgie, Cleo, and Willie cluttered the surface. Mugging for the camera, her friends wrapped their arms around her in every picture. A wicker basket filled with ticket stubs from movies, concerts, and plays stood among the photos. The ragdoll she won at a carnival that came through

Philly her senior year in high school slouched against her eighth-grade spelling bee trophy.

Stroking the doll's hair, Geneva blinked away the tears that pricked her eyes. Her friends were the best a girl could hope for. She would miss them, but once settled, she would write them each a letter explaining her decision. Cleo was ecstatic, since the USO thing was her idea.

Cleo was the boldest of her friends. Short and scrappy, she came along late in her parent's marriage and was the only girl in a house full of boys. She learned early how to hold her own among her rambunctious brothers.

Geneva's throat thickened. Close friends were good, but what would it be like to have a sister? Someone in whom she could confide, and who would support her goals instead of squashing them.

The clock downstairs chimed three times.

"Three o'clock! Enough reminiscing. The taxi won't wait for me, and neither will the train." She removed a sheet of paper from her pocket—a note to her parents. After drafting multiple versions, she settled on a concise paragraph that asked her parents forgiveness for leaving home and refusing to marry Thurgood. She would leave it in the silver platter by the front door where the incoming mail was stacked.

Grabbing her suitcase, Geneva opened the door and stifled the desire to skip down the stairs. Instead, she gripped the railing and slowly walked the treads. No sense proving Mrs. Butler right by falling.

She crept through the dining room where she could access the kitchen. The cook should have gone to the market by now, so it should be empty. If she slipped out the back of the house, perhaps none of the other staff would see her leave. She pushed on the swinging door and jumped.

Bernice sat at the table with a cup of tea. Drat! It was the housekeeper's break time.

Geneva stiffened her spine and clenched the suitcase in her hand. "I'm sure you know about my argument with Mother and Father, so you shouldn't be surprised."

The housekeeper's mouth gaped, and she jumped up from her chair. "Pardon my forwardness, miss, but you can't go. It would break your parents' hearts."

"I doubt that very much." Geneva's chest tightened. "My father was crystal clear about his feelings if I moved out, and heartbreak was not one of them."

"I'm trying to help. You're young and don't understand your parents are trying to do what is best for you." Bernice alternately bunched then smoothed her apron. "I've worked here many years, Miss Geneva. Since right after your parents married. They didn't love each other immediately, but they learned to. Just like you will learn to love Mr. Mayfield. I know your mother was against her match, but she did her duty."

Shivers snaked down Geneva's spine. "What duty? What are you saying?"

Bernice cleared her throat. "As a servant, I'm talking out of turn, but I must urge you to reconsider leaving. You know your parents' marriage was arranged by your grandparents, but did you know your mother met your father for the first time on their wedding day? She was in love with another man, but she broke off their relationship and married your father."

Geneva pressed her hand to her roiling stomach. Waves of nausea threatened to unseat her lunch. She stared at Bernice. Was she telling the truth? Geneva searched the housekeeper's face for signs of deceit, but found none.

Dropping the suitcase, Geneva sagged against the door. Her mother married her father despite loving someone else. Why would she do that? Did she regret her choice? Was she living a happily-ever-after life and wished the same thing for her daughter?

Thurgood had threatened to ruin her father. Perhaps the vile man was blackmailing her dad, and his life-ruining information was behind her engagement.

Should she stay and obey her parents?

Was Dad's reputation more important to him than his daughter?

Geneva reached for her suitcase. Would her parents give her the answers to her questions if she asked them?

Outside, an automobile horn blew. Her destiny had arrived in the form of a taxi. Did she have the strength of will to grasp it?

Chapter Six

The bus rolled to a stop, and its door popped open with a hiss. Geneva followed a burly man off the vehicle. Studying the street sign at the corner, she secured her bearings. Hours spent pouring over the Baltimore map paid off. The USO must be two blocks east and one block south. She lifted her chin, slung her pocketbook over one shoulder, and marched down the sidewalk.

Bright, mid-afternoon sunlight warmed her back. Her heels clicked against the concrete. Oily asphalt shimmered in the heat. The train ride from Philly last night gave her plenty of time to think about her choice to leave her parents without talking with them one more time. The fact is she would not be marrying Thurgood. And she would be making her own decisions from now on. Mother and Father would be hurt. Yes, but in a few months she would be able to talk to them as an independent woman.

To prevent getting lost, she had splurged on a taxi from the station to Mrs. Sutherland's boarding house, her new home. But now that she was settled, it would be the bus from now on.

A whippoorwill flew past and called out. Geneva cocked her head. Two squirrels scampered up one of the trees lining the walkway. Their chattering brought to mind her new roommate. While the two of them prepared for bed, Evie talked about everything from the family farm to the invention of nylon stockings. The one saving grace was that she hadn't probed Geneva for personal information.

Flexing her hands and rotating her shoulders, Geneva grimaced. Perhaps spending several hours this morning weeding the Victory garden on her first day in town wasn't the best idea, but Mrs. Sutherland seemed to appreciate the help.

"And the work makes me feel useful."

A man in front of Geneva turned and glanced at her. She waved. "Just talking to myself, sir."

He sped up, and she grinned. He must think she was crazy.

The USO building came into view. Well-dressed women and men in uniform wandered in and out of the building. Geneva hurried inside and approached the receptionist. "Good afternoon. You were here the day I interviewed. Miss Winchell, yes?"

The woman smiled. "Correct. Welcome aboard, Miss Alexander."

"Thanks. I can't believe I'm finally here." Geneva squinted at a sign across the room. "Where do I report?"

Miss Winchell pointed to the entrance. "You want the Club building. It's behind this one. To find it, you'll need to exit the front door. Once outside, turn left and follow the walkway to the first intersection. Turn left again and go to the second building with the blue metal roof. Enter through the double doors and ask for Devon Royal. He's the coordinator for productions." She made an exaggerated motion of fanning herself. "You'll like working with him. Your supervisor, Mrs. Katz has a meeting downtown. She'll meet with you tomorrow."

"Thanks for your help." Geneva wiped damp palms on her skirt. She squared her shoulders and strode to the door. Following the receptionist's directions, she maneuvered to the front of the club. Faint music wafted through an open window. The sound of voices and thundering feet enticed her to a set of doors marked "Theatre."

She pushed open the door.

Music blared. Chaos.

The accompanist hunched over the piano banging out Benny Goodman's "Sing, Sing, Sing." A group of eight dancers performed an intricate routine on the stage, while a stocky man in khaki pants and a white shirt clapped the rhythm. "One-two-three-four. That's it, ladies. Don't slow down, now. One-two-three-four." Three women in identical fuchsia dresses studied a sheaf of pages and whispered together. Two little girls hunkered down on the floor in the far corner with a game of jacks. Their giggles split the air. In another corner, several older girls practiced dance steps. An elderly man dozed at one of the tables, a small dog of indeterminate breed lying at his feet.

Geneva's heart quickened. *Thank you, God, for this opportunity. Help me serve you in this place.* With a sigh, she dropped into a nearby chair to wait for the dancers to finish their routine.

"One-two-three-four. And freeze-two-three-four. Hands up-two-three-four. And bow-two-three-four." He cut off the pianist, and the performers rose, their faces flushed and beaming. "Excellent. The number is really coming together." He glanced at his watch. "Let's take five before we start the Andrews Sisters' piece."

Geneva stood and ran her tongue over dry lips, and then made her way toward the stage. When the man turned, she faltered for a moment. Giving herself a mental shake, she continued to the front of the room. She proffered her hand. "I'm Geneva Alexander, your newest recruit."

His warm, slightly calloused hand engulfed hers. "Welcome, Miss Alexander. My name is Devon Royal. I coordinate the performances at our little outpost. I'm assuming they sent you here because you have some sort of talent." He tilted his head and seemed to study her. "What do you do?"

Tingles shot up her arm. She extricated her hand and stifled the urge to rub her skin. Thurgood never affected her like that. Perhaps it was her lack of experience with men.

He smiled, and her heart sped up. Whatever the reason for her reaction, she liked it.

"I will primarily serve as a junior hostess, but Mrs. Butler said you could use more singers. That's why I'm here."

"What sort of singing?"

"Almost anything. I grew up singing in the church choir, and I periodically perform solos. I'm not great at jazz, but I love big band numbers."

"Swing music, huh? Me, too." He rubbed his hands together. "How about if you sing me a few bars to give me a handle on your style."

"I beg your pardon?"

"I need to know your range. Sing the first verse of 'Chattanooga Choo Choo' or 'A String of Pearls.' I don't care which one." He glanced at the pianist. "Pick a song, Sammy, and let 'er rip."

The man worked his way up the keyboard with a chromatic scale. "How about 'Pearls?' What key, honey?"

Perspiration formed at Geneva's hairline, and the hummingbirds took flight in her stomach for the second time that day. What had she expected? Of course, he wanted an audition. She smiled at the accompanist, lips trembling. "The key of A will be fine."

"As you say, doll."

He played the introduction, and Geneva took a deep breath. Closing her eyes, she began to sing. The tension in her shoulders drained away as the music transported her. Lost in the notes, she continued singing after the piano quit, her voice filling the cavernous room. When she finished, applause broke out. Geneva opened her eyes.

Devon's face lit up. He clapped with the rest of the folks. Face heating, Geneva swiped at the tears of joy that threatened to spill down her cheeks.

The noise abated, and Devon swept his arm toward Geneva. "Hey, everybody, I think we just found our new lead singer."

The applause started again, and someone whistled. Geneva ducked her head. *Dear God, don't let this go to my head. I want to serve you, but it feels so good to be appreciated.*

Devon shouted above the noise. "All right, folks. Break time is over. Next on the agenda is the Andrews Sisters' number. Pipe down, so the girls can practice." He nodded to Geneva. "Grab a pencil and paper and make a list of every current song you know. After rehearsal I'll review it with you, and put together a repertoire for the new show. Then--"

The door opened with a bang. "Geneva, gather your things. We're leaving."

Geneva's head whipped around toward the voice. Her vision swirled. Thurgood! How had he found her?

Chapter Seven

Geneva's heart thudded in her ears, and she swayed against the piano. She gripped the instrument to keep from falling as her knees buckled. Her eyes darted between Thurgood's smug smile to the unreadable expression on Devon's face. "Thurgood, what are you doing here?"

"I told you. I've come to take you home. This ridiculous little field trip is over. You've unnecessarily worried your parents, and you've embarrassed me." He frowned. "And we can't have that, can we?"

"I'm not leaving. I've made a commitment to the USO, and I plan to honor that."

"You made a commitment to me first. I believe that trumps your current situation."

Devon cleared his throat, and Geneva's face warmed. "I'm sorry for airing our grievances in public."

"Why don't I give you two a few moments?" He squeezed her shoulder, then cupped his hands around his mouth and shouted, "All right, everyone, show's over. Clear out for ten minutes, then we'll get back on schedule." He winked at Geneva and followed the murmuring crowd as they exited the rehearsal hall.

She pressed her lips together and glared at Thurgood. He could bully her all he wanted, but she was staying.

"You really must work on your attitude, Geneva. Belligerence doesn't become you. Now, pick up your pocketbook and get in the car. We'll stop by that shabby boarding house and collect your suitcase." He snapped his fingers. "And be quick about it. I haven't got all day."

"How dare you! First of all, I did not make a commitment to you. That was my parent's doing. Secondly, I'm of age, therefore any agreement they made on my behalf is null and void. I will not be going home with you, and I certainly will not be marrying you. I'm sorry you've made a wasted trip to Baltimore. You can be on your way."

His face darkened, and he strode toward her. Gripping her arm, he dragged her toward the door. "You may be of age, my dear, but you will honor your parent's contract with me. Do not make a spectacle of yourself any more than you already have. We have reputations to uphold, and I won't have you be perceived as a shrew."

Geneva wrenched herself from Thurgood's grasp. "You're hurting me, Thurgood. I'm sure you don't want me to inform my father about your treatment of me. You must leave, before this situation worsens."

He sneered and performed a mock bow. "My apologies. I am distraught that you left Philadelphia without a word to me or your parents and have turned up at this vaudeville production. It's unseemly, my dear. Given time, you'll realize that."

"I don't believe you are truly upset, and even if you are, there is nothing inappropriate about what I'm doing. The USO is an upstanding organization with a mission to support and encourage our troops. It is important to me to do my part for the war effort, more than simply rolling bandages or raising money. These young men deserve our help." She crossed her arms then winced when her flesh, tender from his grip, protested. "I'm staying, and nothing you can say will change that."

"I went to a lot of trouble to find you, and you will come with me."

"I doubt that. Bernice made it clear she thought I was making mistake, that I should stay home and become your wife. I'm sure she notified my parents as soon as they returned home. They would have used their money and contacts to track me through the taxi service." She shook her head. "You don't want me. You're just angry because I had the audacity to turn you down."

"You're much more of a firecracker than I anticipated. Your father led me to believe you were a docile creature. Obviously, he thought that would go a long way in sealing the deal. No matter, it won't take long to change your behavior."

Geneva shuddered. He was worse than she'd imagined. "Listen to me. I'm not changing my behavior. I am not going home, and I am definitely not marrying you. You need to leave, or I will call the authorities and have you removed."

A sardonic laugh burst from his lips. "Don't make empty threats, my dear."

"It's not an empty…"

"Enough of this verbal sparring! You will put aside this nonsense and come with me."

Geneva felt his breath on her cheek and straightened her spine refusing to let him see her flinch.

Thurgood narrowed his eyes and leaned closer. "You will do as I say. Do you know why? I can ruin your father, have him hanged as a matter of fact, which would leave you and your mother to fend for yourselves. You would lose everything, scraping to find food and shelter. Society would turn its back on you, no one would take you in."

"Hanged?" Geneva clutched at her throat. "What are you talking about? Father has not committed a crime."

"That's where you're wrong, my dear. Let me tell you the story of your father's past. Brace yourself; it's a sordid tale." His mouth twisted in an ugly grin. "Your father is not who you think he is. His real name is Erich Jellicote, and he was born in Toledo, OH. There was an incident with a young lady when he was fresh out of college, and he was convicted of rape."

Geneva gasped, and she stumbled against a nearby chair. She fell into the seat and stared at Thurgood, dizziness threatening to overtake her.

"Yes, rape. Sentenced to hang, he somehow managed to escape and fled to Philadelphia where he met and married your mother, and eventually did quite well for himself." He shrugged. "I would have thought he would have kept a lower profile, but perhaps he felt his money would insulate him if he was ever discovered. Simply put, Geneva, if you don't marry me, I will expose your father, and he will be executed. Do you want that on your conscience?"

Swallowing against the waves of nausea that swept over her, Geneva rose. She lifted her chin. "You're lying. I don't know why you would create such a horrific story about my father, but it's not true."

"It is true, and when you and I are married, your parents will no longer be necessary."

Her eyes widened. "Why would you marry someone who loathes you?"

"For the money, my dear, this is a business arrangement."

Geneva swung her arm and slapped Thurgood's cheek. "You are a sick, sick man, and I won't let you execute this fiendish plan. I'll see you dead first."

Chapter Eight

"Police. Open up." Heavy pounding shook Geneva's door.

Geneva bolted upright in bed. A chill swept over her, and her heart pounded. "What's going on?" She threw back the covers and slammed her feet on the floor.

"Miss Alexander, we know you're in there." The knob rattled.

"I'm coming! I'm coming!" She jumped up and grabbed her robe off the chair. Sliding her arms into it, she ran to the door praying she wouldn't trip. Two uniformed officers stood in the hallway. The taller of the pair gripped a billy club and glared at her. His partner grabbed the doorframe and leaned across the threshold, his head moving from one side to the other as though he were looking for something.

"What's wrong?"

Was that a fuchsia dressing gown? She blinked and strained to see. A head covered with pin curls peeked around the policemen. She opened her eyes wider. Her landlady.

"Mrs. Harmon, what—"

"I'm Detective Lazarus." The shorter man stepped closer to her, blocking Mrs. Harmon, "and this is Officer Mawson. May we come in? We need to ask you some questions."

Voices murmured in the corridor as her fellow boarders spilled into the hallway. Her face warmed. What would they think of her being visited by the police?

She stepped back and gestured to the patrolmen. "Come in."

The men filled her tiny living space. With a last look at Mrs. Harmon, Geneva closed the door. She wiped her damp palms on her robe. "What can I do for you, gentlemen?"

Lazarus and Mawson stood ramrod straight next to the piles of clothes she had tossed onto the floor last night. She cringed, and her heart raced.

Lazarus scowled. "Where were you between the hours of ten o'clock last night and four o'clock this morning?"

Geneva stared at her unmade bed. "Last night?"

"It's not a difficult question, Miss Alexander. Where were you?"

"Here. I was here, sleeping. After a full day's rehearsal I was exhausted."

"Tell us about the argument with your fiancé. That probably wore you out, too."

"How do you know about that?"

"Answer the question, please."

Her stomach clenched, and she wrapped her arms around her middle. "Yes, I argued with Thurgood, but he's not my fiancé. When he arrived at the USO facility he demanded I pack my things and return home with him. I was embarrassed by his boorish and dictatorial manner, and I told him so. Despite what my parents and he claim, we are not engaged, therefore he has no say over my activities."

"When was the last time you saw him?"

"During our disagreement. He stormed from the theatre after screaming that our conversation wasn't over. I can only assume he plans to return during this morning's rehearsal." She shuddered.

Detective Lazarus narrowed his eyes. "Continue."

"After Thurgood left, Devon…that is…Mr. Royal continued running through the various acts. We finished well after six o'clock. I stopped by the market to pick up some bread and cheese for dinner and came right home. I fell asleep shortly after nine and awoke when you knocked on my door."

Geneva cocked her head. "What is this all about? Is Thurgood missing? Is that why you are looking for him? I have no idea where he is."

"He's not missing, Miss Alexander. He's dead."

Her knees buckled, and she dropped onto the mattress. Gaping at the policemen, Geneva covered her mouth with cold fingers to quell the nausea that swept over her. Thurgood was dead? How would she know anything about it? Her eyes widened. Did the police think she had killed him?

Swallowing, she clenched her clammy hands together in her lap. "He was alive the last time I saw him. As a difficult, overbearing man, perhaps he angered the wrong person."

"There are lots of *difficult* people, Miss Alexander. They don't end up dead because of it. Someone had it out for him. Are you that someone?"

"No!" Geneva leapt to her feet and clutched her robe closed. She stiffened her spine and glared at the two policemen. "I had nothing to do with Thurgood's death, and it's entirely inappropriate for you to be in my room while I am in my night clothes. Please leave, so I can get dressed and go to the USO."

"We'd be happy to take you to the station where it's more *appropriate.*" Mawson's lip curled around the word, and his face darkened. "You're not going to the USO until we've finished questioning you. Is that clear?"

Speechless, she nodded. Should she call her parents? No. They had spurned her when she moved out of the house and would have no interest in helping her. What about Mr. Royal? Would he come to her aid or would he fire her? There was no one to turn to. She was on her own. Blinking back her tears, she sighed. "If you would be kind enough step into the hallway for a few moments, I will get dressed and go with you to the police station."

"Don't try anything funny like crawling out the window. We've got back up outside."

"You have my word—"

A knock sounded at the door, and Geneva jumped.

Mawson turned the knob and frowned at the portly man, impeccably dressed, holding a briefcase, standing in the hallway. "Who are you, and what do you want?"

Bowing, the man rubbed his fingers over his black, bushy mustache. "Good morning, officers. My name is Rolf Zelinsky, and I am Miss Alexander's attorney. You will cease and desist from questioning my client. She needs time to prepare herself for the day and notify the USO of her delay. I'm sure you appreciate the need to do so." He glanced at his glittering, gold watch. "We will arrive at your facility in exactly ninety minutes. Any objections?"

Lazarus turned to Geneva. "This is your lawyer?"

"I've never seen him before in my life. I don't have an attorney."

Zelinsky patted her on the shoulder. "You do now. I've been retained by a mutual friend to handle your case."

"But how did you know—?"

"Tut, tut. Don't say another word, young lady. Now, these officers will be on their way, and I'll wait outside while you take all the time you need."

"Yes, sir."

Lazarus held up one of her monogrammed handkerchiefs. "And I'll be taking this, since it's identical to the one found underneath Mr. Mayfield."

Chapter Nine

Exhausted from spending hours in the police station the previous day and a night of dreams filled with Thurgood, Geneva sidled closer to the woman next to her on the stage. "Irene, I'm not familiar with this song. Are you?"

Pursing her lips, the leggy brunette frowned. "'Here Comes the Navy' is sung to the tune of 'Beer Barrel Polka.' Where are you from? Everyone has heard the Andrews Sisters sing it."

"No talking, ladies." Devon's voice echoed through the rehearsal hall. "Okay, let's begin. Remember, this is in cut time." He nodded to the pianist then clapped his hands. "One-two-three-four."

Her face warming, Geneva blinked back tears that threatened to spill down her cheeks. Irene was usually warm and friendly. Did she know about Geneva's trip to the police station yesterday? Had the girls been told about Thurgood's murder? Chin trembling, she stammered through the lyrics.

Devon made a slashing motion with his hand. "Hold up, everyone." He turned toward Geneva. "Miss Alexander, would you like to sit this one out? You seem to be struggling to keep up."

She pressed her lips together and shook her head.

"Are you sure? Because we've only got today and tomorrow to get this right."

"I'm fine, and in order to memorize it, I need to rehearse it." She glanced at the troupe. "I promise I'll be ready in time."

Most of the girls nodded and smiled, but Irene and the woman to her left scowled. Crossing their arms, they looked at their feet. Geneva sighed then straightened her spine. What had she done to annoy these two? Were they really that unhappy she didn't know the song? "Irene, would you like me to move?"

"What?"

"You seem upset with me. If Mr. Royal says it's okay, I could switch positions with someone."

The woman glanced at Devon who stood with his hands on his hips. She tucked a stray lock of hair behind her ear and mumbled, "No, you can stay here."

Devon's eyebrow quirked, and an exaggerated grin broke out across his face. "So, we're okay, now? Miss Alexander? Miss Cromwell?"

Geneva and Irene dipped their heads in agreement, and Devon raised his arms. "Excellent, let's start again from the top." He tilted his head toward the pianist. "Maestro?"

The accompanist snorted a laugh and trilled the piano keys then banged out the first four notes of Beethoven's Fifth Symphony. *Dum, dum, dum, dum.* He widened his eyes in mock surprise, and the girls snickered.

Devon shook his head. "Sober up, wise guy."

Cracking his knuckles, the pianist composed his face into a serious expression, then played the introduction to the Andrews Sisters' piece.

Tight harmonies filled the auditorium, and tension seeped from Geneva's shoulders. A balm to her weariness, the melody filled her heart. *Thank you, God, for music.*

Thirty minutes passed as the ensemble repeated the number several times, working on dynamics and choreography. By the fourth time through the piece, Geneva had memorized the notes and could focus on the dance steps which were blessedly uncomplicated, allowing her to keep her promise to Mrs. Butler not to fall off the platform.

Devon fisted his hand indicating the song's cutoff. "Good work, people. You too, Miss Alexander. You seem to be keeping up. Let's take a fifteen-minute breather, then I'll hand out a new song."

Groans peppered the air.

"Quit complaining. This is for our boys. Besides, you'd be bored performing the same stuff over and over."

A few of the dancers chuckled, and conversation buzzed. Geneva made her way to the steps. Pressing her palm against the wall, she crept down the stairs and sat at the nearest table. "Am I cut out for this intensive preparation for performing in nightly shows?" She massaged her neck, huffing out a breath. I have to be after what I said to Mother, Father, and Thurgood.

Thurgood. She swallowed a sob. He was not a nice man, but he didn't deserve to be killed. Who was angry enough to want him dead? She froze. Yesterday's questioning made it seem like the police suspected her, and Irene and Sally certainly treated her like she had done something wrong. What if she was charged with the crime? Would her parents help her or would she be on her own?

"Miss Alexander, do you have a moment?" Devon's voice punctured her chaotic thoughts.

"Yes, of course." Her face warmed. "I'm sorry about flubbing the song at the beginning of rehearsal."

Seating himself, he waved his right hand in dismissal. "Not a problem. I've been getting some flak from a couple of the girls about favoritism. I'm sorry to have hurt your feelings, but I wanted to put that nonsense to rest." He scooted his chair closer. "I wanted to speak with you about yesterday. You must be distraught over the murder and the police's treatment of you, yet you have been a trooper by showing up for rehearsal and giving it your all."

"I don't really want to talk about it. Ignoring the situation won't make it go away, but when I'm here…singing…practicing…it takes my mind off the worry. Well, partly."

"I understand. Music touches a part of our soul that nothing else does." He smiled. "I want to help you. That's why I secured my friend to represent you."

"About that. It's very generous, and I want to pay you back."

"No need. He owes me a favor, and he's doing it pro bono. But we need do our part to prove your innocence. As the man's fiancée, you're probably a prime suspect."

"I—"

"Miss Alexander, telephone call!" One of the stagehands waved at her by the telephone hanging on the far wall.

Moisture dampened Geneva's palms. Was it the police again? Who else would be calling her? She licked her lips.

Devon stood and held out his arm. "We're in this together."

She met his warm gaze, and her heart picked up speed. She didn't have to go through this alone. Tucking her hand in the crook of his elbow, she allowed him to lead her across the room.

She put the receiver to her ear. "Hello?"

"It's time to come home, young lady." Her father's bombastic voice blasted through the phone, and she flinched. "You are embarrassing yourself and the family with this situation. First you run off to become a singer, which is entirely inappropriate, and now I find out that your fiancé has been murdered. It's a disgrace. What do you have to say for yourself?"

"Father, I—"

"I'm sending a car for you. Pack your bags and be ready to leave."

"I have responsibilities here, Father. I'm sorry you're distressed, but I can't come home."

"Can't or won't?" Sarcasm colored his words.

"Does it matter? You taught me to take my commitments seriously, and I've committed to serving our troops through the USO. I'm not going back on my word."

"Show me some respect, daughter. Family comes first. Plenty of other girls could take your place. You need to come home. Your mother is quite upset."

"I'm sorry, Father, but I've made up my mind, and nothing you say will change that."

"Fine, then you'll just have to get out of this jam yourself."

The phone clicked, and the dial tone buzzed in her ear. She hung up the receiver then wiped her eyes and sniffled. Why was her father being so domineering? He was often strict, but rarely unreasonable. There had to be something she didn't know.

Devon held out his handkerchief, and she dabbed at the dampness on her cheeks. "I'm sorry to be blubbering like this."

"It's been a rough couple of days, and your father wasn't exactly supportive."

"I guess you couldn't help but hear him."

Shrugging, Devon buffed her gently under the chin. "Looks like it's just you and me, kid. We'll find the dirty rat who did this."

Geneva giggled, and the tightness in her chest eased. "Perhaps we should add Jimmy Cagney to the show's lineup."

"Nah. I'm a behind-the-scenes kind of guy. And we've got to clear your name. It seems we can't count on the cops to get it right. What do you say? Partners? He extended his arm.

She shook his hand. "Partners." Could a music director and a half-blind girl find a killer before the police arrested her?

Chapter Ten

Geneva sat in the rehearsal hall staring at the petite blonde on the stage. Her shoulder-length, cornsilk was coiled into soft victory rolls, and her face wore a wide grin. She swayed to the music as her sultry voice purred the words to last year's hit, *Do You Care*. Closing her eyes, Geneva let the notes wash over her. Perhaps if she could lose herself in the song, she could forget that her life had turned upside down in a matter of days and she would have to prove her innocence in a murder investigation. Sighing, she wrapped her arms around her middle.

"Can you believe Dinah Shore stopped by our little ol' USO? If I had known she was coming, I'd have worn something different to practice. She's swell, don't you think?"

Heart skipping a beat, Geneva's eyes flew open. One of the girls who hadn't treated her like a pariah since Thurgood's death stood nearby, hands on her hips. A towel was draped around her neck, and her dark hair was scraped back in a haphazard ponytail.

"Yes, if I was half the singer she is, I would have headed to Hollywood too. I heard she got turned down a bunch of times before they teamed her up with Frank Sinatra."

Nodding, the girl leaned against the wall. "He's dreamy. I love those blue eyes of his." She fanned herself with an exaggerated wave of her hand. "That Dinah's a smart one. Did you know she graduated from Vanderbilt? They don't take just anyone, you know."

"I wonder if she'll talk to us, or if they'll keep us away from her. I'd love to shake her hand and tell her how great she is."

"We can only hope." The dancer shrugged then held out her hand. "By the way, I'm Ethel. I don't think we've officially met yet. That Devon keeps us hopping, doesn't he?"

"I'm Geneva. That he does, but I'd rather be busy. Makes me less homesick."

"Pardon me for saying, but why on earth would you be homesick? That boyfriend of yours was an overbearing loudmouth, and from what I hear your father isn't much better."

Geneva's face warmed. "It's complicated. And I miss my close friends. There are five of us that have known each other since grammar school."

"Well, that I can understand. But this is a new chapter in your life, a great opportunity. I want to be a Rockette, and being part of the USO might just get me in the door. Know what I mean?"

"I never thought that joining the USO might help toward a career. Certainly gives me something to think about."

"All right, girls, make your way to the stage." Devon's voice bounced off the plaster walls. "Miss Shore has graciously agreed to do a couple of numbers in tonight's show before she catches her plane to England to perform for our boys. She'd like you ladies to sing back up. What do you think about that?"

The roomful of women leapt from their seats, and chairs squealed against the wooden floor as they hurried to the platform. Murmuring and laughter echoed throughout the hall, and the women's feet thundered up the stairs and across the boards.

Dinah smiled at the troupe. "Thank you for joining me. I'm honored to be part of your program. I thought we'd do 'I Hear a Rhapsody.' Do y'all know that song?"

The ensemble clapped their hands, and the pianist played the first few bars of the piece. Dinah nodded. "Seems like we're all in agreement. I'll take care of the verses. Y'all will pick up at the chorus." She snapped her fingers in rhythm. "One-two-three-four. One-two-three-four. How about we try it at that tempo?"

Music poured from the piano as the accompanist played the introduction. Geneva pinched herself then grinned. Yep, that hurt. She wasn't dreaming; she was singing with Dinah Shore. She'd have to write Cleo and tell her about it. As supportive as her other friends were, Cleo was the one who regularly reminded her she could be anything she wanted to be.

She nibbled her lower lip. If only she could believe that.

Ethel elbowed her, and Geneva joined the rest of the performers in singing the refrain. If she didn't pay more attention, she was going to get herself fired. She tossed a grateful smile at her new friend and focused on blending her voice with Miss Shore's.

Cleo was going to flip.

"Okay, that's a wrap! Best rendition yet, ladies." Devon glanced at his watch. "Be back here in three hours for a quick warm-up before getting into your costumes."

The women chattered among themselves and strolled away in pairs and trios. Geneva wandered to a small table in the wings and grabbed a towel to dab the perspiration from her face. The heat from the lights was brutal, one of the downsides to being on stage. Another table held several pitchers of water surrounded by a crowd of glasses. She poured herself a drink and tried not to guzzle it, but the cold liquid soothed her parched throat, and she drained the container in seconds. Filling the glass a second time, she held the chilled surface to her face and closed her eyes.

"You have a lovely voice."

For the second time since breakfast, Geneva's eyes flew open, and she gulped. What was wrong with her hearing? She hadn't heard anyone approach. "Uh, Miss Shore, thank you. That's quite a compliment coming from you." She ducked her head and rubbed at the condensation on the side of the glass.

"I don't say things I don't mean, honey. You've got a gift, and I saw your face. You obviously love to sing. You're entranced by the music, become one with it. Don't be one of those talented people who can't get ahead in this world. Watch out for yourself, honey. No one else will. Got that?"

Geneva looked up. Dinah seemed to be studying her, waiting for an answer. Tongue-tied, Geneva nodded.

Dinah raised her eyebrow and tilted her head. "I can't hear you."

Licking her dry lips, Geneva cleared her throat. "Got it. I appreciate your encouragement, Miss Shore."

"Call me Dinah. Everybody does." She patted Geneva's arm. "Now I don't know about you, but I'm about worn out from rehearsal, so I'm going to lie down for a bit. You should do the same. Performing is a marathon, and you've got to grab rest when you can."

"Yes, ma'am."

Chuckling, Dinah shook her head. "Honey, I'm older than you by a long shot, but save your ma'am's for when you meet Mrs. Roosevelt." She sauntered off the stage without a backward glance, and Geneva huffed out a breath. Dinah Shore had spoken to her! Told her she had talent. Cautioned her to watch out for herself.

God, thank you for what seems like a confirmation. Is it okay to work with Devon on finding Thurgood's killer?

##

Thirty minutes later, Geneva stood in front of the door to Thurgood's hotel room with the concierge. She held a handkerchief to her face and wiped away the crocodile tears she had worked up to convince the young man she was Thurgood's grieving fiancée. "Thank you for letting me into Mr. Mayfield's room. I won't be long."

"Certainly, Miss Alexander. I probably shouldn't let you in until the police release the room, but I'm sure a few minutes won't matter. We're all sorry for your loss. If there's anything else I can do for you, don't hesitate to let me know." He pushed his key into the lock and turned the knob. Swinging open the door, he gestured for her to enter. "Will you be all right in here on your own? I really should get back to the front desk, but I can remain if you need me to."

"No, I'll be fine."

"Just be sure to lock the door when you're finished."

Geneva nodded and blotted her cheeks. "Thank—." Her voice cracked, and she swallowed heavily. "Thank you."

She'd lied to Ethel, telling her she was going for a walk, and now she'd lied to the concierge. She hadn't told Devon of her plans to search the hotel room either even though he'd offered his help. Would he be angry she'd left him out?

The young man sauntered down the corridor, not seeming to notice her nervousness. She fumbled with the latch then managed to secure the door. She rotated her neck and massaged the tension from her shoulders before she swept her gaze around the room. Still declared a crime scene, the room had not yet been cleaned by the housekeeping staff. The sheets had been stripped from the bed and piled on the mattress. Two of the dresser drawers hung open with clothing dangling over the edge. Leave it to Thurgood to unpack, even though he'd only planned to stay the night.

Some of their arguments came rushing back. His face dark with anger, a snarl curling his lips. He didn't love her. Why was he so upset at her leaving? Was it a matter of pride?

Voices sounded in the hallway, and she cringed, her heart ricocheting in her chest. Were they coming in here?

Footsteps approached and then faded. Safe. For now.

Focus, Geneva. You'll not find anything while wallowing in memories. She turned to her left and began a methodical search. Starting with the oak desk, she pulled open the top drawer and frowned.

Empty.

"What did you expect? A vital clue in the first place you looked?" She rolled her eyes, and moved to the mirrored vanity. One glimpse of her guilt-filled reflection, and she avoided the mirror while she checked each compartment.

The bottom drawer refused to budge. She tugged on the carved glass knob with no success. Something must be caught inside. Sitting back on her heels, she surveyed the room, and her gaze fell on a hanger peeking out from the armoire. Geneva rose and grabbed it. Wrestling with the satin padding, she finally tore the material away from the wire frame. She untwisted the metal and poked it into the tiny space above the drawer.

Pushing and wiggling the steel while shimmying the drawer, she gritted her teeth. She could do this. With one last Herculean effort, she shoved the tool further, and a thump sounded from inside the furniture. The drawer slid open without a hitch. Geneva peered over the edge and gasped.

A slim, white compact lay at the bottom. Elisabeth Arden. Not her brand.

How had the police missed this?

Was it there before Thurgood checked in, or had he spent the hours after their disagreement in an assignation?

Chapter Eleven

Applause filled the auditorium. Geneva grinned at Ethel. The last two days had been filled with extra rehearsals, a welcome diversion. The police hadn't returned since their initial visit to her apartment, but that reprieve wouldn't last long. Despite her lawyer's intervention, the authorities made it clear during her interview she was a strong suspect.

Her lawyer. The words didn't easily roll off her tongue.

She sighed. Devon had hired the man and wouldn't take any money from her. Not that she had enough to pay Mr. Zelinsky' exorbitant rate. She had given up her cushy allowance when she left home. Frowning, she rubbed her forehead. Devon didn't seem to have much money either. How did he afford an attorney?

Ethel poked her, and Geneva pasted a smile on her lips. The crowd soon rose and dispersed, the curtain closing with a swish. Fanning her face with her hands, Ethel said, "Another one in the hopper. The audience seemed to like the new routine."

"I hope so. We certainly work hard enough on it. I didn't think I'd ever get the hang of that combination ball-change-and-heel-turn bit. I'd rather just sing, you know?"

"You're not the only one who struggled with that move. A couple of the girls in the second line worked on it after last night's practice. This isn't Broadway, but Devon seems to want a professional-level show."

"The troops deserve it. I may not be able to see them from the stage, but I know they're young. Very young. And they may not survive the war. We need to provide the best entertainment possible."

"Too bad you can't see them. There were some real lookers out there."

Geneva sighed. No need to be attracted to any of them. Good looking or not, none of the men would want to be saddled with a girl who might soon be blind.

Ethel's hand flew to her throat. "Oh, Geneva. I'm sorry. That was insensitive of me. Frankly, I forget your vision isn't good."

"Apology accepted." Geneva smiled. "I like knowing you don't remember about my eyes. It makes me feel less like the oddball that I am."

"You're not—"

"Sure she is, and it has nothing to do with her vision."

Geneva swung around. Naomi and Bridget stood at the bottom of the stairs, arms wrapped around each other's shoulders. She held out her arms, and they rushed up the steps and enveloped her in a hug. Swallowing against the lump in her throat, she tightened her hold on them.

Ethel cleared her throat. "I take it you know these girls."

Pulling out of her friends' embrace, Geneva pivoted. "These gals are two of my best friends from home." She looked back at them. "I can't believe you're here. What made you decide to come?"

Naomi grinned. "This may have been Cleo's idea, but we think it's swell you're helping out here. It took a lot of guts to defy your folks and that creepy Thurgood. We wanted to see one of the shows, and we pooled our gas rations to drive up."

"Wow, that's true friendship. I don't know anyone I'd give up my rations for." Ethel flipped her charcoal-black hair over her shoulder.

"We've known each other forever. There's nothing we wouldn't do for one another," Bridget said.

"Nothing?" Ethel looked skeptical.

"Yep." Naomi giggled. "One time in high school, our other friend Cleo, hung a sign in front of the school protesting something." She waved her hand. "I can't remember what it was. Anyway, someone tattled to the principal that it was Cleo, and he was going to suspend her for several days. But each of us went to his office and confessed to the deed. So he had five girls all claiming responsibility. He was not happy."

Ethel raised her eyebrows. "What happened?"

"He kept trying to get us to confirm that it was Cleo, but none of us would budge, so he suspended all of us."

"How awful."

Naomi shook her head. "Not really. That kind of made us martyrs in the eyes of the student body, so we became quite popular after that. Of course, our parents grounded us for weeks, but it was worth it."

Geneva grinned. "Definitely. And I'd do it all over again."

"I've never had friends like that. You're very lucky, Geneva."

Bridget looped her arm through Ethel's. "Any friend of Geneva's is a friend of ours, so now you do." She rubbed her stomach. "Enough chatter. I'm starving."

"You're always hungry," Geneva and Naomi said in unison, then chuckled.

Gesturing to the counter at the back of the room, Geneva buffed Bridget's shoulder. "If truth be told, I could use something to eat myself."

The girls threaded themselves through the crowd to stand in line. Ten minutes later, with waxed paper-wrapped sandwiches in hand, they managed to find an empty table in the corner. They ate in silence for several moments.

Naomi laid her food down and dabbed her lips with a napkin. "Not bad for canteen food,"

"We've got a couple of large farms nearby, and one of the farmers provides chicken and eggs, and the other, fresh produce. Because of that the rationing doesn't affect us as badly as elsewhere."

"How are you holding up, Geneva?" Bridget patted Geneva's arm. "This situation with Thurgood's murder has got to be upsetting you, yet here you sit munching on dinner."

"I try not to think about it, but it's been hard. I still can't believe he's dead. I didn't like the man, but he didn't deserved to be killed."

"What do the police think?" Naomi asked.

Geneva blew out a loud breath. "They think I did it. Or at least that's the way it seems. And I was asleep at home, so I don't have an alibi."

Bridget rolled her eyes. "If you did it, don't they realize you would have made sure you had an alibi?"

Shrugging, Geneva rubbed at a scratch on the table with a trembling finger. "I'm not privy to their thoughts about that. But I need to figure out who killed Thurgood. That's the only way I can prove my innocence. Devon has agreed to help me. I wish I knew where to start looking."

"What about his business associates? I've heard my dad complain about Thurgood's money-making schemes, as he called them," said Naomi.

"We never discussed business, I'm not sure who would want to do him harm."

"Would your father know?" Bridget set down her glass with a thunk.

Geneva shivered. *Was he involved? Had Thurgood already approached Father with threats to ruin his reputation? What would he do to prevent that from happening?*

Bridget and Naomi exchanged a glance, and Geneva narrowed her eyes. "What?"

"Well, it could be nothing, but on the other hand it might be a lead," Naomi said.

"Tell me. I've got nothing." Nothing, unless her father had removed the menace.

"Bridget and I were at Burke's Restaurant a few days ago, and Thurgood was there."

"Not surprising. That's one of his favorite places to eat."

"He didn't seem to be having a good time." Naomi frowned. "He was dining with an older man we didn't recognize. And he wasn't Thurgood's usual type of crony. The man's suit was out of date and worn, almost as if he couldn't afford anything nicer. He was overdue for a haircut, too."

"The Depression left a lot of people with financial issues. You shouldn't judge," said Bridget.

"It was just an observation." Naomi gave a dismissive wave. "But here's what you really need to know. The two of them were arguing something fierce. They tried to keep their voices down, so we couldn't hear much. But then the man jumped up from his chair and said, 'Stay away from her or you'll be sorry.' Sounds like a motive to me."

Chapter Twelve

Geneva shivered and pulled her jacket closer to ward off the chill of the unseasonably cold day. However, inside her white cotton gloves, her palms slicked with moisture as she approached the brick bungalow. Nearly identical to the other homes that lined the street, its manicured lawn and gardens hinted at the hours of labor. Not one, but two Cadillacs waited in the driveway.

Back-to-back meetings with Hollywood agents prevented Devon from accompanying her. It would have been nice to have his confident presence, but she couldn't put off the investigation, even though he told her to wait for him. He was unhappy she'd chosen to move ahead anyway.

She glanced at her watch. Nearly noon. Would the Emerys receive her this close to lunch? Her stomach rumbled. Having boarded the first train of the day from Baltimore to Philly, she hadn't taken time for breakfast, and her empty belly protested.

"I should have called ahead." Geneva shook her head. "And say what? I heard you had an argument with Thurgood Mayfield, and I think you might have killed him. Can you prove otherwise?" Tugging at her coat, she sighed. "Maybe I should have had one of the girls come with me."

"Are you going to come through the gate or stay on the sidewalk talking to yourself?"

Geneva's head whipped up, and her gaze fell on a dark-haired man standing on the covered porch of the bungalow. His face held a mixture of amusement and interest. Dressed in a double-breasted suit, he rotated a gray fedora in his hands.

Huffing a deep breath, Geneva straightened her spine and lifted the wrought iron latch. She pasted on a smile, one she hoped the man would read as genuine. Could he hear her heart thundering in her chest?

Squinting at her, he cocked his head. "I know you, don't I? You're Wayne Alexander's daughter."

"Yes, sir."

Gesturing to a pair of rocking chairs, he said, "No one else is home. Would you care to have a seat outside?"

Geneva sat in the nearest rocker. "That would be nice. You have a lovely home, and your gardens are beautiful."

He lowered himself to the second chair. "How did you manage a trip over here on your own? I understand from your father that your vision is quite poor."

She smoothed her skirt as her face warmed. Why would her father broadcast her situation to his friends and make it sound worse than it was? He was usually more private than that. Meeting the man's gaze, she shook her head. "My eyesight is not as bad as Father made it out to be. I have a sort of tunnel vision and need to be careful not to make any sudden moves that could put me in a precarious situation, but I manage to navigate just fine. I've joined the USO in Philadelphia as part of the entertainment troupe. In fact, that's where I've come from." She snickered. "My sense of direction has never been good, even when I could see perfectly."

Mr. Emery chuckled. "You're a brave young lady."

"Not as brave as our boys going overseas. That's why I had to do something for them, even though it's not much. Just a little singing and dancing and conversation. What they are doing is so important, fighting evil." She shook her head. "I can't imagine how they feel."

"No, you can't. I was in the Great War, and it was nightmarish. Those boys will never be the same."

"Thank you for serving, sir."

Mr. Emery waved away her comment as if it was a pesky fly. "Enough talk of war. Why did you come? Certainly not for a social call."

"No, sir. This isn't a social call, but I'm not sure where to start."

"Why not start at the beginning?"

"That would take up too much of your time." Geneva shrugged. This man seemed warm and gracious. Surely he couldn't be a killer. "It's about the argument you had with Thurgood Mayfield."

He froze in the chair and stared at Geneva. "What do you know about that, and what business is it of yours?"

"Three of my friends were in the restaurant when it occurred. They couldn't help but hear it. The two of you were…er…quite vocal."

Mr. Emery's face darkened. "Then if they heard everything, what else could you possibly want to know?"

"That's just it. They didn't hear everything, so I'd like to ask you some questions, if you don't mind. It's very important, sir."

"How on earth can my disagreement with Mayfield hold any significance to you?"

Geneva plucked at her skirt, then laced her fingers together to keep from fiddling with her clothes. She leaned toward the older man. "Thurgood is dead, Mr. Emery. He was murdered in a hotel in Philadelphia. The police think I did it, and I have to prove to them I didn't."

"What? Murdered?" Mr. Emery reared back. "Are you sure?"

"Quite sure, sir. He was stabbed. I was questioned extensively about the incident."

Mr. Emery scrubbed at his face then jumped out of the chair and began to pace. He mumbled to himself and seemed to tabulate something on his fingers.

"Sir, are you willing to talk to me about your dispute with Thurgood? Please. I must prove my innocence." Geneva's voice quavered, and she wiped away the tears that coursed down her cheeks.

"At my expense?" Mr. Emery strode to her and stopped within inches of her knees. He crossed his arms. "You want me to give you some clue that implicates me in his death? I'm afraid I can't do that, because I didn't kill him."

"I don't want you to get into trouble, but I need to give the police more information about Thurgood. About his life and his business dealings. Then they would realize there could be other suspects besides me. I didn't kill him either." She reached toward Mr. Emery, her hand suspended in mid-air. "Please...help me."

He dropped into the vacant rocker. "You were engaged to him. What can I tell you that you don't already know?"

"We weren't engaged. He and my parents both wanted the union, but I didn't. And the few times we went out...well...he talked a lot, but it was either vacuous compliments about me or bragging about what he would do once he had the money that came with our marriage." She shuddered. "Frankly, I didn't listen to most of what he said."

"My estimation of you has improved, Miss Alexander. It's seems you understand what a scheming, manipulative weasel he is…was." Mr. Emery stared at her for a long moment then cleared his throat. "All right, I'll tell you about the argument. Several months ago, Thurgood came to me and asked if he could court my daughter, Raine. He had met her at a couple of social events and claimed he was smitten. I refused his request and thought that was the end of it. Two weeks ago, I discovered that he had been seeing Raine behind my back. He had talked her into meeting him at various locations, a picnic, a walk in the park. Nothing too unseemly, but they didn't have my permission, and without a chaperone…well…it was too much."

He slumped in the chair. "My sweet girl was being hoodwinked into thinking this man loved her. He didn't care for her. Not remotely. Fortunately nothing happened between them. But that's more than I can say for the poor string of women he's ruined."

Geneva closed her eyes. Thurgood had been true to his word and sought other female companionship. She meant nothing to him. Should she be relieved or insulted? Even if she didn't want to marry the man, it hurt to be trifled with. Swallowing past the lump in her throat, she smoothed her dress. "The altercation was about him seeing your daughter?"

"Yes, I told him if he ever approached my daughter again, he'd be sorry. He sneered at me that he had no interest in her, but he would ruin me if he so chose, and that I should think twice about threatening him. He is a ruthless businessman. I have no doubt he could make things difficult for me with a few well-placed lies and half-truths."

"Is it possible that your daughter went to him after that?"

"No, she has been with her aunt in Pittsburgh. Why do you ask?"

Opening her pocketbook, Geneva pulled out the compact and handed it to Mr. Emery. "I found this in his hotel room. Could it be Raine's?"

His large hands dwarfed the tiny container. He gave it back to her. "No, this doesn't belong to her."

"You know your daughter's makeup that well?"

"My daughter doesn't wear powder. It gives her a rash, so that compact cannot be hers."

Geneva stuffed the item into her bag and rose, blinking against the tears that threatened to fall again. A dead end. "Thank you for your time, Mr. Emery. I'm sorry to have bothered you."

"Leave this investigation to the police, Miss Alexander, but tell them this: he was a callous and vindictive man, and any number of his business victims would have reason to do him in. But should you choose to handle this yourself, find the man who was wronged, and you will have your killer."

Head down, Geneva trudged down the stairs. She had no way to find the men that Thurgood duped. Would she ever prove her innocence?

Chapter Thirteen

Geneva's head throbbed. Sammy Kaye's "Daddy" blared from the jukebox over the buzz of conversation punctuated with bursts of laughter. Fortunately guests were required to smoke outside, so she didn't have to face the noxious fumes of tobacco. However, aromas from a dozen floral perfumes tickled her nostrils. She wiggled her toes and winced. Nearly every soldier or sailor she had danced with trod on her feet.

The windows were open, but no breeze fluttered the curtains or bathed the mob in fresh air. Perspiration trickled down her back as she slithered through the crowd toward the counter. Raising her hand at the soda jerk, she said, "Billy, please tell me you still have some lemonade. I could drink a gallon."

The young man blinked at her through his thick glasses and grinned. He held up his index finger. "Don't go 'way." He disappeared through the swinging doors behind him. She picked up a napkin from a nearby basket and blotted her damp forehead. A trip to the ladies' room to powder her face was in order.

At the moment, her purse held two compacts. She still had the one she found in Thurgood's room. Her cheeks warmed remembering their conversation in her parents' living room. What motivated him to arrange a marriage knowing full-well he intended to conduct numerous affairs? How many women were willing to enter into a relationship with a man who had a wife? Was his death tied to his depraved behaviors?

Three days had passed since she'd spoken with Mr. Emery, and no new leads had surfaced. Her heart pounded. What was she going to do?

Billy returned with a frosty glass filled with pale yellow liquid. "Fresh squeezed, Miss Alexander. Sure to quench your thirst."

"I owe you one, Billy."

He blushed to the roots of his hair and ducked his head. "Any time."

Lifting the cold glass to her lips, Geneva resisted the urge to gulp down the refreshing drink. As she turned toward the writhing throng of dancers, a large man in an army dress uniform bumped her shoulder and the sugary liquid sloshed down the front of her dress.

"Oh!" She put the glass down then plucked the drenched clothes away from her skin.

He grabbed a fistful of napkins then seemed to realize he shouldn't use them to clean up the mess. Frozen, he stood with his hands outstretched. "Please accept my apologies, miss. I'm terribly sorry." He shoved the paper cloths into her hands then reached into his pocket and withdrew a roll of bills. "Let me pay to have the dress washed. It's the least I can do."

She dabbed at her dress then gave up. Her bodice was saturated and no amount of wiping with the flimsy napkins was going to change that. Waving her hand in a dismissive gesture, she shook her head. "There's no need for that. It will come out in the laundry." She snickered. "Besides, I had the foresight to wear a cream-colored dress, and the liquid blends in. No one will ever notice."

"I doubt that very much, but it's kind of you to say." He proffered his crooked arm. "I'm Lieutenant Klondike. Would you care to take a walk around the building? It's too stuffy in here for my taste."

"It's nice to meet you, Lieutenant. I'm Geneva Alexander but a walk with you is against the rules. Junior hostesses aren't allowed to be alone with a man."

"Again, I must ask your forgiveness. I meant no disrespect."

"We can go to the library. There will be a chaperone there and it's a quiet place to talk."

His smile lit up his face, and she tucked her hand into his elbow. Waving at Billy she led the soldier to the west end of the room and out the door. The Wedgewood blue carpet muffled their steps as they sauntered through the corridor admiring the watercolor paintings on the walls.

The noise from the recreation hall faded as they entered the bookshelf-lined room. Three round tables with chairs filled the area to the left of the door. A foursome occupied one table playing bridge. At another, a sailor sat writing a letter, his brow furrowed in concentration.

To their right were several clusters of upholstered chairs. No sofas—it wouldn't do for the men and women to sit together.

Geneva led him to a pair of chairs away from the record player wafting the strains of a piano concerto.

He gestured for her to seat herself first, then he lowered himself onto the opposite chair with a sigh. "Thank you for suggesting the library. I'm not a dancer and shouting to be heard isn't my idea of holding a conversation."

"What would you like to talk about, Lieutenant?"

"Are you allowed to tell me about yourself?"

"Not really. We're not supposed to get too personal. But I can tell you that I'm from Baltimore, and I've been here about a month. Sometimes it feels longer. I love to sing, and it's been a blessing to entertain the troops."

"We appreciate what the USO does for us. I've already been to Europe once, and I can tell you from experience that combat is scary. Anything to pick up the boys' morale is wonderful."

"Where did you serve?"

"I can't say."

Geneva smoothed her skirt. "Of course. I shouldn't have asked."

"It's only natural to want to know." He chuckled. "We're supposed to make conversation, but there are so many topics that are off limits, it's a challenge, yes?"

She giggled. "Yes!"

"How about if I describe an exciting incident involving the black market here in the States? I was in the wrong place at the right time."

"As long as you won't get into trouble."

"Nah. I'll leave out the particulars." He leaned toward her and rubbed his hands together. "It was a dark and stormy night...," he whispered.

Shaking her head and grinning, Geneva crossed her arms. "I read that novel, too. Try again."

He wiggled his eyebrows. "Well, actually it was. I was on patrol with one of my buddies, and we became disoriented in the darkness. We took several wrong turns and ended up near the docks. It must have been two or three o'clock in the morning. Anyway, we stumbled on some guys who were stealing supplies from one of the warehouses."

Her eyes wide, Geneva gasped. "What did you do?"

"Fortunately, my sergeant remembered passing a police box a couple of blocks back, so I kept an eye on the thieves while he phoned for help. About ten minutes later, the cops showed up and took down the whole lot of them, including the ones inside the building. My captain told me later they were part of a black market ring, and when they were informed what they were doing was considered treason and they could be executed, they started singing like, um, like you girls and gave up the big boys."

"Was that around here?"

"I can't tell you."

"Right. It's so hard to believe Americans would do that do each other."

He shook his head. "Not really. There are lots of folks who will do anything to make an extra buck, especially the amount you can rake in on the black market. It's dangerous. A bad decision or partnership can get you killed, but you can earn a lot of loot. I guess they think the payoff is worth the risk."

"How much loot?"

Lieutenant Klondike narrowed his eyes. "You wouldn't be thinking of doing something foolish, would you Miss Alexander?"

She bolted upright. "Not at all. I'm just trying to understand how much money would make a person risk his life like that."

"We're talking hundreds of thousands of dollars, perhaps even millions. Enough to set someone up forever if he got out with his skin intact. But as I said, one wrong move..." Klondike drew his finger across his neck and winked.

Icy tentacles trailed across Geneva's shoulders. She shuddered. Thurgood's desire for money—was it strong enough for him to be willing to enter the black market? How could she find out if that's what got him killed?

Chapter Fourteen

Charred remains of the roller rink loomed ahead of Geneva. Whiffs of acrid air still clung to the burned-out shell. Clutching her pocketbook close to her chest, Geneva tiptoed toward the building. The ease with which she'd found a group of criminals operating so close to the club was alarming. Since her chat with Lieutenant Klondike last Saturday night, she'd made a few discreet inquiries among the girls and had found a link to the black market. Apparently the lieutenant was right about his assessment of people and their greed. How quickly her life had changed since leaving home.

She paused to survey the area surrounding the abandoned roller rink. A fire had destroyed all but the coat room and front lobby. The owner had chosen not to construct a new facility—perhaps the war rendered the business useless. A breeze fluttered through the trees that lined the parking lot, their leaves waving in mock greeting. Her tongue stuck to the roof of her mouth, and her heart skittered. Pressing a hand to her stomach, she took a deep breath. Then another.

"Come on, girl, you can do this. Tramping around Baltimore in the dark with disintegrating eyesight isn't the smartest thing you've ever done, but you've come too far to turn back now." She stiffened her spine and resumed her trek toward the decrepit structure, mindful of the debris littering the asphalt. Did the black marketers realize how cliché they were by operating out of a vacant, broken-down building? Had they watched too many Hollywood movies?

A nervous giggle escaped, and she clamped her lips together. Devon had promised to be her partner in proving her innocence, and having him with her would have provided her security but he probably wouldn't have agreed to her scheme of pretending to be a customer so she could quiz the criminals about Thurgood.

Geneva circled the blackened hulk. No sign of anyone. She picked her way over the uneven ground and entered the lobby. Darkness enveloped her, and she stretched out her arms.

"Hello?" Her voice sounded muffled and tentative. She cleared her throat. "Is anyone there?"

Nothing. She was alone.

Inching her way out of the rink, Geneva returned to the parking lot. She held her watch up to her eyes, but the moonless night shrouded the dial. How long should she wait?

Time passed, and her back ached from standing. She shifted to one foot, and then the other. The hair on her neck prickled, and she froze. Were they watching her?

Footsteps sounded. They were coming! Gripping her pocketbook tighter, she held her breath. A shadowy figure approached, flashlight sweeping the terrain in front of him and along the buildings on each side of the street. Should she identify herself?

The beam cut through the darkness, and she shrank against the lone tree in the lot. Surely if it was the man she was here to meet, he wouldn't stroll up the sidewalk as if on a walk in the park. Who was the flashlight-wielding man, and didn't he know there were blackout restrictions?

Closer and closer he came. The glow from his torch raked across the front of her hiding place, and the glare blinded her. She winced. *Please, Lord, don't let him find me.*

The light rested on her body, and she slumped. Why should God keep her safe when she had intentionally put herself in danger?

"Ho! I'm a police officer. Who are you and what are you doing here at this hour?" The light remained fixed on her as he approached.

She exhaled a shaky breath. A policeman. God had taken care of her despite her stupidity. *Thank you, Father.*

"Answer me, young lady." His deep voice rumbled.

"Uh...I'm Geneva Alexander. I'm...uh...with the USO."

"Right. And why would you be traipsing around the city unchaperoned in this seedy place at this hour of the night? Certainly not part of your USO responsibilities."

Tears welled in her eyes, and her face warmed. "No, sir. I was supposed to meet someone...er...a friend but he didn't come, and it got later and later. I have trouble seeing, and when it got so dark, I didn't know what to do."

He peered at her, seeming to determine if she was telling the truth. Would he believe her? Better to let him think she was fast rather than a traitor.

"The Miss Alexander who is a suspect in a murder investigation? That Miss Alexander?"

Geneva stomped her foot. "I'm only a suspect because you people aren't out looking for the real murderer. Thurgood Mayfield was a despicable, deceitful man, and I refused to marry him. But I had no reason to kill him. From what I can figure out there are lots of people interested in seeing him dead. Why don't you and your cronies investigate them?"

The office chuckled. "You're a feisty one. Let me give you some advice: if you want to be considered innocent, stop pussyfooting around in places where you don't belong, places where nice people don't come." He gestured down the sidewalk. "What is your address? To keep you out of further trouble, I'm going to escort you home." Wagging his finger at her, he said, "And don't let me catch you doing anything like this again, Miss Alexander."

##

Geneva unlocked the door to her room and slipped inside. Sighing, she tossed her pocketbook on the chair and shrugged out of her jacket. She hung it on the coatrack then ran her fingers through her hair. Tonight was a bust, but it could have been much worse. Listening to the policeman's lectures about putting herself in danger, staying out of the case, and letting the detective do his job was a small price to pay for her foolishness. No need to tell Devon about her escapade.

Turning toward the bed, she stepped on an envelope. The package was lumpy, and her name was scrawled in pencil on the outside. How had she missed that?

She bent to retrieve it, then went to her desk and opened the drawer. Rummaging through papers, receipts, pencils, and loose change, she searched for her letter opener. A gift from her friends for her last birthday, the curved blade featured a sterling silver handle engraved with her initials. Where was it?

Sighing, she closed the drawer and tore off the top of the envelope. She peeked inside and gasped. Her letter opener lay in the bottom with a note. Withdrawing the paper, she unfolded it.

WE SAW YOU WITH THE COP. DON'T TRY TO CONTACT US AGAIN. IF YOU TELL THEM OR ANYONE ELSE ABOUT US, IT WON'T GO WELL FOR YOU. WE KNOW WHERE YOU LIVE AND WE CAN EASILY FRAME YOU FOR MURDER. OR WORSE.

Chapter Fifteen

Heart racing, Geneva stood in front of the rehearsal hall grasping the handwritten note. After a sleepless night, the bus ride from her boarding house to the hall had been interminable. Her hands trembled, and she swallowed a sob. The black-marketers had been in her room. Touched her things. How had they gotten in without the landlady's knowledge? She froze. Would they really frame her for Thurgood's murder?

"Get a hold of yourself, young lady." She yanked open the door and marched inside. With any luck Devon was already at work. He would know what to do.

Her heels echoed as she strode through the building. She rounded the corner and nearly stumbled with relief. The light was on in his office. He was in. She hurried forward and stopped at the threshold.

Devon looked up and cocked his head. His forehead wrinkled as he dropped his pencil and rose to his feet. "Geneva, what are you doing here so early?"

Mutely, she held out the letter.

He circled the desk and took the paper. Concern filled his face. "Forgive my manners. Please, have a seat. You look distraught. Can I get you some water?" He drew her toward the chair, and she sank into it as her knees buckled.

"Thanks, but I couldn't drink anything right now. I didn't know who else to turn to. You said you'd help."

Seated in the chair next to her, he read the note then laid it in his lap. "No wonder you're upset. You must be terribly frightened. I'm glad you came to me."

She sagged in her seat. He was going to help her. Opening her pocketbook, she withdrew a handkerchief and dabbed the perspiration at her hairline then used it to wipe her damp palms. "What are we going to do? They think I know things, but I don't. That's why I wanted to meet them. Find out if Thurgood was in league with them. Now, they are threatening me. How do I solve this case? What do *I* know about catching a killer?" Her voice rose an octave, and she winced at the sound.

Reaching forward, he took her hands in his. "I promised you we'd tackle this thing together, but we shouldn't put ourselves in danger. However, there's no reason why we can't give the police a hand at finding new clues." Smiling, he tucked a stray strand of hair behind her ear.

His fingers grazed her skin, and her breath caught. Did he care for her in a special way, or did he treat all his entertainers with a gentle fondness?

Blinking, she pulled away. It was best to keep her distance. Even if he did like her, they could never be more than friends. He didn't deserve to be saddled with her and her eventual blindness. "Thank you, Devon." She spoke primly. "Where do we start?"

He dropped his hand. Face reddening, he cleared his throat, then pushed back his chair and stood. He pointed to the chalkboard on the wall. "Let's figure out what we already know and where the gaps are. How does that sound?"

"Like a great idea, but do you have time to do this? I should have thought of that before I came rushing in. You probably have more important things to do than helping the new girl get out of a jam."

"As a matter of fact, I don't, so let's get started."

She nibbled her lower lip. He was a good man. Why wasn't he married? Any woman would be lucky to have him.

"Geneva, are you ready?" His face held a question.

Now it was her turn to blush. She sat up straight and nodded. "I'm sorry. This is all so overwhelming."

"Would tomorrow after practice be better?"

"No, I'm fine. Really. The sooner we assemble the data, the sooner I can prove my innocence."

Devon rubbed his hands together then picked up a chalk stub. "Excellent." He drew two vertical lines, then wrote *Thurgood* on top of the left column. In the middle, he scribbled *Facts* and on the right *Questions*. Crossing his arms, he turned to face her. "First, we'll brainstorm what we know about your fiancé."

"He was never my fiancé."

"Right. Sorry."

She smirked. "You're forgiven."

He chuckled and pointed to the board. "Time's a-wasting, Miss Alexander."

"Thank you for trying to introduce some levity into this awful situation." She folded her hands and peered at the board. "Under Thurgood you can put womanizer. He made it quite clear during our conversation that he has had numerous…uh…liaisons."

The chalk scratched on the board as Devon wrote. "Okay, and I'll write black market with a question mark. His association with them seems strong. Also, what about his relationship with your family or other people you know?"

"I had assumed there were good feelings between them for Father to arrange our marriage, but Thurgood alluded to having information about my father that was unsavory. He may have threatened Father, perhaps even blackmailed him."

"But a daughter is everything to a man. Would he approve of your marriage to such a despicable person?"

Geneva shrugged. "It may have been the lesser of two evils."

"I hate to say this, Geneva, but blackmail would give your father motive."

She reared back in the chair. "No."

"We have to consider all possibilities." His voice was soft. "Did your father have opportunity? Did he come to Baltimore?"

Shaking her head, she said, "Not that I know of. Thurgood claimed Father sent him, so theoretically he was still in Philly. I could check with Mother. Put that under Questions."

"Good girl. Now, you're thinking. What else?"

"Write down his argument with Mr. Emery and the compact I found in his hotel room. Don't forget the handkerchief the police found. How did the killer get it, and who hates me enough to frame me?"

"All good questions." Devon snapped his fingers. "What about Thurgood's family? Didn't you tell me he has a sister? Would she be willing to share any information that might be useful?"

"I forgot about Florence. Does she even know about his death? She left home without telling her parents where she was going."

"How do you know that?"

"She also joined the USO. We saw each other the day we applied."

"I can find out where she is through the national office." He scrawled sister - USO under the Questions column. "We should also investigate his business relationships. I'll see what I can find out. Unfortunately, they would be more likely to speak with me since I'm a man."

Geneva rolled her eyes. "Irritating, but true. Once you find Florence, I can talk to her." She gestured to the board and sighed. "There's nothing under Facts."

"Don't worry. It's still early in the investigation. It makes sense there are more questions than certainties. Something will pop up."

A knock sounded.

Geneva and Devon turned toward the door where a man stood gripping his bowler in both hands.

The man bowed. "My name is Leon Kelly. I'm one of the desk clerks at the hotel. I'm so pleased to find you, Miss Alexander. I heard you were arrested and thought you were in jail, so I came to speak to Mr. Royal. I have information that may help you in finding who murdered that nasty Mr. Mayfield. I don't believe you committed the crime."

Geneva's hand flew to her throat. "What?"

Mr. Kelly nodded and tugged at his collar. "It was late, just before eleven o'clock, on the night he was killed. I know that because it was almost the end of my shift."

Devon narrowed his eyes at the man. "How do you know Miss Alexander?"

"I came to one of the shows and saw her. When she sings, there is such joy on her face. Then her picture was in the paper, and I recognized her."

"Fine, go on."

He dipped his head. "All right. Mr. Thurgood came into the lobby and sat in the corner farthest from the door. Moments later, a man came in that I know for a fact is a dealer in the black market. The man handed Mr. Thurgood a small box, like one would get from a jeweler. Before Mr. Thurgood turned away, I saw him open the box, but I couldn't see what was inside. He seemed unhappy with the contents, and the two men appeared to argue about the item. A few minutes later, the man held out his hand, and Mr. Thurgood slapped a thick envelope into it."

"How do we know you're telling the truth? Why didn't you go to the police with this information?"

A shadow passed over Mr. Kelly's face. "You'll just have to believe me. I don't trust the authorities. My son died in their custody, and no one ever took responsibility for the deed. If you're not careful, the same negligent police work will put Miss Alexander in jail for a crime she didn't commit."

Chapter Sixteen

Squinting against the sun's glare, Geneva shielded her eyes and lingered at the bottom of the stairs leading into the police station. The warmth of Devon's hand on the small of her back brought little comfort. If her peripheral vision were better she'd be able to see his face and discern his mood. Perhaps he'd only accompanied her out of pity.

She pressed her lips together to prevent the sigh in her chest from escaping. Dawdling was of no benefit. It was best to get this meeting over and done with. She squared her shoulders and climbed the steps.

Devon opened the door then followed her inside. He removed his fedora as they made their way to the front desk where a flame-haired sergeant sat scowling at a stack of paperwork. No doubt he would rather be fighting crime on the streets than shuffling reports.

"Excuse me, sir." Geneva's voice broke the silence. "I'm here to see Detective Lazarus. My name is Geneva Alexander."

The sergeant flicked his gaze between her and Devon several times before shoving a logbook and pencil toward them. "Sign in, then park yourself over there." He jerked his head toward several well-worn, wooden chairs lining the wall.

She scribbled her name on the sheet before handing the pencil to Devon who added his scrawl. Tucking her pocketbook under her arm, she turned toward the uncomfortable-looking seats and shook her head. She glanced at Devon. "I'll stand, thanks."

"I think that's best, but let's move to the window."

The sergeant scraped his chair back and stood. "Suit yourself. It might be a while." He lumbered through the doorway, and his footsteps faded.

Geneva stared out the smudged panes at the blur of activity on the street. Behind her, Devon paced. Would the detective be interested in the information she brought, or would he see it as an attempt to divert his attention from her as a suspect? Her stomached clenched. A wave of dizziness swept over her, and she braced herself against the wall.

Devon rushed over and wrapped his arm around her shoulder. "Perhaps you should sit."

She held up her hand. "I just need a minute. The detective needs to see a strong woman, not one cowed by fear and perceived guilt."

"Perceived or real, Miss Alexander?" Detective Lazarus's voice held contempt and judgment.

Her head whipped up, and she whirled toward him. Pulling away from Devon, she crossed her arms. "How about if we discuss this in your office, Detective? I have information you should find of value."

He narrowed his eyes and studied her. She refused to flinch or look away. Scowling, he gestured down the corridor. "As you wish, Miss Alexander. I assume you'll be joining us, Mr. Royal?"

"Absolutely."

Lazarus led them into his office and dropped into the chair behind his desk. Geneva eyed the rickety-looking ladder-back chairs before lowering herself onto the seat. Did the department have any chairs that were produced during this century?

"Where's that fancy lawyer of yours, Miss Alexander? Does he know you're here?"

"I will notify him about our conversation."

"You seem confident that I won't arrest you here and now."

Geneva bolted upright. "For what?"

"Impeding a homicide investigation. If you have information, as you claim, you've obviously continued to poke around on your own. I know about your little jaunt to the roller rink. Did you think the officer who found you wouldn't report the incident?"

Her face warmed, and she sagged against the chair. "I hoped he wouldn't." She peered at Lazarus through tear-filled eyes. "Are you going to incarcerate me?"

Devon leaned forward. "See here, Detective. You know Geneva didn't kill the rogue. Are you using her for bait or a diversion so the true killer will lower his guard? You can't keep threatening to arrest her. Either you have enough evidence or you don't."

Lazarus barked a harsh laugh. "Who are you to tell me what I can do? I can hold the threat of arrest over your pretty little girlfriend's head for as long as I want. If she's not guilty, she has nothing to worry about."

Devon frowned. "I wouldn't be so sure about that."

"Look—"

"Gentlemen, please stop!" Geneva struggled to her feet. "Detective, I apologize for getting in the way. I didn't mean to, how do you say it, impede the investigation. I'm simply trying to prove my innocence. Will you hear me out?"

"Sit down, Miss Alexander." Lazarus heaved a loud sigh. "I will listen to what you have to say, but I am serious that you must stop delving into this crime on your own. If you did not kill Mr. Mayfield…"

"I didn't."

The detective held up his hand. "Let me finish. As I was saying, if you didn't kill the man, and the real murderer feels that you are hot on his trail, I have no doubt he or she will strike again. Do you understand what that means? He or she could kill you to prevent being identified."

Geneva's heart raced, and her breath came in gasps. Her vision swirled, and firm hands pushed her head between her knees.

Devon whispered into her ear. "Breathe slowly. In. Out. In. Out. What happened to my strong, independent woman?"

His woman? Warmth filled her, and her head cleared. She pushed herself upright. Digging into her pocketbook, she pulled out her handkerchief and pressed it against her eyes long enough to absorb her tears. She shoved the cloth back into her bag and cleared her throat. Devon was right. She could do this.

"Forgive me, Detective Lazarus. I was momentarily overcome. It won't happen again. Are you ready to listen?"

He stared at her for a long moment, then dragged a pad of paper closer and grabbed a pencil from a chipped drinking glass. "This had better be good."

She nodded and recounted the desk clerk's visit. At the mention of the jewelry box exchange and angry words that followed, Lazarus's eyes widened, but he kept silent. When Geneva finished, she sat back and licked her dry lips.

Devon squeezed her hand. When she looked at him, he gave her an encouraging smile.

"That's quite a story, Miss Alexander. Why should I believe the man? He couldn't be bothered to report this to the police directly. What does that say about him?"

"He doesn't trust the police."

"Has he been a *guest* of ours?"

"No, but his son was and died in jail. Mr. Kelly says it's your fault."

"My fault? Who is this Mr. Kelly…wait…Leon Kelly?" Lazarus's face darkened, and he dropped the pencil. "His son was Andrew Kelly?"

Geneva shrugged. "I don't know."

"But it appears you do, Detective." Ice crystals coated Devon's voice. "Perhaps Miss Alexander does have a right to fear being unjustly accused or her case mishandled, after all."

Lazarus scrubbed at his face then steepled his fingers on the desk. "Not that I owe you an explanation, but I will set your mind at ease. Yes, Andrew Kelly died in our custody. He was a CO, a conscientious objector, and two of the officers on duty the night took exception to his *philosophy*. They claimed he fell down the stairs, but when we presented the medical examiner's evidence indicating he had been beaten, and that the blow to his head was made with a billy club, they confessed to the deed. They have been discharged and now sit in cells awaiting trial."

"How does that help Miss Alexander?" Devon asked.

"It proves that we take murder seriously, even when it is perpetrated by our own. Miss Alexander will get a fair shake. I will turn over every rock to determine who killed Mr. Mayfield." He raised his eyebrows. "Do you think you could convince Mr. Kelly to speak with me? We didn't find a jewelry box on Mr. Mayfield or in his room. Perhaps Kelly can give us further insight into where we might locate the item."

The pressure in Geneva's chest released. "So you believe me when I say I didn't kill Thurgood."

"Frankly, Miss Alexander, there appears to be a line forming of people who could have murdered the man, but I am not ruling anyone out at this time, including you. And I meant it when I said I would arrest you for impeding the investigation if you meddle."

Geneva trembled. The detective still suspected her. She had no choice but to continue the investigation on her own. *Would her efforts be successful before the killer found her?*

Chapter Seventeen

Thunder rumbled overhead, and the skies darkened with angry clouds. Geneva huddled under the east piazza of Independence Hall waiting for Devon. Not wanting to be overheard in the theater, she had invited him to sit in the square outside the famous building to discuss updates in their investigation. However, the weather put a damper on that. Would her plans fail as well?

Peering around the edge of the building, she scanned the men and women scurrying along Chestnut Street looking for Devon. None of the pedestrians glanced toward the historic, red brick structure flanked by Congress Hall to the west and Old City Hall to the east. Did they not appreciate the majestic bell tower that soared above them? Sword sheathed, the statue of John Barry stood guard at the other end of the square.

Lightning flashed. Rain poured from the heavens. She flinched and pressed closer to the brick façade. Checking her watch, she sighed. Had Devon changed his mind about helping her?

"Geneva!"

She turned toward the voice.

Devon waved from across the street. With the other hand, he clamped his fedora on his head as he dashed toward her. He ducked into the piazza and removed his hat. Shaking off the moisture, he grimaced. "What a day this has turned out to be. Sorry I'm late. The phone rang just before I left, and the call took longer than expected."

"Is everything all right?"

"It will be. One of our deliveries was held up coming out of Canada. We're on the same side in this war, you'd think the authorities would make it easy crossing the border."

"I didn't realize you did business outside the U.S. Is the delivery important?"

He shrugged. "Important enough. But I've got things under control."

Geneva studied his face. He seemed to be avoiding her eyes. The USO headquarters provided items that facilities couldn't get locally. What sort of product could he possibly be importing? He had been gracious since she arrived; an all-around good guy, but was he something other than he appeared?

Gesturing to the bench against the brick wall, he said, "We've got a murder to solve. Much more imperative than my problems. Let's figure out where we are so far."

A chill slithered up Geneva's spine as she sat on the unforgiving, wooden bench. Could she trust Devon? The stiff set of his shoulders and the wrinkle on his forehead said he was upset. Was she reading too much into his posture?

He dropped onto the bench and leaned toward her. "Geneva? You seem a million miles away. Everything is going to work out. We'll find the killer and prove your innocence."

She shrank back, and his face reddened. He ducked his head and rotated the damp fedora in his hands. "Uh, if you'd rather I didn't help you…"

"No…I mean yes, I'd like your assistance." She wrapped her arms around her middle and hunched into her coat. The conversation was not going as she had rehearsed in her mind.

A gust of wind drove the cold rain between the columns and into her face. Geneva gasped and jumped up from the bench. Scrubbing at her face with wet palms, she sputtered.

Devon reached into his pocket and yanked out a handkerchief. He wiped the dampness from her skin, his eyes dark with concern. With a wry smile, he handed her the damp linen. "I don't want to ruin your makeup, maybe you should take over. Are you all right?"

Their fingers met, and she shivered. Dipping her head, she pressed the cloth to her cheeks and forehead. Devon must think she looked frightful. Sighing, she pressed her lips together. What did it matter? He'd help her find Thurgood's killer, and that would be that.

"Geneva?"

She froze as she focused on the handkerchief in her hands. The blue plaid pattern was the same as Thurgood's. Hadn't he claimed they were specially made? How could Devon have an identical one? She didn't have the courage to ask him. Pinning a smile on her face, she pushed the cloth into his hands.

Maybe Thurgood had lied in an effort to seem important, and Devon's hankie was a coincidence. Or not. Only time would tell. Pushing that clue to the back of her mind, she lifted her chin. "I'm fine. You must be tired of rescuing me."

"Not at all. It's been my pleasure, although I've not done very much."

"That's about to change." She crossed her arms. "Now, let's compare notes, so we can determine our next step."

"Right." He tucked the handkerchief into his pocket and guided her back to the bench. "You'll be happy to know I've heard back from USO headquarters about Florence. She's here in Philly at the other USO facility."

"There's another location? I thought the one on Broad Street was the only location in the city."

"To be honest, I forgot about it. They're over on 30th Street."

Geneva's heart sped up. Hopefully Florence could shed some light on Thurgood's activities. "Can we go see her?" She climbed to her feet. "I've got enough money for bus fare. It wouldn't take us long to get there, and we could be back in time for tonight's rehearsal."

Devon laid his hand on her arm. "Not so fast. She's in the hospital. Apparently there was some sort of incident and the backdrop for one of their skits fell on her. Her arm is broken, and she has a concussion. They're keeping her for observation."

"How did it happen? Do they think it was an accident?" Eyes wide, she stared at him. "Maybe whomever killed Thurgood is now after his sister." Geneva's knees buckled, and she staggered against Devon.

He wrapped his arm around her shoulders and eased her onto the bench. "That's a big leap in logic. Let's not jump to any conclusions."

Devon released her, and she missed the warmth of his body. "What else could it be?"

"Clumsiness, ineptitude, or a simple mistake. We can't read more than that into the situation until we investigate further."

She sagged against the bench. "You're right. I'm jumping at shadows and seeing villains around every corner. Who else can we contact?"

Devon rubbed his jaw for a moment, then grinned. What about Thurgood's business partner? Surely he of all people knows what Thurgood was up to." He glanced at his watch. "It's too late now, but if we set out first thing tomorrow morning, we could be back by mid-afternoon. Plenty of time to get you into costume for the show.

An idea sprang to mind. Nodding, she tilted her head. "Would you mind giving back your handkerchief? The least I can do is wash it for you."

"You don't have to do that."

"I would feel better if you let me."

He shrugged and handed her the gaily-colored linen.

Did her innocence hinge on a small scrap of fabric?

Chapter Eighteen

The train shimmied and danced on the tracks as it hurtled south toward Baltimore. Geneva gazed out the window at the blurry landscape that shot past. Devon sat beside her, his head tipped back against the seat and his eyes closed. The car was full of passengers, mostly women and children. The muffled clickety-clack of the wheels melded with the buzz of conversation.

She glanced at Devon's profile, his normally animated face peaceful and still in sleep. The lines at the corner of his eye spoke of his penchant for jokes and laughter. A lock of dark hair fell over his forehead, and she stifled the urge to smooth it into place. How could she be drawn to him one minute and the next suspect him of killing Thurgood?

Sighing, she crossed her arms and looked away. *Dear Father, please guide our search. Detective Lazarus doesn't seem interested in finding the real killer. I don't know whether or not to trust Devon. Is he what he appears? Or does he deserve an Academy Award for his acting the part of a good Christian man?*

Cocking her head, she waited for an answer or a feeling that God was listening. Silence met her. She shook her head and hunched into the seat. Did He not care? Was He too busy with the war to bother with her minuscule problem? Perhaps to Him it was small, but if she couldn't prove her innocence, she would spend the rest of her life in prison, shredding her family's reputation. Her parents would never forgive her.

A baby cried out, and Devon's eyes flew open. "What was that?"

She smiled. "One of our tiny, fellow travelers is unhappy with the accommodations." Jerking her head toward the red-faced infant whose forehead was wrinkled in a deep frown, she shrugged. "Aren't we all? I could use a change of scenery myself."

He sat up and rubbed his face, then ran his fingers through his hair, causing it to spike in several directions. Again resisting the urge to fix the unruly strands, Geneva dug into her pocketbook and drew out her compact. She handed it to him and pointed to his head. "You're a bit travel-weary yourself."

Popping open the small makeup case, Devon peered into the mirror and shuddered. He smoothed his dark locks then turned to her and winked. "Better?"

Her lips turned up. "You are much more presentable, sir."

He dipped his head and grinned. "That is good news, m'lady. We must be presentable." He closed the lid with a snap and returned the compact. Climbing to his feet, he held out his hand. "I'm feeling a bit peckish. Would you care to accompany me to the dining car?"

Geneva grasped his fingers, and allowed him to help her rise. A tingle spread from the tips to her elbow. Did he feel that? She peeked in his direction as he released her hand. A dull flush bloomed on his cheeks, and he pressed his lips together. Apparently so.

"I could use a bite to eat myself." She slid between the seats, and he gestured for her to lead the way. The train rocked and swayed. She clung to each seatback as she traversed the narrow aisle.

Three cars later she swung open the connecting door and staggered into the dining car. Crisp, white cloths covered tables graced with carnation-filled vases guarded by uniformed porters. Silverware and crystal gleamed. Brass sconces and overhead lights brightened the mahogany paneled room. Green shades rolled above each window waited to shield passengers from the sun's rays as necessary. One could almost imagine there wasn't a war on.

Slipping into the nearest seat, Geneva laid her pocketbook on the windowsill. Devon dropped into the opposite chair.

A server arrived on silent feet. "Good afternoon, miss, sir." He proffered the menu card then filled their goblets with water. "I'm afraid we have a limited selection of entrées today. Rationing, you know."

Geneva frowned. In the blink of an eye, reality came crashing back. Life was not as difficult for the Americans as it was for the Europeans, but she longed for the day when her choices were not dictated by deprivation. "What's your recommendation?"

He bowed slightly. "It's a bit early for lunch, but the potato soup is quite filling, and we have a vegetable stew that has been popular. Both come with fresh-baked bread."

"The stew sounds wonderful. Do you have any coffee?"

"We do." He leaned closer and whispered, "But it's nothing you want to drink." He straightened. "May I recommend a cup of tea?"

"All right."

Devon returned the menus. "I'll have the same. Thank you, my good man."

Dipping his head, the waiter took the cards then made his way toward the galley.

"I appreciate you coming with me, Devon. Thurgood's partner would most likely not talk to me without your presence. Mr. Claymore is old-fashioned that way. A woman's place is in the home, and all that."

"It's my pleasure. I'm sorry for the reason we're spending so much time together, but getting to know you has been wonderful. You're not like other girls."

Geneva's chest tightened, and her face warmed. Why did she have to blush at the slightest provocation? He must think her a ninny.

Reaching across the table, he took her hand and stroked the back of it with his thumb. Her flesh tingled, and her stomach quivered. At this rate she'd never be able to eat her meal. "You flatter me, Devon. I'm a simple girl from Baltimore."

"That's what makes you special. I don't want all the razzmatazz I see in most of the girls. They're trying to be something they're not. You're down-to-earth and genuine. Hard to find in the entertainment field."

She sipped her water then set down the glass and rubbed at the condensation. "What about you? Are you a simple man? I don't know anything about you."

"Fair enough." He withdrew his hand and steepled his fingers. "I was born and raised in Manayunk which is only a few miles north of Philly. My father worked as a mechanic in one of the textile factories. He kept the machines running and managed to hold his job during the Depression, but his wages were reduced and we sometimes found ourselves in one of the soup lines."

"Oh, Devon. How awful."

He shrugged. "It wasn't as bad as all that, but I left as soon as I finished high school. I tried my hand at a bunch of jobs and ended up as a junior manager at the Earle Theater on Market Street. Have you ever been?"

"No. Coming to work at the USO is my first trip to the city."

"You're missing out. We'll have to see about going sometime. The biggest names in show business have appeared there. I met Eddie Cantor, the Dorsey Brothers, and Duke Ellington, just to name a few."

"Why leave that for the USO?"

He dropped his eyes and rubbed at the condensation on his glass. "After Pearl Harbor I tried to enlist, but got rejected because of my asthma. It's ridiculous really. I guess the military can afford to be choosy, so they decided they could win this war without me. I sulked for several months, and then a friend of mine suggested I could do my bit by keeping up troop morale. So I applied, and here I am."

"You've nothing to be ashamed of. Supporting the soldiers and sailors is important."

His face darkened, and he glared at her. "Not as important as killing those lousy Jerries."

Her smile faltered.

"I didn't mean to growl at you. I may have nothing to be ashamed of, but I'm often avoided by people. Girls won't date me, and older folks look at me with pity. It's as if they think I'm 4F on purpose."

"God has a reason for keeping you home."

Devon slumped in his chair. "I wish I knew what that was. I'm a believer, but it's been hard to sustain my faith with all that's happening in the world. How can God allow Hitler to become so powerful and take so many innocent lives? Does God care about mankind anymore or is He going to leave us to our own devices? If that's the case, we're doomed."

"He cares, and I think we'll ultimately win this war against evil. We may never understand why things happen. I mean, why did Thurgood have to die and why is God letting me be considered a suspect in his murder? I lie awake at night wondering what kind of good can come from this, and I get angry. Then in the light of day, I cling to the truth that He's holding me in His hand, and whatever happens will be okay."

"You're an amazing woman, Geneva. You have more faith than I ever could. Thurgood died because of something he did. I'm sure of it." He swallowed heavily and dropped his gaze. "I, ah, have something to tell you." He rubbed his jaw. "I knew him once. Not very well, and it was a long time ago."

Geneva bolted upright in her chair. "What?"

Devon nodded. "I'm sorry I haven't mentioned our association before now. We were both at Harvard studying business. We had a couple of classes together, and he barely gave me the time of day. He was too busy being big man on campus and ruining more than one life in the process."

Her eyes widened. Devon knew Thurgood. Why hadn't he told her? Did he have something to hide? He had kept that information from the police, too. "What do you mean?"

"I tried to get into one of the social clubs, and he blackballed me and a couple of the other guys. He said we weren't the *quality* individuals the club wanted in their ranks. What he meant was that we didn't have the right pedigree, but he made it sound like we were troublemakers." He barked a harsh laugh. "It didn't take long for word to get around. We were blamed for a number of pranks that we had nothing to do with. Then the Academic Dean's office was broken into, and President Josiah Quincy's walking stick was stolen. Thurgood suggested to his connections that I was part of the scheme."

"Were you arrested?" Geneva's voice was barely above a whisper.

"No, but I was summarily dismissed although there was no proof I was involved. The stick was later found in a closet, thanks to an anonymous tip." Devon's hands fisted, and his nostrils flared. "Thurgood was a despicable man, and he deserved what he got."

Geneva licked her lips and shuddered. Was Devon's anger at Thurgood strong enough for him to kill?

Chapter Nineteen

"Mr. Claymore is tied up. Please have a seat." The gray-haired secretary gestured toward the corner of the opulent room where a cordovan leather couch and two burgundy upholstered chairs nestled below a window draped with burgundy curtains. Potted plants graced the accent tables, and oil paintings covered the walls.

Geneva exchanged a glance with Devon who shrugged before guiding her to the sofa. He sank into one of the vacant chairs. She fiddled with the strap on her pocketbook and sighed. "Do you think he'll see us? Maybe we should have made an appointment."

"Nonsense. It's better to show up unannounced. He has to come out of his office at some point, and we'll be here."

Typewriter keys clacked in staccato rhythm, stifling any possibility of further conversation. Geneva clenched her fists and studied the pattern in the Persian rug at her feet. Why had her father's wealth been so important to Thurgood? He and his partner seemed to have plenty of money if their lobby was any indication.

A sharp buzz filled the room. The secretary pressed a button on the wooden box on her desk and spoke into it, "Sir?"

"Please clear my schedule. I'm leaving the office."

"Mr. Mayfield's fiancée is here with a Mr. Royal. They've asked to see you."

Silence.

"Mr. Claymore?"

"Yes, fine. I can spare a few minutes, but then I must depart for an appointment."

"Very good, sir." The woman rose and walked to the cherrywood door on one side of the foyer. Opening it, she said, "Mr. Claymore will see you now."

Geneva scrambled to her feet and hurried to the doorway before Mr. Claymore could change his mind. Devon was close behind her. They crossed the threshold, and she froze. Gaping, she surveyed the office. Dripping with crystal, sculptures, and art, the room's luxury outstripped that of the lobby.

Thurgood's partner stood behind a six-foot square gleaming mahogany desk, completely cleared except for a cobalt-blue Tiffany lamp. Mr. Claymore's black horn-rimmed glasses magnified his brown eyes. His charcoal-colored suit, complemented by a gray tie and matching pocket handkerchief, fit as if hand-tailored.

Claymore dipped his head in greeting. "Miss Alexander. How nice to see you, but your timing is unfortunate. I have an important commitment for which I cannot be late. I'm sure you understand."

Geneva blinked. "Uh, yes, well…"

"We won't take too much of your time, Mr. Claymore, but we have something important to discuss about your partner's murder. I'm sure *you* understand." Devon put a hand on the small of her back and nudged Geneva forward until they were directly in front of the desk.

A muscle in the man's jaw twitched as he glowered at them. "I've already spoken with the authorities. I don't owe you any sort of explanation."

"The police continue to pursue Geneva as a suspect. We'd like to provide them with the names of other people who might have had a motive to kill Thurgood."

Geneva sagged against Devon. Would this nightmare never end? "Please, Mr. Claymore. You've known my family a long time, since before I was born. Won't you help me?"

He peered at her over his glasses. "I'm a very busy man, Miss Alexander. Especially now that Thurgood is gone. I've had to take on his duties and his clients in addition to my own."

Her head throbbed and tears threatened. He made Thurgood's death sound like an inconvenience. Did the man have no compassion? "Mr. Claymore…"

"Look, Claymore, murder takes precedence over a business meeting. Wouldn't you say?" Devon scowled. "All we're asking for is a few minutes of your time. I'm sure if we went to the police and let them know you acted like you were hiding something, your schedule would get a whole lot more cramped."

"You wouldn't dare. I'm not hiding anything. That's preposterous."

Devon tugged at Geneva's arm. "Let's go. We want to get back in time to see Detective Lazarus before he leaves for the day."

"Wait!" Mr. Claymore dropped into his chair. He pulled out an engraved pocket watch and glanced at it. "You have fifteen minutes. That's truly all I can spare."

"So talk fast." Devon seated himself, and lifted his chin.

Geneva dug out her notepad and pencil. Flipping to a fresh page, she gazed at Mr. Claymore as she sat.

He huffed out a breath then settled his spectacles on the bridge of nose. "Frankly, Miss Alexander, you'll need several pages to list the people Thurgood angered. I had repeated conversations with him about the need to curb his arrogance in dealing with clients and associates. His—how shall I say it?—social interactions were also an issue."

"Why not fire the guy?"

Mr. Claymore shook his head. "He was a partner in the firm. I could have bought out his portion of the company, but I don't have that kind of liquidity at the moment."

He ran a finger around the inside of his collar. "You should put your father's name at the top of your list, Miss Alexander. I was stunned when he arranged the union between you and Thurgood. The two of them argued on a regular basis, and Thurgood seemed to have the upper hand. About three weeks ago while strolling with my wife, I came upon them in Federal Hill Park. We were exploring one of the many passageways under the park. The pair emerged from a shaft near the east end."

"Father grew up nearby, so he is quite familiar with the tunnels. But why would he meet Thurgood there?"

Shrugging, Mr. Claymore crossed his arms. "They were startled to see me, of course, and ceased all conversation, but your father did not look the least bit happy. He tried to convince me they had inadvertently stumbled upon each other, but I don't believe that to be true. Neither would discuss it with me, so I let it drop."

With a trembling hand, Geneva wrote her father's name on the paper. "What of your other partners? Was he disagreeable with them as well?"

"Yes, indeed. He was a risk taker, and often brought proposed investments to the company that didn't match our philosophy. When the recommendations were voted down, he would often get nasty. He seemed to take the decisions personally."

Devon raised his eyebrow. "Thin-skinned, was he?"

"Rather, yes, but also passionate about his work. He was not the easiest of men to get along with, but he was very good at what he did." Mr. Claymore's face darkened. "However, recently he put the company in a bind when he withdrew funds without approval. When I approached him about the situation, he laughed in my face and told me to relax." Claymore pounded the desk. "Relax! Do you know how much trouble we could get into with the authorities? There are regulations that must be adhered to. That sort of rogue behavior is unacceptable."

"What did the other partners say about this?"

"They don't know about it. When Thurgood promised to return the money, I agreed not to tell them about it."

Devon cocked his head. "And did he replace the money?"

"Part of it. The rest was due the day he died." Mr. Claymore pushed back his chair and stood. "That's all the time I have. I really must go."

"But, you've only given me my father's name. Surely there are others."

"That's the best I can do. As for cuckolded husbands and boyfriends, you'll have to search elsewhere for those names. I'm sorry to be so blunt, Miss Alexander, but that is the reality of it." He marched across the office and opened the door. Snatching his hat from a hook on the wall, he turned at the threshold. "Please see yourselves out."

Geneva gaped as he disappeared from view. "My father isn't speaking to me. We can't get any information from him. And if what Mr. Claymore said about the money is true, Father doesn't know about the unapproved withdrawal."

The secretary appeared in the doorway. "But I do."

Devon's head snapped up. "And you're willing to share the information?"

She nodded. "I'm sorry to say this, Miss Alexander, but the money wasn't for an investment like Mr. Claymore said." Her face pinked. "It was used to pay off the family of a girl Mr. Mayfield got in trouble. The girl's father was furious. Thurgood offered him ten-thousand dollars, and the man took the payment, but he made lots of threats. Perhaps he made good on one of them."

Chapter Twenty

Geneva dropped onto the hard, wooden chair backstage as chaos ebbed and flowed around her. Set movers wrangled backdrops into place with thuds and bangs. Musicians tuned their instruments while singers warmed up their voices and the air with soaring harmonies. The staccato tread of footsteps added hints of percussion.

Ethel appeared out of the gloom, her skirt fluttering as she walked. "Hey, honey, I've been looking for you. Why're you hiding out?"

"I thought it would be better to be alone. I'm not much company at present."

"That's hard to believe. You're always so positive."

"Not today. I'm beginning to wonder if I made a huge mistake. First, I joined the USO and my parents practically disowned me, then the man who I didn't want to marry was killed, and the police think I did it. I should never have come to Philly."

"Nonsense. Your parents will come around, and the real murderer will be found."

"I hope you're right. Devon…er…Mr. Royal and I have been trying to figure out who really did it, but all we've discovered so far are dead ends."

Eyes widening, Ethel grinned. "Devon, huh? Lucky you. He's swell looking."

"It's nothing like that. We're just friends. Besides, I'm not sure I can trust him. He said some things—"

"Sure, honey. Whatever you say." She waggled her eyebrows. "I wouldn't mind being *just friends* with him."

Geneva swatted Ethel's arm. "You goose."

"I got you to smile." Ethel sat in the vacant chair next to Geneva and clasped her hands in hers. "All kidding aside, I can help, too. Like it says in Ecclesiastes, 'And if one prevail against him, two shall withstand him; and a threefold cord is not quickly broken.' I can be your other cord."

Geneva's breath caught. "You're a believer?"

"Yeah, probably not the best witness on earth, but I'm a Christian. Have been since I was a little girl." She shrugged. "Maybe you're the reason I was assigned to Philly. I asked to go to Boston because my sister lives there."

"You think God is involved that closely in our lives?"

"Absolutely! He's beside us every step of the way. I'm sure it may not seem like it now, what with your fiancé's murder and all, but God has a plan, and it's gonna work out for the best."

"You'd really help me? You could be putting yourself in danger."

Ethel squeezed Geneva's hands. "We're in this together. I don't plan on taking any unnecessary risks, but surely we can dig around in places the police can't. I bet people who won't talk to the authorities would talk with us."

"That's true. Yesterday, Mr. Claymore's secretary gave us information that we never would have gotten if we hadn't gone to his office. Maybe I'm making assumptions, but I don't think she passed that clue on to Detective Lazarus."

"See? You're already ahead of the game."

"Ahead of what game?"

Geneva's head whipped up. Devon stood behind Ethel, his eyebrows drawn together. Her face warmed. She had been so engrossed in her conversation she never heard him approach.

"You shouldn't eavesdrop, Mr. Royal." Ethel wagged her finger at Devon. "It's not polite."

"If you don't want to be overheard, perhaps you shouldn't talk in a public place." Devon mimicked her stance and flashed a grin. "Seems like you girls are being awfully secretive. Anything I should know about?"

Ethel looked at Geneva. "Should we tell him?"

Taking a deep breath, Geneva nodded. "In for a penny. In for a pound."

"Fine." She grinned at Devon. "I'm the newest partner in the sleuthing team of Alexander and Royal. I'm going to help get to the bottom of this murder."

"Are you, now?"

"Yes, sir. Geneva is my friend, and I'm not going to let her go to jail for something she didn't do. I can get people to tell me just about anything." She put her hand on her hip, tilted her head, and batted her eyelashes. "On account of I'm so charming."

Devon chuckled. "Yes, you are, but we'll need to divide and conquer. Three of us is a bit of a crowd to question someone."

Ethel's face fell. "You're right, but I don't want to be left out."

"You won't be. I have a very important task for you." He glanced over his shoulder then back at Ethel. "I need you to chat up the girls. Find out what the other troupe members saw or heard around the time of the argument and what they told the police. See if they witnessed Thurgood after he left the theater, at the hotel, or anywhere else he might have been after the altercation."

She gave a mock salute then hugged Geneva. Peeking at her watch, she jumped up. "We've got an hour before the performance starts. No telling how many people I can natter with. Take care of our girl, Mr. Royal." Ethel ducked behind the curtain, and her footsteps faded.

Geneva sighed. *Will this really work out, Lord? Will I be proven innocent? Or is it your plan to incarcerate me?*

Devon sat in Ethel's empty chair. "If anyone can ferret out information, it's Ethel. The others love her." He nudged Geneva's shoulder. "But enough about her. I searched you out because I have news. Florence Mayfield has recovered enough to speak with us. She's not due to be discharged for several more days. Do you want to head to the hospital tomorrow?"

"That *is* news. How did you find out?"

"I called in a favor. A friend of a friend is a nurse there."

"Isn't she breaking the rules by telling you about Florence?"

He shook his head. "She didn't give me specifics about her condition, only that she's been moved to a regular room."

Geneva nibbled her lower lip. Would Florence be able to shed any light on her brother's activities or would she clam up despite their falling out? And what about Devon? He had been so kind and seemed genuinely interested in helping her, but his handkerchief gave her pause. Why would he have one identical to Thurgood's? He claimed his were specially made for him. Had Devon stolen it from Thurgood after killing him? Was the incident at college with the two of them enough motive for Devon to murder?

Her stomach clenched, and perspiration broke out along her hairline. Too many unanswered questions.

"Geneva?"

She blinked and turned to Devon. "This is so overwhelming. I don't know what to do."

He reached for her hand, and she drew back. Surprise flitted across his face. "We'll take this one day at a time. We could take the nine-thirty bus if you wanted to arrive when visiting hours start at ten o'clock. Or we could wait until after lunch if you'd like to sleep in after tonight's performance. It's up to you."

"What if I want to go by myself?"

"Uh...that would be fine, but I figured you might want company. As you said, you're overwhelmed."

"To be honest, Devon, I don't know whether to trust you or not. You withheld the fact that you knew Thurgood in college and that there were ill feelings between the two of you. What else haven't you told me?"

"Nothing. There's nothing else. And I didn't tell you about Thurgood because it was a very long time ago. It has nothing to do with his murder."

Willing her knees not to buckle, she rose and gripped the back of the chair. "It has everything to do with the case. It's a motive for killing him. Surely you see that."

His face darkened. "No, I don't. We were college kids. It was a long time ago." He reached for her then pulled back and jammed his hands into his pockets. "Listen, Geneva, I care about you. A lot. More than I should as your director, and I want to help you get out of this mess. I hope you'll let me. That you'll believe me when I say I didn't kill Thurgood."

She rubbed her forehead. Should she believe him? He had been a gentleman since their first meeting. Perhaps she was jumping to conclusions. If they took the bus, they'd be in public. She would be safe, wouldn't she? *Lord, help me.*

"Miss Alexander? Where are you? I was told you were here." Detective Lazarus's voice echoed through the vacant theatre.

Geneva flinched. *Is this you helping me, God?*

She followed Devon to the edge of the platform, and he waved. "Onstage, Detective. But frankly, Miss Alexander doesn't have time for you. She needs to get into costume for the performance. In fact, our audience should be here any minute."

Lazarus paused at the bottom of the steps. "She needs to make time. I'm conducting a murder investigation."

"We're well aware of that, but she is an integral part of tonight's acts. Do you want to explain to our troops why we have to do an abbreviated show because you couldn't wait until after the performance to speak with one of their favorites?"

Scowling, the detective blew out a loud breath. "Going to play hardball, are you?"

"Call it what you will, but my first responsibility is to the men who are fighting for our freedom. I respectfully ask you to wait until after the production. Who knows? You may even enjoy it."

"Fine." Lazarus seemed to speak through gritted teeth. "But rest assured, Miss Alexander, I'll be watching you the entire time and will expect you to meet me *immediately* following the show. Understood?"

Chapter Twenty-one

The forest-green curtain came down on silent pulleys, the hem's gold fringe dancing in the muted light. Just before the fabric blocked her view of the applauding audience, Geneva caught sight of Detective Lazarus. His ramrod posture and clenched hands on his lap told her what she couldn't see on his face. He did not enjoy the performance and couldn't wait to arrest her for a crime she didn't commit.

When the curtain rose to shouts of "Bravo," Geneva executed a wooden curtsy along with the other performers. Would this be her final show? Her last evening as a free woman? Shuddering, she rubbed her arms and locked her trembling knees to keep from falling. The curtain lowered, and the back stage lights came on. She squinted against the glare.

Ethel rushed to her, forehead wrinkled in a frown. "Are you okay, honey? You don't look so good."

"I—"

Sweaty stage hands tromped across the boards amid the cobalt-blue dressed dancers who trotted off stage. Someone bumped into her from behind, and Geneva stumbled. Firm hands grabbed her shoulders. She remained upright. Her skin tingled at the warmth seeping through her sleeves.

"I've got you." Devon's voice rumbled.

How did her body know before she did that it was Devon who held her? "Thank you. I'm fine, now."

His brown eyes seemed to search her face, seeking the truth. "Are you sure?"

She pasted on a smile. "Not really, but I will be. Can you stall the detective? I'd like to change into my street clothes."

Ethel winked. "It would be my pleasure to take that responsibility."

"You'll just have to find another task, missy." Detective Lazarus strode toward them, his trench coat flapping behind him. He pointed at

Geneva. "When I said *immediately,* that's what I meant. I allowed you to perform. Now, it's time for you to answer my questions."

Hands on hips and lips set in a pout, Ethel moved between Geneva and the officer. "I don't see how waiting a few minutes will hamper your interrogation. She already told you she'd help. Now, why don't you prove me wrong that you're not a gentleman and let Geneva change out of her costume?"

Lazarus shook his head. "This is a murder investigation, not a social call."

The left-wing curtain swayed, and the well-dressed, portly figure of Rolf Zelinsky appeared.

Geneva glanced at Devon who wore a satisfied grin on his face. "Devon?"

"I telephoned your lawyer during the show. Mr. Zelinsky should be with you any time you're being questioned by the police." Devon glared at Lazarus. "I'm sure the detective would have gotten around to reminding you of that."

His mouth set in a thin slash, Lazarus gave a curt nod.

"Nice to see you again, Miss Alexander." Mr. Zelinsky smiled, and his teeth showed bright against his bushy, black mustache. His navy-blue, pin-striped suit peeked out from his open, black cashmere overcoat. He gripped a worn, leather briefcase in one hand, his bowler in the other.

Geneva licked her lips and heaved a soft sigh. Devon had contacted her attorney. Surely he would prevent any sort of miscarriage of justice. Wouldn't he?

Mr. Zelinsky's gaze swept the group and came to rest on Detective Lazarus. "A compromise is in order. We understand the imperative nature of the case. In light of that, Miss Alexander will relinquish the opportunity to change her attire, if you will move this conversation to a private location within the theater where she can be seated in comfort. Of course, I will be present during the discussion."

The muscle in the detective's jaw twitched as he glared at the lawyer. Geneva held her breath. Would he agree to the terms?

Detective Lazarus swung his gaze at Devon. "Where would you suggest we meet?"

"There's a room downstairs with a couch and some comfortable chairs. I'll show you the way." Devon gestured toward upstage right.

"After you." Lazarus made an exaggerated bow.

Devon tucked Geneva's hand in the crook of his arm and leaned close to her ear. "Mr. Zelinsky will ensure this meeting is handled by the book. If Lazarus had a solid case against you, he'd have arrested you prior to the show. He's fishing. Don't let his overbearing manner get to you."

Trust him, My child. He's a good man and has your best interests at heart. As do I.

Geneva sagged against Devon and gripped his arm. He patted her hand, and she bowed her head, allowing him to lead her downstairs. *Thank you, Father. Forgive my unbelief. Help me rest in You and Your plan.* Warmth filled her. Straightening her spine, she lifted her chin.

She tugged Devon closer and said in hushed tones, "With the detective breathing down our necks, there's not much time to talk, so I'll say this quickly. I'm going to go out on a limb and trust you. We'll visit Florence together tomorrow, but I also want to follow up with the family who was paid off for their daughter's situation. Can you make the necessary arrangements, please?"

He responded with an imperceptible nod, and she pressed her free hand against her throat. Her pulse slowed beneath her fingers. If only she could get the squadron of crop dusters in her stomach to stop doing barrel rolls.

When they reached the room, Devon swung open the door, and Ethel grabbed Geneva in a one-armed hug. She murmured, "I'll keep gabbing with the girls and let you know what I find out." Cocking her head at Lazarus, she dropped into a mock curtsy. "I'll leave you to it, Detective. I have much to do before the night is over." She pivoted on her heel, and with an exaggerated swaying of her hips, she retraced her steps and disappeared around the corner.

Geneva lowered herself one of the lumpy cushions of the blue floral couch and crossed her ankles. Smoothing her skirt, she laced her fingers and laid them in her lap. Devon stood by her side, his hand resting lightly on her shoulder. With a grunt, Mr. Zelinsky wedged his girth into one of the vacant Queen Anne chairs.

Detective Lazarus leaned against the doorjamb and ran a hand over his Brylcream-slicked hair. He pinched the bridge of his nose and took a deep breath. "All right, Miss Alexander. Let's get on with this."

"I'm ready, Detective."

"First, I apparently need to remind you to leave this investigation in my hands. I received a call from Mr. Claymore. He indicated you went to see him and demanded that he give you the name of anyone he suspected had a motive for killing your fiancé. You could impede the case if you don't stay out of it. Do you understand?"

Geneva pressed her lips together and nodded.

"Good." He pulled a pencil and small, spiral-bound notebook from his breast pocket. "Now, what are the names Claymore gave you?"

"I beg your pardon?"

"I need the list of names Thurgood's partner gave you."

She sighed and shook her head.

"He didn't say anything?"

"He—" Geneva's voice broke, and she cleared her throat. "Only one—my father. He said there were others...husbands...who might have a reason to do Thurgood in, but he didn't know who they were." She'd keep the clue from Mr. Claymore's secretary to herself. She understood the detective's threat, but that didn't mean she had to obey him.

"Your father, eh? That puts an interesting spin on things. What do you know about his relationship with Thurgood?"

She frowned. Unwilling to share her theory that Thurgood might have been blackmailing her father, she said, "Not much. It must have been good for him to consider marrying me off to the man."

"Don't talk to your father about this. I'll pay him a visit."

"That won't be a problem. My father and I aren't on speaking terms at the moment. He took exception to my disagreeing to the union. And he is most unhappy with my decision to join the USO. He's still rather Victorian in his beliefs."

"I see. Well, we've followed up on the engagement ring. We were able to get into Thurgood's safety deposit box at the bank and found the item along with a receipt for the purchase. We contacted the jeweler, and he confirmed it was a legitimate sale."

Devon cocked his head. "Then why did they argue?"

"Thurgood had the ring custom made and claimed there were flaws in it, so he wouldn't pay the agreed-upon price. The man offered to correct the defects, but your fiancé said he'd take the piece off the man's hands at a lower price, and if that wasn't acceptable Thurgood would ensure everyone knew about the man's shoddy workmanship."

"That sounds like something Thurgood would do. There probably isn't anything wrong with the ring," said Geneva.

"There's not. We took it to another jeweler, and he inspected it. Said it was exquisite, and he couldn't find any blemishes on it." Detective Lazarus narrowed his eyes. "Was Thurgood in the habit of giving you gifts—flowers, candy, jewelry?"

Geneva barked a harsh laugh. "Thurgood loved no one but himself, and least of all me. That is why I refused to marry him. I don't need to be taken care of, and I will not marry a man I don't love or who doesn't love me. He made it perfectly clear he was offering a marriage of convenience, although certainly not convenient for me. He only gave me an item when it seemed to be in his best interest. He made sure there was an audience when he presented me with anything."

"You didn't answer my question. What sort of gifts did he give you?"

"A few bouquets, a book of poetry, and a bracelet. Nothing of great value."

"What did the bracelet look like?"

"A thin gold chain with a heart charm. There was a tiny diamond in the center of the heart. Frankly, it seemed a gift better suited to a young girl, not a grown woman."

"So, nothing expensive?"

"Get to the point, Detective." Mr. Zelinsky rolled his eyes. "Miss Alexander has already indicated what sort of presents the deceased gave her."

"Fine." Detective Lazarus dug into his pocket and withdrew a diamond-and-emerald-encrusted bracelet. He dangled it from his fingers, and the half-carat stones glittered in the light. "This was also in the safety deposit box."

Geneva gasped.

He raised his eyebrow. "It appears you are familiar with this piece. Care to tell me about it, Miss Alexander?"

She stared at the detective, her mouth working, but unable to speak.

Devon stroked her hair, and she turned toward him, tears welling in her eyes.

"Miss Alexander, I don't have time for your theatrics. What do you know about this bracelet?"

Shifting her wide-eyed gaze back to the detective, she whispered. "It belongs to my mother. She thought she lost it while at a company function several months ago."

Chapter Twenty-two

Gliding along the Route 40 bypass in a leather-seated Buick was a welcome change from the smoke-filled, crowded bus that wobbled and bumped over the macadam. Geneva was content to use public transportation from Baltimore's Penn Station, but Devon insisted on paying for a cab. Truth be told, she appreciated his generosity.

She straightened her skirt and perused the brick row-house on Bel Air Road where they would find the young woman and her family who had been paid off by Thurgood. Five concrete steps led up to each of the three identical homes that stood shoulder to shoulder. Three pairs of narrow, single-pane windows seemed to watch her from above the wrought iron screen doors. Crowned with peeling, cream-colored dentil molding, the structure held the tired air of a trio of down-on-their-luck society girls.

The curtain in one of the upstairs windows of the center house fluttered, and a young woman pressed her face to the glass. She smiled and waved before disappearing from view. Moments later, she pushed open the screen door and shielded her eyes from the glare of the noon sun. "Are you Mr. Royal and Miss Alexander who called last night?"

Trying not to stare at the young woman's pregnant belly that strained against the yellow-and-pink floral dress, Geneva nodded.

Devon cleared his throat. "Is your father at home?"

She gestured for them to enter. "He's in the kitchen just finishing his lunch and won't be happy that I showed myself at the door, but I can't be bothered with what the neighbors think. It's not like we live in Riverside or Federal Hill."

"Thank you for seeing us on short notice." Geneva ascended up the stairs and stepped into the house with Devon close on her heels. "We'll try not to take too much of your time."

"Time is something I have plenty of." She stroked her swollen middle. "Until this baby decides he or she is ready to enter this world, I don't go anywhere. It's nice to have company." She extended her arm. "By the way, I'm Thelma Flanders."

Geneva grasped her hand. "I'm Geneva."

Thelma gestured toward a faded brown sofa littered with gold-and-green throw-pillows. "Please, have a seat. Would you care for a glass of lemonade?"

"No, thank you." Devon shook his head. "We'll be going to lunch after our visit."

She nodded and lowered herself into one of two vacant walnut cane chairs. The wood creaked in protest, and she blushed.

"Wouldn't you prefer the couch, Miss Flanders?" Devon remained standing.

"You're very kind, but the cushions swallow me whole, and I have difficulty getting up."

Heavy footsteps approached, and a tall, lanky man with a mop of graying hair appeared in the doorway of the living room. Large ears poked out through his shaggy curls. "Welcome to my home. I'm Lyndon Flanders. You must be Miss Alexander and Mr. Royal."

"Yes, sir. Thank you for your willingness to speak with us," said Devon.

Mr. Flanders wiped his forehead with a handkerchief. "Has my daughter offered you refreshments on this hot day?"

"Yes, sir. We declined."

"Very well, then let's begin." He stroked his daughter's hair before seating himself in the vacant cane chair to her right. His mouth twisted, and a frown wrinkled his forehead. "You wish to discuss Thurgood Mayfield."

"Yes, sir." Geneva kneaded her fingers then slid them under her legs to keep them still. She tipped her head toward Thelma. "We know this is a delicate matter, but it is important to find out the extent of your contact with him in recent days."

"There hasn't been any." Mr. Flanders massaged his jaw. "I went to his office about three months ago when my daughter came to me about her condition. I demanded that he do right and marry her. He refused and offered me a large sum of money to take care of the situation and go away quietly. We…uh…argued, but in the end, I realized that a union with that man would be wrong. I agreed to the payment, and he said he had to move some money around but that he would make good on the promise. About a week later I received a cashier's check for ten-thousand dollars."

Devon leaned forward. "You haven't spoken with Mr. Mayfield or gone to see him within the last few days?"

"No. I just told you I haven't. Why don't you believe me?"

"Because Thurgood has been killed, and you have a motive."

"Mayfield is dead?" Mr. Flanders jumped up from the chair and began to pace. "When did this happen?"

"Two weeks ago, today," said Devon.

Geneva blinked. Had it really been only fourteen days since this nightmare began? It seemed like a lifetime.

Flanders stopped behind Thelma and put his hands on her shoulders. "If you're suggesting I had something to do with his death, you'll have to look elsewhere. I'm glad the man is dead, now he can't harm another young girl. But I had nothing to do with his murder. My daughter and I were at the hospital." He pinked. "Thelma was in a bad way. We thought she was losing the baby."

"Can you give us the name of the hospital?" Devon sounded skeptical.

"Maryland General on Madison Street. My name will be on the emergency room register."

"You seem to be doing better, now, Miss Flanders. I'm glad," said Geneva.

"I am. The doctor didn't put me on bed rest, but I do have to take it easy." Thelma reached up and patted her father's hand. "I would not have wished for this pregnancy to happen, and I'm ashamed that I allowed myself to be sweet-talked by Thurgood, but God is making something good of this."

Geneva widened her eyes. How could anything associated with Thurgood be good?

##

The astringent stink of chemicals flavored the air as Geneva entered Pennsylvania Hospital. Fatigue clung to her muscles as she tromped toward the front desk. The one hour train ride back to Philly from

Baltimore had seemed much longer as she reviewed the conversation with Thelma and her father. Other than confirming his alibi at Maryland General through some smooth talking by Devon, the trip had been a waste of time. One less suspect, but no additional clues.

Behind the desk sat a snowy-haired woman dressed in a somber, gray dress. Round, tortoiseshell glasses surrounded her eyes. She looked up at Geneva and Devon, her pale lips pinched in a tight grimace. "May I help you?"

"Yes, ma'am. I'm here to visit Florence Mayfield."

The woman's gaze flicked between the two of them. "Miss Mayfield is in serious condition. Only family members are allowed to see her at this time."

Geneva swallowed and squared her shoulders. "I was engaged to her brother before he…uh…passed away." *God, forgive my lying.*

"And this young man is…?"

"Devon Royal. He escorted me from Philadelphia."

Sliding the registration book toward Geneva, the receptionist frowned. "Please sign in. You have fifteen minutes." She waved toward the wooden chairs lining the white walls. "Mr. Royal, you may wait over there."

"Yes, ma'am." He squeezed Geneva's hand in a reassuring gesture, and the receptionist raised an eyebrow.

Devon stared at the woman until she broke eye contact. Pointing to the hallway on her left, she said, "Go down this corridor, and Miss Mayfield's room is the third door on the right. If you're not back in fifteen minutes, I will send a nurse to get you."

Her stomach fluttering, Geneva nodded then followed the directions to Florence's room. She stood in the doorway for a moment and took a deep breath. Would her friend help or would this visit also be a wasted trip? Wiping damp palms on her skirt, she walked toward the bed.

Florence turned, and a wan smile broke out on her face. "Geneva, what a nice surprise. How did you know I was here?"

"I needed to speak with you, and my…er…boss spoke with the people at USO headquarters, and they told him where you were assigned. When he contacted your post, they informed him of your injury." Geneva patted Florence's shoulder. "What happened? Do the doctors say you're going to make a full recovery?"

"I was rehearsing when one of the back drops fell and knocked me over. It hit my head and banged me up a bit. I've got a concussion, so they're keeping me for observation. With any luck, I'll be out of here in few more days. I'm bored to death." A shadow crossed her face, and her lower lip trembled. "I'm assuming you heard about Thurgood."

"Yes, how are you holding up?"

Florence shrugged. "I'm sad for him. He didn't used to be so awful, you know, arrogant and domineering. When we were growing up, he would play with me no matter what I wanted to do. He would participate in my tea parties or read me stories. When we got older, he'd take me to the pictures. That all changed when he came home from college." She cocked her head. "I know you didn't love him, but I thought you'd at least attend the funeral."

"I should have for you and your family, but I couldn't. The police were watching me. They still are. That's why I'm here. I don't mean to burden you with my troubles, but they think I killed him, and I have to prove that it wasn't me."

"The police suspect you killed Thurgood?" Florence tried to push herself upright and winced. She flopped against the pillows, her face white. "Did you give them reason to think that?"

"No!" Geneva dropped into the vacant chair and clenched her hands. "We had an argument the night before he died. He came to the rehearsal hall and demanded that I go home with him. He left, and I thought that was the end of it. He was killed sometime that night, and one of my handkerchiefs was found underneath his body. The police say that puts me at the scene, but I wasn't there. I didn't do it."

"Then why did they find your hankie?"

"That's just it. I don't know, but I'm going to find out." She grasped Florence's hand. "You believe me, don't you? Will you help me?"

Florence stared deep into her eyes for a long moment.

Geneva waited, heart skittering. She couldn't say anything. Her friend would have to make up her own mind. *Please, God, help her see my innocence.*

"Yes, I believe you, but I don't know how I can help you." She gestured to her prone form. "I'm useless until they spring me from this joint."

"You don't need to go with me, just answer some questions." Geneva glanced at the watch pinned to her bodice. "We don't have much time. I was only given fifteen minutes for our visit."

"What could I possibly know?"

"Perhaps more than you realize. Can you think of anyone who would want to harm Thurgood or that he argued with?"

Lost in thought, Florence tapped her index finger on her front teeth. Moments later, she snapped her fingers. "About a month ago, I heard him on the telephone with someone. I don't know who it was, but it could have been Mr. Claymore. He often came for dinner, and the two of them would bicker. From what I could hear, it seemed Thurgood owed him a significant amount of money because of some sort of business deal that went sour. At first, Thurgood tried to placate the man with promises to recoup the man's money with another investment, but that didn't seem to be going over well. A couple of times I could hear the man's voice coming out of the receiver, and he sounded very angry."

"Angry enough to kill?"

Florence's eyes widened in her ashen face. "Yes." Her voice was barely above a whisper. "He said he'd make sure Thurgood didn't get away with any more fraudulent schemes."

Chapter Twenty-three

The platform vibrated as a troop train thundered into the station. Wind from the hurtling behemoth whipped Geneva's hair around her face. She waved away the dust and debris that flew into the air, and coughed. The oily tang of diesel fuel mingled with sweet perfume as she threaded her way through the crowd of USO girls toward the front of the train. Porters shouted over the din of men's voices and women's giggles.

She had decided to join the girls who accompanied the men on the buses from Penn Station to the USO facility—anything to keep her mind off Thurgood's murder and the investigation.

Jostled and pushed, she escaped to the edge of the mob. Taking a deep breath, she folded her hands and waited for the chaos to dissipate. Ethel and one of the new performers appeared among the sea of faces. Geneva waved, and they squeezed between the crush of bodies to reach her.

Ethel dabbed at her face with a lace-edged handkerchief. "What a scorcher. On days like this, I miss the cool weather we have in the mountains of West Virginia." She huffed a large breath. "Geneva, I don't think you've met Claire yet. She's from down your way somewhere."

Claire smiled. "Nice to meet you. Ethel said you're from Philadelphia. I'm from King of Prussia."

"Small world, isn't it? I visited Valley Forge National Park numerous times with my friends. We love the hiking trails."

"I'm not much of a hiker, but my husband and I often picnicked in the fields. I wonder if we were ever there at the same time as you. Crazy to think about that, huh?"

"You're married. Did your husband get called up?"

"Yes, right after Pearl Harbor." Claire's mouth turned down for a second, then her face brightened. "He's Navy, and if I'm interpreting his letters correctly, he's somewhere in the Pacific. Hopefully, some nice

USO girl is boosting his morale. That's why I joined. Seemed only fair to help someone else's husband or son."

Geneva's heart tugged. What would it be like to have a man who loved her to write letters to? Just because she hadn't wanted to marry Thurgood didn't mean she was averse to marriage. Were a husband and children in her future? *What are Your plans, Lord?*

"Are you married, Geneva?" Claire tilted her head.

"No. Perhaps someday." If she could find a man who didn't mind a woman who would eventually go blind.

"God will provide a mate, don't you think? That's how it happened with my Ian. I wasn't even looking to get married."

Shrugging, Geneva murmured a noncommittal sound. A tall, angular enlisted man sauntered toward the three of them, and she gasped. "Orville Harcourt, is that you?"

He grinned and swept her into a tight hug before setting her down. "Ginny, you're so grown up. I haven't seen you since we graduated high school."

Her face warmed, and she tucked a stray hair behind her ear. "What a thing to say. Our school days are long behind us. And I go by Geneva, now."

He tugged at his uniform jacket. "You'll always be Ginny to me. I guess you're right about how long it's been. Who knew I'd be wearing one of these?" Glancing over his shoulder, he asked, "What are you doing at the station? Is your husband here?"

She shook her head. "No husband. Guess I haven't found the right guy. I'm with the USO."

"That's swell. You always could sing like an angel." He chucked her under the chin. "Glad to see you using your talent instead of being cooped up at home."

Ethel jabbed Geneva with a sharp elbow and batted her eyelashes. "So, you going to stand around and jaw all day or introduce me to your dreamboat friend."

Claire giggled, and Geneva rubbed her rib where Ethel had made contact. Grinning, Orville tucked a thumb under each armpit and rocked back on his heels. "She thinks I'm a dreamboat."

Geneva rolled her eyes and slapped Orville's shoulder. "Apparently her vision is worse than mine."

"Says you." He clicked his heels then bowed. "Corporal Orville Harcourt at your service, miss."

Ethel executed an exaggerated curtsy. "Ethel Kettler, and this is my friend Claire O'Shaughnessy. Would you like to escort us to the bus, Corporal?"

"It would be my pleasure." He crooked his arms. "Unfortunately, I only have two arms available, but I can solve that problem." Pursing his lips, he produced a piercing whistle. "Hey, Stockbridge. Come lend a hand."

A stocky, curly-headed young man trotted over to them. "How may I be of service?"

"Quit being so serious, Stockbridge. This is my friend Ginny…er…Geneva, and two of her USO sisters. I need help escorting them onto the bus, and I thought you were just the man for the job. Girls, this is Private Billy Stockbridge."

Billy snapped a salute and crooked his elbow. "I'd be delighted to volunteer for this mission, sir." He winked at the women. "He's not really my superior, but he likes it when I call him sir."

"Keep it up, Stockbridge, and I'll find another *volunteer.*"

Geneva tucked her hand into Billy's arm and laughed at the easy banter between the two men. They were headed to a combat zone soon, and yet their spirits seemed high. Without knowing it, they had boosted her morale. She watched Orville flanked by Ethel and Claire saunter toward the bus. The girls giggled and fawned over him. That wasn't her style, but she'd do what she could to make Billy feel special.

"Have you known Orville long, Geneva?"

"Long enough. His family moved to Baltimore when he was a sophomore in high school. He had trouble fitting in and I did too, so we gravitated toward each other. Nothing romantic. Just pals. We lost track of each other after graduation."

"I imagine it's swell to see him again. What are the chances of that happening?" He peered down at her. "Do you have a fella?"

"No, but I'm not looking for one." His face fell, and she patted his arm. "But we can be friends, just like I am with Orville. Isn't that better?"

He looked skeptical.

"Before you shove off give me your address, and I'll make sure you get letters from lots of the girls. Then you can have your pick." She patted his shoulder. "Now how did you meet Orville?"

They climbed onto the bus and found seats across the aisle from Orville and the girls. Billy removed his cap and folded it over his belt. He settled into the chair and laced his fingers. "He was my roommate at University of Maryland. He studied chemistry, and I was an economics major, but we got on thick as thieves. We both got jobs in Washington, DC, and when he told me he was going to enlist, I decided to join him. We've been lucky so far to be in the same unit."

"I'll bet you have lots of stories."

Poking the back of Billy's head, Orville frowned in mock anger. "Don't spill the beans, or I'll have to share some bits and pieces about you."

"I was only going to tell her about the times you were a hero."

Orville snorted a laugh. "Yeah, there are so many of those."

Billy chuckled then sobered up. "Even before you enlisted. How about when you saved Leona Ferguson from old octopus arms?"

"You would have done it too."

"But I didn't, and I know she'll be forever grateful to you."

Waving a hand in dismissal. "Enough about me. Why don't you girls tell us about the USO? This will be our first stop at one. Will we really see some of the big Hollywood stars?"

Geneva clasped her hands. "If you're lucky. Dinah Shore came through last week, and she was wonderful. We sang with her during the show finale. I'm not sure if there's anyone famous on the schedule today. We could ask Devon."

"Devon?"

Ethel pressed her palms against her cheeks and cocked her head. "Our dreamboat of a director. He's sweet on Geneva, but she refuses to believe it."

Orville chuckled. "I thought I was your dreamboat. Is that what you call all the men in your life?"

"Only if they deserve the title." Ethel smirked. "And you, my young corporal, definitely do."

He reddened to the roots of his hair. Geneva grinned. After being ignored in high school, Orville warranted the attention Ethel was pouring on him.

Claire leaned over to him and whispered, "It may not seem like it, but she's harmless."

His face deepened in color, and Ethel pinked as well. "I didn't mean to embarrass you, Orville. You seem like a real nice guy."

"A real peach," Billy said. "Not like that big-time operator, Mayfield."

Geneva froze as a wave of nausea swept over her. Surely he wasn't talking about Thurgood, but she had to know for certain. She licked her dry lips and pressed a hand against her stomach. "Mayfield?"

"That Jane-crazy guy."

Ethel giggled. "English, please, for us girls who don't know all your *military* terms."

"A guy who is overly fond of women. In this case, the tomcat who was trying to have his way with Leona."

Closing her eyes, Geneva took a deep breath. With that description, the man could be Thurgood. "What's his first name?"

Billy's eyes filled with concern. "Hey honey, you don't look so good. What gives?"

Gripping Billy's arm, Geneva swallowed against the lump growing in her throat. "I'll be fine." She spoke through tight lips. "What is the man's first name?"

"Something highfalutin like Taswell or Tyrone. I can't remember."

"Thurgood?" Geneva spit the name out.

He slapped his forehead. "That's it. Do you know him?"

Ethel gasped. "Yes. He was her fiancé, or at least trying to be. It's a long story. He's dead, and the police think Geneva did it." She covered her mouth and spoke from between her fingers. "I shouldn't have blurted all that out, huh?"

The boys' eyes widened, and Geneva sighed. So much for a normal evening of socializing.

Billy patted her hand, an encouraging smile on his face. "Do you want to talk about it, or should we pretend we didn't hear Ethel?"

"There's not much to say. Everything Ethel said is true. I'm trying to prove my innocence, but I'm not having much luck."

Orville frowned. "I'm not surprised he ended up in a bad way. He was a smooth operator and often took advantage of people, especially with get-rich quick schemes. His antics probably caught up with him. Someone acting out of vengeance."

"He was like that even in college?" Geneva asked.

"Yep." Billy grimaced. "No one could ever prove that he had fraudulent intentions which is why he was never thrown out of school. He always seemed to be one step ahead of the authorities. When I called him on it once, he commented that life was all about having a back-up plan. Sounds normal, but the way he said it made it seem sinister."

Geneva shivered. No doubt it had been. This time Thurgood's plan failed, and perhaps the phone call Florence overheard was the key. It was definitely time to visit Mr. Claymore again.

Chapter Twenty-four

Two days later, Geneva and Devon climbed the stairs up to the main entrance of the brownstone building that housed the plush offices of Mr. Claymore. She rotated her neck to release the stiffness caused by riding on the train for more than an hour. The trips between Baltimore and Philadelphia were wearing, but necessary if she was going to find Thurgood's killer.

Devon pressed the button to call the elevator and gave her a smile. "You've got to be exhausted, Geneva. You could have taken last night off from performing."

She shook her head. "I appreciate that, but it's not fair to the other girls. Besides, sitting around gives me too much time to think about this awful situation."

"We'll get to the bottom of it. I promise you."

How could he say that? Was he simply trying to encourage her or was he holding something back again?

The elevator doors parted, and a burgundy-uniformed operator gestured for them to step inside. "Floor, sir?"

"Twenty-two."

"Very good, sir." The man pressed the appropriate button, and the brass panels closed with a bang. A minuscule bump, and the car glided upward.

Geneva bowed her head and nibbled her lower lip. Rocking on his heels, Devon shoved his hands into his pants pocket. When he moved, the earthy smell of his cinnamon-scented bay rum aftershave wafted toward her. She took a deep breath then silence filled the tiny space.

Time crawled. The elevator nudged to a stop, and the bell pinged. "Your floor, sir."

Geneva and Devon exited the elevator, and the sound of their feet echoed through the tiled corridor as they walked to the elegant office. She rubbed her damp palms against her skirt then clasped them together. Why couldn't she be more self-assured? She told her parents she could handle being on her own. Of course, she hadn't expected to be a murder suspect. Straightening her spine, she pressed her lips together and sent a silent plea toward heaven. *Lord, please give us some sort of clue.*

Devon grabbed the brass knob and opened the mahogany door. Geneva studied the names etched in the opaque glass before she crossed the threshold. Alexander, Claymore & Mayfield. Should she be surprised Thurgood's name hadn't been removed? Was the firm keeping his death a secret from their clients?

Her footsteps were muffled on the Persian carpet as they approached the secretary whose rhythmic clacking on the typewriter battled Bing Crosby's voice warbling "I Don't Want to Walk Without You."

The woman looked up, hands poised over the keyboard for a second before she twirled the knob on the radio, and Bing's voice faded to a whisper. Her eyes narrowed. "Miss Alexander and Mr. Royal, do you have an appointment? Mr. Claymore isn't here."

Geneva's chest tightened. She rubbed her temples. "When will he return? We've come a long way to see him."

"He's out of town on business. I can't say when he'll be back."

"Can't or won't?" Devon's face was set in a mulish expression.

"I beg your pardon."

"Listen, you…"

Geneva laid her hand on Devon's arm to cut off his words. She pasted on a smile. "I'm sure your job is quite difficult, Miss…?"

"Paxton."

"Doing your own tasks as well as juggling Mr. Claymore's schedule and the assignments he gives you. We greatly appreciate your help during our last visit. We don't want to put you in a tenuous situation, but this firm seems to be an integral part in our investigation. And secretaries know *everything* that goes on behind closed doors."

"I am the most senior secretary, and the partners rely on me heavily." Miss Paxton preened. "But I can't release any privileged information."

"Of course, they rely on you. We don't expect you to breach any confidentiality, but perhaps there is something off the record you might be able to share." Geneva stifled the urge to look at Devon. "Don't you want to help find the person who killed poor Thurgood?"

"*Poor* Thurgood?" Sarcasm colored Miss Paxton's words. "He was a lot of things, but deserving of pity is not one of them. Difficult and scheming, he angered more than his fair share of people, and he never treated me with respect. I'll do what I can to help because I like you, Miss Alexander, not because I feel sorry for the man."

Geneva blinked at Miss Paxton's vehemence. "Thank you. I appreciate anything you can tell me."

The woman opened the top desk drawer and withdrew a pencil and small notebook. She flipped the pad to a clean page and began to write. After a moment, she laid down the pencil and studied the paper. She tore it from the book and handed it to Geneva. "The two names at the top of the list are men with whom Mr. Mayfield was working on new investments. He had disagreements with both of them at one time or another, and the deals involve a significant amount of money. That's the best I can do for you. Please don't ask me for any further information."

"I understand, Miss Paxton. I'm grateful for your assistance." The door to the suite opened, and Mr. Claymore appeared at the threshold.

His eyes widened, then his face darkened for a moment before his expression settled into pleasant neutrality. "Miss Alexander, to what do I owe the honor of your visit?"

"I had some additional questions, Mr. Claymore. May we have a moment of your time?"

He glanced at Miss Paxton, then jerked his head toward the door behind her desk. She jumped up and slipped into his office without a word.

Devon frowned. "Apparently, we won't be staying long, Geneva. Isn't that what you're saying, Mr. Claymore, by leaving us out here?"

"I'm a busy man, Mr. Royal, and the two of you arrived without an appointment. The fact that I'm giving you any of my time is generous. If you recall, I suggested that you leave the investigation of Mr. Mayfield's demise to the police. I fail to see how badgering me about his activities in this firm is of any use. Our clients value their privacy, and until I receive an official subpoena for information, my lips are sealed." He glowered. "Especially to you, young lady. Does your father know you've been traipsing back and forth on the train?"

Geneva's heart raced. "Is Father here?"

"No, he's rarely in the office, but that's not your concern." Mr. Claymore stepped aside and gestured toward the corridor. "Now, you must go. I have a company to run."

Devon huffed a breath. "You're being less than forthright, Claymore, and your rudeness to us doesn't hide that fact. Eventually, whatever is going on in this firm will come to light."

The setting sun cast shadows across the sidewalks as Geneva and Devon plodded toward the boarding house. He insisted on seeing her home. Her face warmed. During the journey back to Philly, the cadence of the wheels against the track and the swaying motion of the train had lulled her to sleep moments after boarding. She awoke to find her head nestled on his shoulder. Her mother would be appalled to discover her only child had slept in public cuddled against a man.

Her back ached, and her head throbbed. When would the nightmare be over?

Devon wrapped his arm around her shoulder and grasped her arm with his hand. "You should have let me pay for a cab. As your friend, I'm concerned you're wearing yourself out." She looked at him, and he winked. "And as your director, I'm worried you won't be able to perform."

She gave him a wan smile. "I'll be fine. I come from hearty stock. It's just been a long day."

"A long few days, wouldn't you say?"

Nodding, she blinked back the moisture that filled her eyes. She sniffled and wiped away a stray tear. "I am tired. The emotional toll seems to be as heavy as the physical weariness. A good night's sleep will make me right as rain."

"Take the morning off. There's no need for you to handle a troop train visit on top of tomorrow night's show."

They reached Geneva's lodging. She stifled a yawn and wavered on her feet. "Thanks. I believe I'll take you up on your offer."

"Excellent."

"Good night, Devon."

Two burly figures dressed in black ran out from behind the bushes next to the house. One of the assailants pushed Devon to the ground, and the other stripped Geneva's pocketbook from her arm. They wore wide-brimmed hats pulled low and stockings over their faces distorted their features. When Devon tried to stand, the muggers brandished knives at the pair. "Don't try anything stupid, Mr. Royal," the taller man rasped.

Geneva clapped a hand over her mouth. Screaming would do no good and only anger the two men.

"Who are you and what do you want?" Devon held his hands over his head in surrender and climbed to his feet. He moved between the attackers and Geneva, shielding her with his body.

"Do you think we're dumb enough to give you our names? Now, listen close 'cause we're only going to say this once. Stop nosing around trying to figure out who killed Mayfield. He got what he deserved. You don't want the same thing to happen to you, do you?"

Trembling, Geneva poked her head around Devon. "What do you mean 'he got what he deserved?'"

"You're one pushy dame. Who do you think you are asking us questions? We were sent to warn you, nothing more. Now, do what you're told and back off. Or you'll be sorry."

"See here, that's no way to talk to a lady. You've done your duty, so get lost." Devon moved toward the man, and the thug swung the knife. It slashed Devon's forearm, and he cried out. Staggering, he fell to one knee as blood flowed from the wound.

Chapter Twenty-five

Geneva shrieked and bent over Devon who moaned.

"Let's get out o' here." The hoodlum jabbed his cohort and the two fled, their booted feet pounding the pavement as they disappeared from sight.

Devon pressed his hand over the torn fabric, but the cut continued to bleed. He peered at Geneva and wavered.

"Help! Help!" She wrapped her arm around his shoulder as she looked up and down the empty street. Where was everyone? Her heart slammed against her chest and her breath came in ragged spurts. "You're going to be fine, Devon." *Would he? Stop. Don't think like that.*

"A handkerchief. Do you have one with you?"

He nodded, his face ashen. "Inside pocket of my jacket." He spoke through clenched teeth.

She reached into his coat, the warmth of his body enveloping her arm, and pulled out the hankie. Another one just like Thurgood's. Pressing her lips together, she shook her head. No time to dwell on the implications. Devon was losing too much blood. "I need to put this directly on the wound. Can you handle that?"

Taking a deep breath, he grimaced. "I'll have to, won't I?"

"I'm sorry if this hurts." She pushed up his sleeve, and he gasped. Blood pulsed from the slash, and she pinched together the edges of the wound. Devon blanched, his skin slicking with sweat. He bit his lower lip and closed his eyes.

Pressing the crisply ironed handkerchief onto his arm, she placed his hand over the hankie then raised his arm. "If you hold that over your head, the bleeding should lessen."

"How'd you learn first aid?" He gave her a crooked grin, his teeth flashing in the fast approaching dusk. "Were you a Girl Scout?"

She moistened her lips, and her heart rate slowed. If he could tease her, perhaps he would be okay. "As a matter of fact, I was, and one of the leaders was a nurse, so she taught us basic first aid. Not that I thought I'd ever use it." A lock of his hair fell over his forehead, and she started to brush it back, but she caught sight of her hands, sticky with blood, and wiped them on her skirt. Her stomached rolled. "Will you be all right if I go inside and get help?"

"Yes, and have someone call Detective Lazarus. He needs to know about this."

"I'll be right back." She climbed to her feet and rushed up the steps toward the house. As she reached the door, it opened to reveal one of the other lodgers and her boyfriend. "Please, help me. My friend has been hurt. We were attacked."

The girl's eyes widened, and the young man glanced toward the street.

"He's there, on the ground." Geneva pointed.

"My name is Gerry McLennon. I'm in med school." He turned toward his girlfriend. "Lorelei, call for an ambulance. The police, too. I'll see what I can do for her young man. And get some clean towels."

"Please hurry. He was knifed." Geneva wrung her hands. "And when you call the police, ask for Detective Lazarus."

"Follow me." Lorelei beckoned to Geneva, and they hurried down the hall. Dizziness threatened to overtake her, and the walls seemed to close in. Who sent the men and why did they warn her and Devon? Did the person who murdered Thurgood think a warning would stop her from trying to prove her innocence?

They entered Lorelei's room. She hurried to a dresser and yanked open the bottom drawer. Pulling out a stack of white towels, she thrust them into Geneva's arms. "Will that be enough?"

"I hope so. I don't want to ruin your things."

"Towels can be replaced. Your boyfriend can't."

"He's my boss."

Lorelei tilted her head. "You seem awful upset. I think he's more than that, but it's none of my business. Now, take these to Gerry, and I'll make the calls."

Geneva gripped the towels to her chest and rushed out of the house. *Please, Lord, keep my feet from stumbling over some unseen impediment.* She clattered down the stairs to the spot where Gerry bent over Devon who was now prone on the sidewalk. A small crowd had formed, and she pursed her lips. Where had they been when she needed them? "Here." She thrust the pile toward the young man.

Moonlight shone on him as he pulled one of the towels from the stack and laid it over the handkerchief blackened with blood. Geneva's stomach somersaulted, and she swallowed against the nausea that threatened to overtake her. She turned away and took a deep breath. A slight breeze lifted her hair and tickled her face.

"More. I need more towels."

Geneva grabbed one from the pile on the ground and handed it to him. "Sorry."

"I understand. Not everyone is cut out to be a medic." He rolled the towel and tucked it under Devon's head. "Better?"

Devon whispered. "Yes. Thank you."

"You're going to be just fine. The docs will stitch you up, and you'll be good as new. You might end up with a scar, but some ladies like that sort of thing."

Geneva squinted at the doctor in the dim light. It was difficult to read his face. "Is he really going to be okay? There is so much blood."

"Knife wounds bleed profusely. Although I'm still a student, I've seen enough to know. I truly believe he'll make a full recovery."

Sirens wailed in the distance. She pivoted toward the sound, and her throat thickened. Devon was hurt because of her. He might have died. She couldn't let him be involved in her investigation any longer. It wasn't safe.

An ambulance squealed around the corner and stopped in front of the house. Medics jumped out of the vehicle and opened the back. They pulled out a stretcher and laid it beside Devon. One of the men waved his arms. "Step back folks. We need room to work."

The crowd shuffled back a few feet, and the man knelt next to Devon. He murmured to Gerry who responded in hushed tones. What were they saying? Geneva stood against the brownstone, arms wrapped around her middle as the trio of men worked.

A dark sedan rumbled toward her and parked. Both doors opened. A uniformed police officer slid out of the driver's side, and Detective Lazarus exited from the passenger seat.

Geneva sagged against the building's cold stone, her body chilled despite the heated air. Who knew she'd be relieved to see the detective? His razor-sharp gaze seemed to take in the entire scene in spite of the darkness. How did he do that?

He strode toward her. He touched the brim of his fedora in a curt greeting. "Trouble seems to follow you, Miss Alexander."

"Through no fault of my own, Detective."

His eyes narrowed. "That remains to be seen."

The medics loaded Devon onto the stretcher and carried it to the ambulance where they loaded it into the back. One of men climbed inside, and the other medic closed the hatch before ducking into the driver's side. Gerry collected the soiled towels while the police officer questioned the throng of people.

Geneva looked back and forth between the vehicle and Detective Lazarus.

He shook his head. "There's nothing you can do at this point, and when we're done I'll take you to the hospital."

She searched his face, then sighed. "Can we talk inside? The people—"

"Sure." Detective Lazarus nodded.

Gerry approached and glanced at the detective who scowled. "Are you all right, Miss Alexander? Lorelei and I can drive you to the hospital."

Detective Lazarus studied the collection of bloodied towels in the man's hands. "I need to take her statement. Who are you?"

"Gerry McLennon. My girl lives in this building."

"Why don't you make yourself scarce for a bit while I speak to Miss Alexander? Don't go far, I'll need your statement too. Only then can you head to the hospital. The docs will be working on him for a while, I imagine."

"Yes, sir." Gerry gestured to the porch. "I'll be up there when you're ready."

Stepping aside, Detective Lazarus allowed Geneva to proceed him into the house. They walked in silence. Her mind raced. What could she tell him that would help him find the attackers? She and Devon must have discovered something, or the killer assumed they had.

Geneva led him to one of the two parlors where boarders could entertain their guests. Unusually empty at this time of night, the room was dimly lit, causing shadows to dance in the corners. The blue brocade furniture was worn, but not shabby. End tables held lamps, candy dishes, and ashtrays. Someone had drawn the blackout curtains against the night, giving the room a sense of coziness.

She dropped into the nearest chair, and the detective leaned against the fireplace mantel. He dug into his coat pocket and pulled out a pencil stub and a notepad. Flipping through its pages, he mumbled to himself.

"Detective, would you please sit? I'm sure towering over me is some sort of technique to make me feel inferior or uncomfortable, but frankly, I'm not in the mood for theatrics. It has been a taxing evening, and I'd like to get to the hospital as soon as possible. So let's get right down to business, shall we?"

His left eyebrow lifted. "You've developed some spunk, Miss Alexander. Or is that your real self coming through? Has the shy, retiring girl been an act?"

Tears gathered in her eyes, and she blinked them away. She straightened her spine. "They are both me. But at this moment, I'm scared and worried, and more than a little fed up with men." She rubbed her blood-stained hands on her skirt. "Thurgood was an overbearing brute. Mr. Claymore has been alternately condescending and difficult. Two men just attacked a friend of mine and took my pocketbook. I didn't kill Thurgood, yet you treat me like a murderer. Perhaps that makes this girl less than gracious."

She glared at him. "Now, can we get busy, so I can get to the hospital?"

He grinned and lowered himself onto the chair next to her.

"I don't see how this is funny, Detective."

"My apologies. I'm not laughing. I simply find your honesty refreshing. After nearly thirty-five years on the force, I can tell when someone is lying or holding something back, and you must admit you've been evasive. To this old policeman, that spells guilt."

Closing her eyes for a moment, she took a deep breath. She dipped her head in acquiescence. "I understand. I was hesitant to share the fact that my parents, who apparently feel I am unable to be self-sufficient, foisted me onto a man who had no intentions of being faithful. In my naiveté, I didn't realize that could be construed as a motive." She lifted her chin. "But I'm not a piece of furniture to be sold off to the highest bidder."

"Well said, Miss Alexander."

Her face warmed. "I didn't mean to subject you to a tirade, Detective."

He shrugged. "Let's begin. Please walk me through your entire evening, bit by bit. I'll interrupt if I need clarification."

"All right, but you may not like what I have to say." She outlined the visit to Mr. Claymore's office, and as anticipated, the detective frowned. He didn't say anything, so she continued, describing the attack. At the memory of the two men, her heart skittered, and her palms began to sweat.

"Take your time, Miss Alexander. I know this is difficult, but the more you can tell me, the better chance I have of catching these two goons."

"I understand, but that's all I remember."

He shoved the notepad into his jacket pocket. "If you think of anything else, no matter how inconsequential it seems, please contact me."

"Yes, sir."

Leaning back, he crossed his arms. "What is your best guess as to who is behind Thurgood's death?"

"You're asking me?"

"Sure. Whether you like it or not, you're the closest person to the situation." He cocked his head. "And you've investigated around a couple of situations I haven't."

Hurried footsteps sounded in the hall, and the uniformed officer appeared in the doorway. "Sorry to interrupt, Detective, but we may have found those two punks. The descriptions match."

"Excellent work. Take them to the station, and I'll meet you there."

The man shook his head. "You need to go to the morgue, sir."

Chapter Twenty-six

The lights above the rehearsal stage baked the top of Geneva's head as she danced to the orchestra's pulsing music. Perspiration trickled down her back. Would practice never end?

Her steps faltered, and Ethel tromped on her foot. "What's wrong with you, Geneva? It's not like you to mess up choreography once you've learned it."

"Sorry."

"Focus, ladies, focus." Devon's voice boomed.

Geneva flinched. Two days had passed since the attack, but the event continued to invade her thoughts. No matter where she was, she continually looked over her shoulder, expecting a menacing man in black to appear. Detective Lazarus didn't owe her a report, but why hadn't he asked her or Devon to identify the man in the morgue to determine if he was indeed one of the assailants. Not that the information would be of any use to her.

Twirling to the right, she bumped into Ethel who frowned and pivoted her to the left.

She nibbled her lower lip and forced her mind to concentrate. Any more mistakes and Devon might pull her from this number. Or worse, the entire show. He had not spoken of the incident, yet seemed as affected by it as she was.

Favoring his arm, he kept it covered with long sleeves despite the summer heat. He seemed to avoid her, but was gracious when they did interact. What was he thinking? Did he blame her? She certainly blamed herself.

She couldn't risk him getting hurt on her account, so she decided to leave him out of the investigation, but here she was whining to herself that he seemed to dodge her every chance he had. *Make up your mind, Geneva.*

Fifteen minutes later, Devon cut off the orchestra. "All right, folks, that's a wrap. Only a couple more kinks to work out of the new routine, and then we should be able to add it to the lineup. Good job. We'll pick up here again tomorrow."

Geneva pulled a hankie from her pocket and blotted the beads of sweat from her forehead. She turned upstage to follow the dancers to the wings.

"Miss Alexander, a moment, please." Devon's voice broke through the buzz of conversation.

Cringing, she took a deep breath and spun to face him. She shielded her eyes from the overhead lights and squinted. It was difficult to read his expression.

He beckoned to her, and she glanced at Ethel who shrugged. "I'll wait for you in the dressing room, then we'll take the bus home together."

Geneva nodded. Better to get this over with, whatever it was. She strode toward the auditorium, hoping to convey a confidence she didn't feel. Why was she so skittish about speaking with him?

She descended the stairs and skirted the departing musicians. Devon stood by the podium, his baton clenched in one hand. A faint sheen of moisture glistened on his pale face. Was his injury bothering him or was it something else?

"Should we sit? You don't look well."

"I tire more easily than I'd like. Who knew a flesh wound could be so debilitating?"

"It's only been two days. You should take some time off." She crossed her arms. "How important is it to add the new number?"

He tossed the wand onto the rostrum. Wincing, his cheeks reddened. "It's embarrassing enough the military won't take me. How pathetic would it be if I'm too hurt to direct a musical production? They don't give purple hearts for that, you know."

Geneva reached toward him then dropped her hand. What right did she have to comfort him with a touch? "Look, I know I don't have an inkling of what you're going through, seeing the men every day, knowing you're not able to join them, but I do know how it feels to think you're a burden. Like a useless lump of clay no one can use."

"Geneva—"

"Let me finish. I'm not saying these things so you'll have pity on me, so don't waste your words. But as awful as this situation with Thurgood has been, I've come to realize God is with me no matter what happens. I've also realized He is supporting me with friends like Ethel and you to help me get through it. I don't understand how He works, but because you're 4F you can be here for me." She ducked her head. "It sounds selfish saying it out loud, but I know He has His reasons whether we understand them or not."

Devon barked a laugh. "So you think God gave me this physical abnormality just so I could be at the USO when you needed me? Surely He could have used someone else of more value."

"No, that's not what I meant at all. I'm saying that as His creation you have value, no matter what your condition, and He can use you to help others." She blinked, then shook her head. "I guess I need to heed my own words. Whenever I think about my impending loss of vision, I question my worth, yet I'm preaching that your condition doesn't make a difference."

He smiled, and the tightness eased in her chest. "I need to confess something, and I hope you won't be angry with me."

Tilting his head, he said, "Yes?"

She licked her dry lips. "Because of what happened in college between the two of you, and your mutual taste in handkerchiefs, I was convinced you were Thurgood's killer."

"That happened a long time ago, and certainly isn't enough of a reason for me to kill a man. But what about my hankies?"

"Thurgood has…had some just like them, and he claimed they were specially designed just for him. I figured you stole them when you killed him."

He rubbed his forehead. "Why would I steal something as trivial as a set of handkerchiefs?"

"I don't know…as a trophy?"

"And then use them for all the world to see? Not likely. Besides, Thurgood lied or perhaps he was lied to by the salesman. They're made by the French designer Rochas. I received mine as a gift from a wealthy friend, but I'm sure Thurgood could afford to purchase his."

Relief swept over her. "So you're not sore at me?"

His gaze softened. "No. You're stuck with me."

She gestured to his arm. "It's too dangerous."

"Which is exactly why you shouldn't be doing this on your own. You're not going to leave it to the police, and we've already agreed to be partners." He winked at her. "And now that you don't suspect me as the culprit, we should be able to work together just fine."

Her face warmed, and he chuckled. "Now, if you're not too tired after rehearsing, let's track down the two men on Miss Paxton's list."

**

Clouds covered the midafternoon sun, casting gloom over Devon and Geneva as they climbed out of the cab in front of an 18th century brick mansion on the outskirts of Philadelphia. She had assumed all of Thurgood's clients lived in Baltimore, so was skeptical that any one of them would travel a distance to harm him. But the first man on Miss Paxton's list resided in Haverford, home of the prestigious Merion Cricket Club. A taxi ride away from Thurgood's hotel.

She shuddered, and Devon grabbed her hand. He looked at her with concern. "Are you frightened?"

"A bit. We're in his house, on his turf."

"We'll be fine. Men like Mr. Bishop don't do their own dirty work. If he is responsible for Thurgood's death, chances are he didn't wield the knife himself. It's more probable that someone like one of the thugs who attacked us was responsible. And even if he did want to kill us, he most assuredly won't do it in his home. Too messy, and he'd run the risk of not being able to cover up the deed."

"You've given this some thought."

"Lots of time on the drive over."

The door opened as they walked the long, slate path to the house. A tuxedoed butler stood at attention, his eyes the only thing moving as he studied their progress. He gestured for them to enter, and they stepped past him. After closing the door with a discreet thud, he led them to a richly appointed parlor. "Mr. Bishop will be with you momentarily."

He left on silent feet, and Geneva glanced at Devon who grinned.

The Wedgewood-blue walls were interrupted by a pristine, white chair-rail. A gilt-framed portrait of stern-looking man in 17th century attire glared at them from above the fireplace. Geneva twirled slowly and almost knocked over one of the crystal vases filled with fresh flowers that graced the sofa's end tables. She righted the object before water could spill onto the gleaming mahogany floor which was covered with a multi-colored Persian rug whose fringe appeared freshly combed. There was more money in this room than she could hope to earn in a lifetime. She'd hazard a guess that rationing didn't impact the man.

In one corner, Devon bent toward the Frederick Remington sculpture of a cowboy on a galloping horse encased in glass on a pedestal.

"A fan of Mr. Remington's work, are you?"

Geneva's heart raced. How long had Mr. Bishop been standing in the doorway? Did everyone in the house walk on cat's feet?

Devon straightened. "A bit. I was fortunate to visit a gallery out west that displayed quite a few of his sculptures and paintings. I admire the sense of unleashed power and energy evident in his art."

"An astute observation. He captured a time when men were men, doing whatever was necessary to possess the land, attain their goals, and be a success. Alas, I own but the one piece. Perhaps, someday…" He stroked his full, dark moustache, then gestured to the cluster of chairs in front of the hearth. "Enough about that. You wanted to discuss my relationship with Thurgood Mayfield. What does that have to do with you?"

They seated themselves, and Devon folded his hands. "As I explained to your secretary when I made the appointment, the police seem intent upon proving Miss Alexander killed him. We are attempting to find the real murderer. Unfortunately, Thurgood was not…uh…well-liked, and the list of suspects continues to grow. We hope your story will help us."

Mr. Bishop stared at them for a long moment. "You're correct. He was a distasteful man, and his business practices left much to be desired. However, he was clever and took measured risks that often produced significant returns. Any investor worth his salt understands those risks. Do you really think it could be one of his clients?"

"That's what we'd like to determine. His poor handling of an investment lost you a tremendous amount of money. How did that make you feel? Are you willing to tell us about that?"

"Not specifically, but I can outline what happened."

Geneva wrapped her arms around her middle. The man seemed very self-assured and at ease. Did he really not care that his net worth had taken a hit?

Mr. Bishop leaned back and crossed his legs. "Thurgood came to me about six months ago with a proposition to invest in an overseas company that was manufacturing an item for the war. The conversion of American dollars to the foreign currency was favorable, and the product was supposed to be up-and-coming technology."

"Overseas?"

Shaking his head, Mr. Bishop said, "No specifics. Anyway, it came to light that the device was not as far along in development as Thurgood led me to believe. The return on investment was going to take longer than anticipated. I was not happy and asked Thurgood to return my money. Before he could do anything about it, the facility was destroyed in a bombing raid, thus rendering the project defunct and the money irretrievable."

"The banks couldn't do anything to help you?"

"America isn't doing business with this particular country."

Geneva narrowed her eyes. "You're in league with the Axis powers?"

Mr. Bishop's face darkened. "Don't leap to conclusions you can't prove, Miss Alexander."

Devon fisted his hands together. "So are you an investor 'worth his salt' or has the loss affected your ability to purchase, say…a couple of new Remingtons?"

"The funds were returned to me, so I'm whole again."

"What? When?"

"It was a bit crass, but I received a briefcase filled with the entire amount I had invested with Thurgood." He looked off into space. "That would have been…not quite three weeks ago. On the Wednesday of the week he died."

Geneva gaped at Devon. The money arrived the day *after* Thurgood was killed.

Chapter Twenty-seven

"Are you sure it was Wednesday? Not Monday or Tuesday?" Geneva pressed her hand against her racing heart that threatened to jump from her chest.

"I'm positive." Mr. Bishop scowled. "Why do you ask?"

"Because Thurgood was dead by then."

"He apparently made arrangements to have the funds delivered before his unfortunate demise. Although it was packed in a satchel, the transaction wasn't totally uncivilized. The young man who brought it was dressed in a uniform."

Geneva frowned. "A soldier?"

"No, like Western Union livery, although I don't think that was the actual company because he wasn't wearing their green uniform. Frankly, I didn't pay much attention. I signed for the package, and he left."

Devon rubbed his jaw. "But would Thurgood trust a pouch full of cash to a delivery boy?"

"It came in a sealed box, and a reputable organization doesn't ask their clients what's in the shipment, only its value for insurance purposes."

"There must be dozens of delivery services in the city." Geneva's voice trembled. "How in the world will we find the right one?"

"I'm not sure we need to." Devon said. "At least, not yet. Either Thurgood really did repay his debt, or someone wants us to think he did, perhaps the killer. Either way, if Mr. Bishop is to be believed, he no longer has a motive."

"I never had a reason to kill the man." Mr. Bishop puffed out his chest. "I have more money than I will ever need. Yes, I was angry Thurgood sold me a bill of goods on this investment scheme of his, but it was only because he assured me it was a sure bet. If he had been honest about it up front, I still would have given him the money, but lowered my expectations about the return."

Mr. Bishop turned and tugged on a beige needlepoint bell-pull.

Within seconds, the door opened and the butler appeared.

"Bring the satchel from my office. You'll find it under the desk."

"Yes, sir."

Silence filled the room, and Geneva dropped her gaze. Devon tapped his foot, breaking the stillness. She laid her hand on his laced fingers for a moment. He flushed, and his shoes stopped moving.

The manservant returned with a leather bag. He bowed and handed it to Mr. Bishop.

"That will be all, Wilson."

"Very good, sir."

Mr. Bishop held out the satchel, and Devon rose to retrieve it. He reached inside the bag and rummaged around, then withdrew his hand and ran it over the outside. Turning to Geneva, he said, "There are no identifying features. Do you recognize it?"

She shook her head. "The few times I ventured out in public with Thurgood, it was for a social event. He never carried any sort of bag."

Devon handed the satchel to Mr. Bishop. "Looks like we're back to square one."

"Perhaps not, young man."

Devon raised his eyebrow, and Geneva held her breath. Mr. Bishop had no reason to help them. They had practically accused him of murder.

"This may be a long shot because the incidents occurred last year, but some men can hold a grudge for a very long time. In fact, Mr. Mayfield should have been reported to the authorities for what happened, but both situations were resolved behind closed doors. I wasn't part of either matter, but I know several of the investors who were."

Geneva sighed. Would this investigation never end? Every clue had been a dead end, and interviewing multiple pompous, rich men like her father promised to be tedious at best. Why did she think she could poke around, ask a few questions, and uncover Thurgood's killer?

"We appreciate any assistance you can give us, Mr. Bishop." Devon leaned forward. "We'll use the utmost discretion."

Mr. Bishop looked down his nose. "You must. These men will take exception to veiled accusations of murder. They are important men of high stature with little tolerance for fools. Should any of them perceive you suspect them of killing Mr. Mayfield...ah...let's just say the conversation wouldn't go well, and you would probably find yourself a guest of Baltimore's finest."

Shuddering, Geneva glanced at Devon who nodded. "Understood, sir. Anything you are willing to tell us would be welcome."

"On the first occasion, Mr. Mayfield borrowed funds from an escrow account. From the little I know, a group of five or six men planned to purchase foreclosed commercial properties, renovate, and either sell or lease them. It was never clear to me what Mayfield used the borrowed money for, and considering the men were going to want their funds sooner rather than later, he was absurd to delve into the account." He shrugged. "But desperate men do desperate things."

Devon frowned. "And charges were never brought? That's seems rather fishy, don't you think?"

"I was not privy to the discussions, but if Mr. Mayfield promised to make amends, the men may have been willing to overlook the infraction."

"I struggle to understand how they could do that, so I'll take your word for it."

"Don't mistake their lack of action for forgiveness or acceptance of his deeds. There obviously was something in it for them to allow this transgression to be swept aside."

"What about the second incident?"

Mr. Bishop pursed his lips. "More despicable than the first, and I'm stunned it also went unreported.

Geneva and Devon exchanged a glance, but remained mute.

"Mr. Mayfield devised a scheme in which he claimed to know the owner of a silver mine out west who was looking for investors. The man supposedly needed new equipment, money to pay laborers, and to process the ore. In return he would give the investors a percentage of the take. How Thurgood managed to convince these businessmen is beyond me. They would have conducted some sort of due diligence, so how did he sell them a mine that didn't exist?"

Geneva gasped. "That's terrible."

"It's not the loss of money that's unforgivable in the financial industry, but the fraud."

"If Thurgood squared things up with you, could he have done the same for the others?"

Mr. Bishop shrugged. "That will be a question for each of those men."

"But how could he return the funds? I understood him to be in economic straits." Geneva's face warmed. "It's one of the reasons he was willing to marry me, perhaps the only reason."

"It certainly begs the question as to where he would have gotten the money." Devon's eyes widened, and he snapped his fingers. "Say, do you think he would have gone to a loan shark and then was killed when he didn't repay his loan on time?"

"Possible, but perhaps unlikely. Despite being the dregs of society, those distasteful men generally keep their debtors alive in order to continue collecting from them. Their henchmen are more apt to harm the poor clod than kill him. But if Mr. Mayfield got belligerent as he was wont to do…"

Geneva closed her eyes. Fraud, loan sharks, henchmen? Her life was quickly becoming as sordid as a Raymond Chandler novel. Should she turn the information over to Lieutenant Lazarus and trust the truth would eventually come to light, or should she risk arrest on an interference charge by continuing to solve the crime?

Considering the killer seemed to have her in his sights, she didn't have time to wait for the lieutenant to get it right. But would she find the murderer before he found her?

Chapter Twenty-eight

Applause thundered through the auditorium. Geneva grabbed Ethel's hand and bowed with the rest of the performers. Her heart warmed as it always did at the end of a show. Singing and dancing for the young men going off to war might not seem important to some people, but she knew it was the last bit of fun many of the boys would have for a long time.

Devon smiled and gave the girls a thumbs-up before turning to the crowd. He waited for the clapping to die down. When silence fell, he said, "Please grab sandwiches and snacks in the canteen and spend some time with the hostesses before the bus leaves for the train station."

Geneva basked in the chatting and laughing of the men as they sauntered out of the music hall, and she followed the dancers backstage to the dressing rooms.

Some of the girls giggled and preened in front of the mirror while others slipped out of their costumes and donned street clothes. Geneva rubbed the heavy stage makeup from her face, then smeared cold cream onto her skin to remove the remaining cosmetics. She grabbed a towel from the teetering stack on the end of the vanity and wiped her face before tossing the cloth into the laundry bin.

Mindful of the clutter her fellow performers had left in their rush to leave the room, Geneva picked her way across the floor to her locker where she peeled off the glittering costume and hung it on the closest rack. Pulling on her favorite blue polka dot dress, she stepped into her black pumps and wished she had a pair of stockings to complete the outfit. Geneva ran a comb through her hair then peered into the tiny mirror hanging on her locker door.

The guarded look in her eyes and her pinched lips indicated that reality was never far away. She was a murder suspect, and she was possibly one clue short of landing in jail for a crime she didn't commit.

After the troops were gone, she would talk to Devon about interviewing the men Mr. Bishop had told them about.

Wrinkling her nose at her partial image, she closed her eyes for a moment and took a deep breath. *Lord, I can't do this without You.* The tightness seeped from the muscles in her shoulders, and she sighed. Why couldn't she rest in God all the time? His peace sure beat the tension and anxiety she constantly carried.

Forgive my unbelief, Father. She straightened her spine, put on her lipstick, and tucked her pocketbook under her arm. Giving herself one last stern look in the mirror, she left the dressing room and hurried to the canteen.

Music and merriment greeted her as she pulled open the door. Ethel waved at her from a table a few feet away where she sat with three Marines. One of the new girls hovered nearby, a nervous smile tugging at her mouth.

Geneva spied an empty chair and dragged it to Ethel's table. She sat and raised her eyebrows at her friend.

"Gentleman, let me introduce you to one of our most popular songbirds, Geneva Alexander. She hails from the fair city of Philadelphia. She's a neighbor of yours, Harvey." Ethel pointed to each of the men. "Harvey, Don, and Stan."

"Nice to meet you." Geneva turned to Harvey. "You're from Philly?"

"Nah, I lived in the cheap seats. Jenkintown." He rubbed at a scratch on the table and mumbled, "You sing real pretty."

Don jabbed him with his elbow. "Harvey, here is the strong, silent type. What he means to say is that solo in the middle of 'Don't Sit Under the Apple Tree' was swell. You're as good as Patty Andrews."

"That's nice of you to say, but I'm just an amateur. Glad you enjoyed the performance. Ethel here can dance up a storm, can't she? A regular Ginger Rogers."

The men nodded, and Ethel's face pinked, but she looked pleased. She waved away the compliment. "So tell us a bit about yourselves, boys. Did you enlist or get a personal invitation from Uncle Sam?"

Stan chuckled. "Don and I enlisted together as soon as we turned eighteen. We share the same birthday and have been friends since grade school. We don't want to miss any of the action, so we joined this party as soon as we were legal." He poked Harvey. "This guy waited for his number to come up."

Harvey reddened to his hair line, but remained mute.

Ethel frowned. "Nothing wrong with that. All you Marines are tough guys no matter who got in first."

"Hey—"

"Let's dance, shall we?" Geneva held out her hand to Harvey. "We can talk about home and all the things we miss about the great state of Pennsylvania."

Tugging at Don's hand, Ethel pulled him to his feet. "That's a swell idea. Stan, you can cut the rug with Marjorie." With that, she and Don melted into the crowd of swaying couples.

Harvey's eyes widened, and his gaze bounced between Geneva and the dance floor. She leaned toward him. "Don't worry, it's easier than it looks. I won't let you fail."

He smiled and grasped her fingers. They rose, and she led him around the edge of the room to the far corner. She placed his hand on her waist then laid her hand on his shoulder. "Fortunately, they're playing something we can waltz to. Follow my lead, and you'll be a pro in no time. It's one-two-three, one-two-three."

"I think I can manage that, Miss Alexander." He grinned. "After all, I'm a tough Marine."

She giggled, and she felt him relax. *Thank you, Lord. Is this what it means to serve You? Helping to ease these young men's fear and homesickness? Surely there is something more important I could be doing?*

Blinking away her thoughts, she asked, "Ready?"

He nodded, and she counted off the beats. After several missteps, Harvey got the hang of the movement, and he twirled her among the other dancers. A swirling rainbow of dresses flowed between the white, blue, and tan of the men's uniforms.

The music swelled around them, and Geneva continued to count the rhythm for Harvey. His grip on her hand tightened, and she tried not to grimace. When he trod on her toes, his face flamed.

"Forgive me. Perhaps I'm not as trainable as I think."

"Nonsense. You're doing fine, but if you'd like to stop…"

"No, a Marine never gives up. I'd like to see this through until the end of the song."

"I admire your fortitude." She grinned. "What else can you tell me about yourself?"

"Trying to distract me, eh? Let's see. After I graduated from high school, I attended college for a year, but it wasn't for me. I'm not too good at book learning. A friend of mine worked at the Pennsylvania Railroad, and he got me a job there. The work was okay, but I was thinking of enlisting when my number came up."

"You didn't seek exemption for doing war work?"

"Nah. Any monkey can do the job I had, so it didn't seem fair to stay home."

The song ended, and a smattering of applause filled the room. Harvey grinned. "Hey, we did pretty swell."

"That we did." Geneva licked her dry lips. Perspiration trickled down her spine. "I'm parched. Do you mind if we take a break?"

He cocked his head. "You're not just saying that, are you?"

She fanned herself. "No. I'm a tad warm and could use something cool to drink."

With his hand on her elbow, Harvey led her to the counter where they slid onto two vacant stools. He raised his finger at the soda jerk. "Two lemonades, my good man."

"Coming right up, sir."

Seconds later, two glasses filled with the frosty drink arrived. Geneva fought the urge to gulp the refreshing drink, instead sipping slowly. She set down the cup with a thunk and rubbed at the condensation on the glass. "Will you go back to the railroad after the war?"

Harvey shook his head. "I plan to stay in the Corps. They've taught me a lot in the few short weeks I've been with them. Even the drill sergeant, who was a tough nut, said I made a good Marine. He's the one who suggested I re-up. Said I could make my way up the NCO ranks." He ducked his head. "No one has ever believed in me like that."

"Not your family?"

His lips thinned, and he shook his head again.

Geneva's heart tugged. She knew what that felt like. Should she remain in the USO after the war? Would they want her? Devon talked about taking his show experience to Broadway, and now Harvey was going to reenlist. Everyone seemed to have a plan except her. Of course, it was difficult to think with a murder charge hanging over her head.

"Geneva!"

She turned toward the voice. Ethel pushed her way through the mass of dancers. "It's your mother. She's on the phone in the office. It's important."

"Mother? What could she possibly want?"

"She wouldn't give me a message. Said she could only speak to you."

"I'm sorry, Harvey. I have to take this."

"Would you like some moral support? I could accompany you."

Laying her hand on his arm, she said, "That's sweet, but things with my parents are...complicated."

"I understand." He patted her hand. "It was an absolute pleasure to meet you, Geneva. I wish you the very best."

"And I, you." She pivoted on her heel and rushed out of the room, racing down the hall to the office. After entering, Geneva closed the door and took a deep breath. She pressed a hand to her frantically beating heart then picked up the receiver. "Hello?"

"You must come home. I need you." Her mother's voice was tight and unnaturally high.

"What's wrong, Mother? You know I'm committed to the USO."

"It's your father. He's in the hospital. The doctors say he's had a heart attack."

Chapter Twenty-nine

Heart pounding, Geneva yanked open the front door to the hospital and rushed to the reception desk, her steps clattering across the tile floor. She bumped into a small table, and the lamp teetered. Grabbing the fixture before it fell, Geneva scowled. Would she ever get used to her failing vision?

The snowy-haired woman behind the desk looked up and put a finger to her lips. "Shh!"

Geneva's face warmed. She smoothed her hair and took a deep breath. "My father's a patient here. Where is his room?"

Her face softened, and the woman nodded. "What's his name?"

"Wayne Alexander. He had a heart attack."

"You poor dear. Let me check my list to see if he's allowed visitors." She pulled a battered clipboard close and peered at the sheet of paper haphazardly clamped under the clip. Her motions were reminiscent of molasses in January.

Stifling the urge to snatch the list from the receptionist, Geneva clenched her fists, the nails biting into her palms. She wrinkled her nose and swallowed. Acrid, antiseptic odors clung to the air. Did all hospitals smell the same? How did the medical staff stand it? Or the patients?

Her gaze ricocheted around the room and fell on an elderly man and a petite, curly-headed girl. He read to her from a picture book, his arm wrapped around her shoulders. Intent upon the pages, the child seemed oblivious to the sadness in the man's voice. He periodically sighed and stroked her hair. Geneva nibbled her lower lip. What terrible news awaited the pair?

"Miss?"

Geneva turned back to the receptionist.

"Your father is in room 305." She pointed to a staircase to her left. "Two flights up and take a right. If you have any trouble, one of the nurses can help you. I pray he'll be all right."

"Thank you." Would the woman really pray for Father? Geneva had prayed during the interminable train ride from Baltimore, and as usual, unbelief battled for supremacy over her faith.

She followed the receptionist's instructions and moments later stood outside the assigned room. A nurse straightened the covers over a man's bulky form, then leaned over and murmured something Geneva couldn't hear. A chuckle rumbled in the patient's chest. Her eyes widened. When was the last time she'd heard her father laugh?

Perhaps this was the wrong room. She glanced at the placard next to the doorframe. Three-oh-five…the correct room. Maybe the man on the bed wasn't Father. Movement in the corner caught her eye, and she spied her mother holding a crumpled handkerchief to her eyes.

Geneva was in the right place after all. Taking a deep breath, she smoothed her skirt then strode through the doorway. The nurse smiled at her and exited the room.

Mother looked up, tears streaming down her cheeks. She held out her arms, and Geneva froze for only a few seconds before enveloping her in an embrace. Never demonstrative, Mother must be desperately afraid for Father's life if she sought a hug.

They clung together for several moments, Geneva relishing the warmth of her mother's arms.

"I'm not sure the situation calls for all this emotion. The doctor says I'll make a complete recovery."

Geneva pulled away and peered into Mother's face. "Is that true? I thought you were upset because there was no hope."

Fresh tears seeped from Mother's eyes. "The doctor says he has to take it easy, but he should be fine. They performed a fluoroscopy and seem to think there is minimal damage to his heart. I'm so relieved, I can't stop crying. This isn't like me at all."

"I like this new you." Father's voice was quiet but steady, and Geneva turned to look at him. He smiled, his eyes crinkling in the corners.

Lord, what is going on here? I don't recognize my parents. Mother's never been anything but stoic, and Father is downright jocular despite lying in a hospital.

Geneva approached the bed. Father reached for her hand and gently squeezed her fingers. "Thank you for coming, Geneva. You're a good daughter. I don't tell you often enough." He cleared his throat. "Actually, I'm not sure I've ever said it, and I'm sorry."

She gaped at him. Devon should be here. He would make the appropriate response. Her mother's tears and her father's apology left her speechless.

Father tugged her toward him. "Would you give your silly old dad a hug?"

"Dad?" *Since when did he want to be called Dad? And he certainly had never referred to himself as silly. Maybe he really was dying, and her parents were once again trying to protect her.*

Leaning forward, she wrapped her arms around his shoulders and pressed her cheek against his whiskery skin. Swallowing against the lump forming in her throat, she closed her eyes. *Lord, please let Father live. We may not always get along, but I love him, and I'm not ready for him to die.*

She shoved a chair closer and sat, head lowered. "I'm sorry I lost my temper and left home, Father. I understand you were simply trying to protect and provide for me. I should have stayed and tried to work things out."

"You had every reason to be upset. I was domineering and difficult. Yes, I wanted you to be taken care of, and I thought marriage was the way to handle the situation, but I should have let you have some sort of say in the matter." He lifted her chin and met her eyes. "Please forgive me."

"And me." Mother approached the bed and laid her hand on Geneva's shoulder. "I've been condescending and overbearing. I'm old-fashioned, and need to accept times have changed. You're a grown woman. We should have treated you like the adult you are."

Geneva's gaze swung back and forth between her parents trying to read their expressions. Both wore smiles and looked at her with love. She hesitated then nodded. "Of course, I forgive you, but I don't understand what's happening here. Why the change in attitude? Is Father going to live or are you trying to let me down easily?"

He caressed her hair. "My sweet girl. You have every right to be suspicious. What we've told you is true. I *am* going to recover, but I came close to death. The experience forced me to reevaluate my life. I was dictatorial with you and your mother, and less than honest in my business dealings. From here on out that's going to change. I'm a new man, and I will make things right. It's what God would have me do."

"God?" Geneva shook her head. She sounded like a parrot, but Father's words stunned her. He attended church, but typically disagreed with Pastor Voyce's messages.

Father's eyes moistened, and he blinked. "You must be struggling to assimilate all of this."

She nodded. "I don't know what to think. I've loved and respected you both because you're my parents, but you've always held me at arms' length. We've never felt like a family. While I was growing up, I…uh…thought maybe you regretted having me, especially after my diagnosis. And now you're embracing me and apologizing. It's a lot to take in."

He pulled her to him into a fierce hug. "Oh, Geneva, we were never more excited than the day you were born. And every day since then you have been a joy. But our actions belied that, and I'm so ashamed. We didn't want you to think we pitied you, but now I see the pain our actions caused you. I don't expect you to trust us right away. We have to prove our love to you."

Studying his face, she searched for signs of guile.

"I understand your skepticism, honey. Lying at death's door brought me face-to-face with who I was as a man. Wondering if I was going to live or die made me realize I didn't deserve for God to welcome me into heaven. So, I prayed with all my strength that He would spare me and give me a chance to make it up to you and your mother. And to those I've wronged."

His lower lip trembled. Pressing his lips together, he sighed. "He was gracious enough to answer my prayer, and I plan to spend the rest of my days making amends and becoming the man He wants me to be. Your faith has been genuine, and you have followed God even during the most difficult days when we first received the news about your eyes. I'm so proud of you, Geneva, striking out on your own. It couldn't have been easy."

"Hearing you say that means a lot to me, Father, but you're right, it hasn't been easy, and as a result, I've changed too. I'm no longer the trusting and gullible young woman who left home. I have friends who accept me for who I am, and they don't treat me differently because of my vision issues. I have responsibilities. People rely on me to do my job." She rose and walked to the window. Standing with her back to the glass, she crossed her arms. "Frankly, I'm more cautious now, so I need to consider everything you've said and decide if I can believe you. I've forgiven you, but trust may not come easy."

Mother stifled another sob into her handkerchief, but Father nodded, his eyes clouding with sadness. "You have every right to be doubtful, and it breaks my heart that I've brought this about. Will you at least stay for a couple of days so we can spend time with you?"

She shook her head. "Now that I know you're all right, I'll return to Baltimore tomorrow. We have a two-day hiatus next week, so I'll come back on Thursday. That will give me time to reflect on everything you've said."

"We look forward to it." Father's face reddened, and he grimaced. "About Thurgood, honey. I'm sorry we forced you into the engagement. In my eagerness to see you settled, I let him convince me he could take care of you. I knew of his arrogance and heavy-handedness, but he promised that he had your best interests at heart and he would do everything in his power to keep you safe and happy."

"How could you believe him?" Geneva barked a harsh laugh. "You must be blinder than me. I talked to Mr. Claymore, and he told me about Thurgood's dishonesty. You had to have known about that, and yet you sold me off to him. I don't understand how you could do that."

Father rubbed his forehead. "I was aware of his…failings, but I didn't think they would impact his treatment of you. And there are other reasons, more pressing than you can imagine." He closed his eyes and shook his head. "I never should have let him have the upper hand. He held my past over my head, threatening to disclose my secrets. I couldn't let that happen."

"What secrets?" Geneva shot a glance at Mother. "Do you know what he's talking about?"

Mother turned toward the window and bowed her head.

Geneva marched to the bed. "Tell me. What secrets?"

"I can't. Not before I make things right."

Her breath caught, and Geneva pressed a hand to her lips. *Was Father's new-found faith a sham or the result of a guilty conscience? Had he killed Thurgood to keep him quiet?*

Chapter Thirty

The following evening, Geneva trudged up the stairs to her room in the boarding house. She rubbed the stiffness from her shoulders then pulled the key from her pocketbook. Her body still vibrated from the train ride. A long soak in a tub of hot water would be divine, but she left that luxury behind with many others when she struck out on her own. She was lucky when she got fifteen uninterrupted minutes in the shared bathroom at the end of the hall.

Letting herself into the room, she hung her purse on the coatrack then quickly unpacked the valise. After tucking it in the bottom of her closet, she stretched out on the bed, gathered the pillow over her head and blew out a deep breath.

Her mind raced. More than a day had passed since her father's comment in the hospital, yet the passage of time had done nothing to lessen the shock that he seemed to have a motive to kill Thurgood. Neither parent would pursue the conversation, so long stretches of awkward silence had been punctuated with Father's questions about her experiences with the USO. She gave up her attempts to get him to talk about the situation and entertained them with anecdotes about the boys who came through on their way to deployment.

"Lord, I'm a mess. I don't know which way to turn. Every clue has proven to be a dead-end until now when it seems like Father could be the guilty party. What did he mean when he said he couldn't 'let that happen'? He won't tell me his secrets. Don't I have a right to know what they are? His withholding information could put me in jail. Doesn't he realize that?"

Tears streamed down her face and soaked the quilt. "Help me know if Father is telling the truth about his relationship to You. I want to be part of a family, but his declaration of being a changed man rings false. It seems too convenient, especially if he killed Thurgood. Does he think a jury will grant him mercy if he claims repentance?" Geneva sat up and wiped her eyes. Sniffling, she said, "I hate being so distrustful. Oh, that Devon were here to talk to. To hug me and tell me everything is going to work out."

Her face tingled, and she pressed her palms to her cheeks. When had she begun to think of him as more than a friend? She couldn't let herself fall in love with him. Disappointment and hurt would come as a result. No man worth his salt would saddle himself with a woman who would end up blind. "Face it, Geneva, you'll live out your days single and unloved."

I love you, My child.

The unspoken answer to her prayer seeped into her soul. She bowed her head and sighed. "Thank You for the reminder, Lord." Warmth spread through her, and she rose. "No more lollygagging. A good scrubbing of this place will get my mind off this nightmare, at least for a short while."

A knock sounded at the door. "Geneva?"

"Mrs. Harmon?"

"Yes."

She barely heard her landlady's muffled voice. "Your young man is down in the parlor."

Geneva opened the door. "My young man? I'm not seeing anyone."

"Mr. Royal. Isn't he your special friend?"

"No, he's my boss at the USO."

Mrs. Harmon's eyebrow shot up. "Yet he comes to your home. A bit late to be receiving visitors, you know."

Geneva squinted at the watch hanging on her bodice. "It's only seven thirty. Please tell him I'll be right down."

"Don't be too long." The woman frowned and retreated toward the stairs.

Glancing at her rumpled dress, Geneva attempted to smooth out the wrinkles. Devon was here, and she looked as travel-weary as she felt. Did he have news about the case?

She hurried to her dresser and grabbed her toothbrush and a comb. Praying the bathroom would be free, she rushed down the hallway. Vacant. Yes! She ducked inside and made quick work of freshening up.

Moments later she headed back to her room and stood in front of the closet.

What to wear? Attired only in her slip, she ran her fingers along the dresses swaying on the rod. "Just pick something, Geneva. It's not a date, for goodness' sake." Her hand came to her favorite lavender-and-yellow polka dot frock. Perfect. She pulled it off the hanger and slid it over her head. The satiny material swished as it settled around her hips. Stepping into her shoes, she plucked her keys from the bowl by the door and exited her room.

Geneva's tongue stuck to the roof of her mouth. Not wanting to look like she had dressed up for Devon's visit, she refrained from putting on lipstick, a decision she now regretted. She pinned on a smile and entered the parlor.

Fedora clutched in his hands, Devon prowled the frilly, blue room. At the sound of her shoes on the wooden floor, he paused in front of the fireplace. A smile lit up his face. "Geneva, thanks for seeing me. You look lovely."

She ducked her head and smoothed her skirt then tucked her hands in the garment's pockets. "Thank you." Aware of the possibility of her landlady hovering within earshot, she gestured to the chairs in the far corner of the room. "Would you like to have a seat?"

"Yes, that would be nice." He waited for her to drop into one of the Queen Anne chairs before lowering himself in the other. He propped his hat on his knee and laced his fingers. "You've returned. Does that mean your father is on the mend? You could have stayed longer if you wished."

"Perhaps I should have, but I'm going back next week. The doctors say he had a minor heart attack, although to me there's nothing minor about it." She shook her head. "They say he'll make a complete recovery."

"That's wonderful. You must be so happy."

Nibbling her lower lip, Geneva shrugged.

He leaned forward and took her hand in his. "What is it?"

Her skin tingled where his warm fingers rested. Her breath quickened. Could he hear her heartbeat thundering in her ears?

Footsteps sounded in the hallway, and she snatched away her hand.

Devon straightened and his face reddened. "I'm sorry. I shouldn't have done that."

"No…it's just…Mrs. Harmon…"

"I understand. There's no privacy. Would you like to go somewhere else?"

She tilted her head. "Devon, why are you here? Don't get me wrong. I'm pleased to see you. It's been an exhausting few days, and I can always count on you to make me feel better, but I don't understand why you've come unannounced at this hour."

His color deepened, and he cleared his throat. Closing his eyes for a moment, he heaved a deep sigh, then leaned toward her again. "I wanted to meet you at the station, but I got caught up at work. Headquarters called to arrange an appearance by Ann Miller. Lots of details to discuss and they wanted things ironed out so they could finalize the visit with her agent tonight. I guess show business people never sleep."

Geneva's eyes widened. "Ann Miller? That's wonderful. When is she coming? Do we get to perform with her or will we get the night off? Can we watch the show?"

Devon chuckled and held up his hands in surrender. "Hold your horses. I'll give you all the skinny."

She giggled. "I'm sorry, but she's one of my favorite actresses. She's beautiful and seems so self-assured. I wish I could be like her."

"You may not have her confidence, but you're just as pretty."

"That's kind of you to say—"

"I'm not being kind. You're the prettiest girl I've ever seen. And more importantly, you're beautiful on the inside. You're gentle and considerate, always putting others' needs ahead of your own. I've seen you with the boys who come through. You treat them as if they're the only guy in the room. You make them feel special." He tucked a strand of hair behind her ear, then ran his finger along her jawline.

She shivered as he dropped his hand into his lap.

"Forgive me." He pressed his lips together. "I shouldn't be so forward, but I care about you, Geneva, more than a director should for one of his performers. I didn't intend to say anything to you this evening. I came to check on how you were doing after the trip to see your dad." He rubbed his forehead. "I've really botched things up, haven't I?"

Pressing a hand against her stomach, she took a deep breath. "No, you haven't made a mess. I…uh…I…have feelings for you, too. I've been fighting them because I didn't think you could possibly like me as more than a friend. My parents made it clear while I was growing up that I'm a burden. Someday, I'm going to be blind. It's only recently that I've realized I don't have to be married to be complete. God loves me just as I am. That's enough for me."

Devon's face glowed. "I'm sorry you'll have to deal with losing your vision, but you see more with your heart than many others see with their eyes. I can be your eyes. With my 4F status, I didn't think any woman could respect me or think of me as worthy of her love, yet you say you care for me. Aren't we too peas in a pod? Both thinking we could never be loved by another."

"Loved?"

He waved his hand in dismissal. "Maybe not love yet." He grinned. "How about strong affection?"

"I can agree with that." She giggled then sobered. "But we can't pursue a relationship until I've proven my innocence. In fact, you should stay out of the case. It's too dangerous."

"Not going to happen. You're my girl, and I'm going to see this through. We're in it together. There will be no more talk of you handling this on your own."

She bowed her head. *Thank you, Lord, for Devon. He's a good man. Help me…us…prove I didn't kill Thurgood.*

He tipped up her chin. "Are you all right?"

"Yes, just thanking God for you and asking for His help."

"Like I said 'stalwart faith.'" He clapped his hands. "What's our next step? Have we spoken to all the investors yet?"

"No, but I think we need to go in a different direction." She blinked away the tears threatening to run down her cheeks. "We need to investigate my father." Her voice broke. "He may have killed Thurgood to hide a secret past."

Chapter Thirty-one

Two days later, Geneva peered at her parents' home through the window of the taxi she and Devon had taken from the train station. So much for waiting until the following week to return to Philadelphia. After a crying jag when she told him about Father's possible motive, she had calmed down enough for the two to discuss ways they could investigate him.

When she admitted she knew the combination to Father's safe because her mother had slipped up once and commented she was flattered he used her birthday, Devon had suggested the audacious plan of examining its contents. He convinced her their actions didn't qualify as breaking in since she had a key to the house. Would she end up regretting her decision to believe him?

He squeezed her hand then kissed her cheek. "I know this is difficult for you, but it's for the best. We need to set your mind at rest about your dad, and we can't do that until we discount him as a suspect."

Her lower lip trembled. "But what if we can't do that? What if we find something that implicates him?"

"We'll ford that stream when we come to it. Meanwhile, you need to appear confident to the household staff, as if you have every right to be in his office. We've already confirmed your mother is at the hospital, but she could come home at any time."

"You seem awfully comfortable with this. Is there something in your past you're not telling me?"

"No, but as a 4Fer I've often had to convey more confidence than I've felt, as if I'm okay with being rejected by the military."

"How terrible."

Devon shrugged. "Enough about me. Let's get this over with." He passed money to the cabbie. "Can you come back in an hour?"

"Yes, sir."

Grasping Devon's hand, Geneva slid out of the vehicle behind him. She took a deep breath and straightened her spine. She could do this.

They hurried up the walk, and Geneva opened the door. Their footsteps echoed on the gleaming mahogany floor, and the housekeeper, Bernice appeared from the parlor. "Miss Alexander, 'tis a surprise to see you. Your mother said we shouldn't expect you until next week. Is everything all right?"

"Yes, fine. Just here on some business."

Bernice's gaze bounced back and forth between Geneva and Devon.

"You remember Mr. Royal. He was kind enough to accompany me on the train." Geneva gestured to her eyes. "My vision, you know."

"Of course. I could arrange for Cook to make some sandwiches."

"That won't be necessary. Please don't let us get in your way."

"You're never in the way, Miss, but that's nice of you to say. I'll be upstairs if you change your mind about wanting something to eat."

"Thank you."

The woman trundled up the stairs, and Geneva jerked her head toward the doorway on the left. Devon nodded. He pulled her into the office.

Geneva froze. While growing up she rarely entered the room. Her father had made it clear she was unwelcome. The tangy scent of Bay Rum mixed with cigar tobacco clung to the air, and she closed her eyes caught in a memory as if it were yesterday.

She was seven or eight years old. The door to the office had been ajar, and she could hear voices from inside, but she was so proud of her latest report card. Surely Father wouldn't mind if she interrupted to show him the column of all As. Pushing open the heavy oak door, she entered the room. An elderly man with mutton-chop whiskers stood near one of the windows, thumbs tucked into his vest pockets and a pipe clenched between his teeth. Shaggy, white eyebrows danced on his forehead as he spoke.

The man's scowl gave her pause, but excited by her news, she skipped to Father's side behind the mammoth desk. Papers and books were scattered on the typically tidy surface. His cigar sat in a chunky glass ashtray, a curl of acrid smoke wafting from its tip. He held a large stack of money in one hand, and when she approached, he shoved it into his top desk drawer.

"I've told you never to come in here." His thunderous voice filled the room, and she flinched. "What could be so important that you dare defy me?"

Her tongue stuck to the roof of her mouth, and she was unable to answer, so she held out the thick piece of paper with a shaky hand. Raising an eyebrow, he snatched it from her then glanced at it before tossing it on the desk. "Your report card? Surely this could have waited for a more appropriate time. Now, get out and don't ever come in here again. Do you understand me?"

She finally found her voice. "But Father I made all A's. I thought you'd be proud."

"Surprised is more like it."

His words cut her like a sword, and her face heated. Ducking her head, she ran from the room, willing herself not to cry.

"Geneva?" Devon spoke from across the room. "Are you okay? You look like you've seen a ghost."

A quivery sob escaped her lips. "You could say that. I was reliving one of the last times I set foot in here. It was not a pleasant experience." She heaved a sigh and fought for composure.

Devon rushed to her side and enveloped her in his arms. "He can't hurt you anymore."

"I know, and he claims he's a changed man. I'm having a hard time believing him."

"You don't have to do this. We can turn the information over to Lieutenant Lazarus and let him follow up." He stroked her hair, and she shuddered.

Pulling away, she shook her head. "No. We came all this way, and no matter how painful the truth is, I must find out what it is."

He drew her to him and placed a kiss on her forehead. "That's my girl. I'll be with you the whole time."

Geneva pressed a hand to her stomach then marched to the portrait of her stern-looking grandfather behind Father's desk. *Did any of the men in her family ever smile?* She swung the hinged frame toward her and began to twirl the knob on the wall safe. As she passed each number of the combination, the tumblers clicked.

She arrived at the last number and pulled down on the handle. The door opened with a muted squeal. Behind her, Devon's breath stopped. She turned and grinned at him. "I was afraid he had changed the combination."

"Me, too, but I didn't want to say anything that might discourage you."

Giggling, she swatted his arm. "That would have been a wasted trip. Thanks for your willingness to come, even if this proves to be a fruitless endeavor."

"I'm sorry your father has hurt you over the years, but you can count on me no matter what. I promise never to cause you pain."

"An unrealistic vow to make."

"Okay, never to *intentionally* hurt you."

Geneva's eyes filled, and she blinked away the tears. What had she done to deserve this man? She smiled and tugged him toward the safe. "Enough coddling me. We need to search this before Mother returns home."

She reached into the safe and drew out the stack of envelopes and folders. Laying them on the desk, she began to sort through them. The top envelope held a wad of cash. Her eyes widened, and she handed the money to Devon who quickly counted it.

"There's nearly three-thousand dollars here. Was your father in the habit of leaving large amounts of cash in the house?"

Shrugging, she said, "I don't know for certain, but he stuffed a large pile of money into his desk the last time I was here."

"When was that?"

"I was just a child, elementary school age."

Devon nodded and set the money aside.

She rifled through the folders that held real estate contracts, powers of attorney, and bank statements and ledgers. "I can't tell if these are important."

"I'll look at them. You see what else is there."

A sealed envelope was all that remained in the bottom of the safe. Should she open it? How would Father react when he discovered she had looked through his personal records? Staring at the outside of the envelope, she fingered the gummed flap.

"You have to open it."

Geneva looked at Devon. "But what if I violate his privacy for nothing?"

"If he's the new man he claims to be, he'll understand. If not..." He hiked his shoulders.

"You're right. It's now or never." She slid a fingernail under the edge and peeled back the flap. Sliding the papers from inside, she flipped through them and gasped. Heart pounding, she returned to the first page and scanned the words. Devon leaned over her shoulder to read, his breath causing her hair to flutter.

Shivering at his nearness, she stopped reading for a moment then forced herself to return to the documents. Moments passed as the pair waded through the legal jargon. Geneva turned over the last sheet and sagged in the chair. "Does this contract say what I think it does? That Father offered Thurgood one hundred thousand dollars to marry me in exchange for a percentage of earnings on any investment Thurgood makes? Is he allowed to do that?"

Devon sat on the corner of the desk and crossed his arms. "It looks that way to me, and it's executed. Not all lawyers are above board, but I can't imagine actually drawing up a contract for a shady deal."

"True. But this is legitimate, right? Why would Father go through with a contract that could potentially yield him even more wealth than he already has, only to kill the source?"

"Seemingly. It would help to know where the money came from. Did he receive it for something, or was he preparing to give it to someone?"

Geneva frowned. "He certainly didn't discuss his financial affairs with me, and I doubt he did so with Mother. Frankly, he made the money, and she spent it."

"Do you see a problem with that?" Geneva's mother entered the room, a haughty look on her face. "What are you doing? You have no right to be in here." Her glance shot to the gaping safe, and her eyes widened. "How dare you open your father's safe."

"I had to, Mother. The police think I killed Thurgood, and I have to prove I didn't."

"And you think rifling through your Father's papers will help? That's a ridiculous notion." Her mother's face darkened. "You put those things back where you found them, young lady."

Geneva stood, contract in hand. The pages crinkled as her grip tightened. "Did you know about this…this…this bill of sale? Father was set to make quite a bit of money with this little agreement between Thurgood and him, pawning me off as if I was some sort of commodity."

Her mother rose to her full height and peered down her nose. "I don't know what you're talking about. We weren't pawning you off. You needed to be cared for because we won't be around forever. Father had your best interests in mind."

"If that were the case, I would have been written in to receive a portion of the benefits. As it is, Father earns a pretty penny from the deal." Tears gathered in Geneva's eyes. "You don't seem to care one iota about my being a suspect. You were so busy reprimanding me about looking at Father's papers, you glossed right over that. Where is the sobbing, shrinking woman now? Was your crying in the hospital an act?"

"Of course not. But I must be strong until your father is discharged."

Geneva narrowed her eyes and studied her mother then bent and gathered the pages into the envelope. "I'm taking these, and you can tell father if you like." She turned to Devon and swallowed against the lump forming in her throat. "I found what I came for. There's no reason to remain."

Her mother strode to the desk and grabbed the envelope. Geneva tussled with her and snatched the papers, knocking her mother's pocketbook to the floor. The bag tumbled open, and the contents spewed out.

Geneva cried out. Amid the gloves, handkerchief, coin purse, keys, and lipstick tubes sat a compact just like the one found in Thurgood's hotel room.

Chapter Thirty-two

Alone with her thoughts in the dressing room, Geneva studied her face in the mirror. Lines bracketed her mouth and creased her forehead. Half-moon shadows hung below her eyes. If the investigation went on much longer, she would look like an old woman. The awful encounter with Mother yesterday hadn't helped either.

It was a wonder Ethel hadn't commented on her appearance yet.

Geneva closed her eyes and wrapped her arms around her middle. "Dear Lord, I'm at a loss as to what to do and whom to believe. Mother's compact is just like the one from Thurgood's room, but as she said, there are thousands sold every day, that she didn't go to see him. Is she involved? She was so awful yesterday, hateful even, but does that make her a killer? Did Father do it, and she's covering up for him? Help me, please."

Hunched into herself, Geneva wept.

Voices sounded in the hallway, and her head shot up. The girls shouldn't find her moping. She dabbed her eyes with her handkerchief, then rubbed foundation on her face. Hopefully, the makeup would disguise her wan visage, although it would be difficult to hide her real feelings from Ethel. Geneva shook her head. That girl was way too discerning.

The door banged open, and several giggling performers clattered into the room. Chattering and kidding each other, a few of them nodded a greeting to her. They busied themselves stowing personal items and pulling out costumes for the first number in tonight's show.

Satisfied with her complexion, Geneva brushed on rouge then added mascara to her lashes. Lipstick would be applied moments before going on stage. She met Ethel's questioning glance in the mirror and smiled with a shrug. Her friend's curiosity would have to wait until they were alone to get the latest on the case.

Geneva rose and went to the costume rack. Fingering the colorful apparel, she found her outfit and pulled it off the hanger. She slipped out of her dress and donned the gold-sequined bodysuit before snapping the shin-length red taffeta skirt overlaid with matching tulle around her waist. One of the girls hummed Dorsey's "I Remember You," and Geneva swayed to the music. Dressing for a show always perked her up.

Ethel walked past and squeezed Geneva's shoulder.

Lord, thank You for friends like Ethel and Devon. Help me rest in You.

A knock sounded at the door. Geneva looked up as one of the front-office girls stepped inside. Molly? Maggie? Margie. Her name was Margie.

"Geneva?" Margie scanned the room, and Geneva raised her hand. "Over here."

"Mr. Royal wants to see you about tonight's show as soon as you have a minute."

What could Devon possibly have to discuss about the performance? "I'll be right there."

"Okay." Having delivered her message, the girl hurried out the door, and it closed with a thud.

Geneva slipped on her shoes, took one last look in the mirror, then hurried from the room and made her way to Devon's office. Engrossed in a telephone call, he scribbled on a notepad, his eyes narrowed in concentration. A lock of hair fell over his forehead, and her fingers itched to put the errant strands back in place.

He glanced up and smiled. Gesturing to the vacant chair, he mouthed, "Won't be long."

She nodded and dropped onto the scarred, ladder-back seat. Her gaze wandered around the cluttered room. Photographs of visiting celebrities who had performed at the club were tacked on the wall behind Devon. A rainbow of costumes draped across a chair brightened the far corner. Two six-foot wooden palm trees guarded the window, and a life-sized papier-mâchè mermaid reclined on the table. Scripts and musical scores lined the bookshelves.

The receiver rattled to rest on the telephone cradle, and she turned back to Devon. He laid down his pencil. "Thanks for coming. I was hoping to catch you before you dressed for the show. I think you should take the night off."

"What?" Crossing her arms, she gaped at him.

"It's been an emotional couple of days, and you must be exhausted from traveling back and forth. I'm sorry I didn't think of it sooner."

"Are you telling me as my director or my…uh…friend."

He chuckled. "You can say it. *Boyfriend.* And that's a fair question. I suppose it's a bit of both. I'm worried about you. You've been under a lot of strain."

"You mean well, but I can't step down tonight. The girls have to rearrange the choreography when one of us is out, and it's not fair to them at the last minute. Being busy and focusing on the routines keep my mind off what's happening. What are my problems compared to the men who are putting their lives on the line? Boosting their morale with some song and dance is the least I can do." She stood and twirled. "Besides, I'm already dressed and made-up."

He cocked his head and seemed to study her face. Apparently satisfied with whatever he saw, he winked. "You're one tough cookie, Geneva Alexander, but as your director I'm telling you if you make mistakes tonight, I'm going to pull you from the next few performances until I feel you're able to do right by us."

She let out a deep breath and pressed her hand to her stomach. With a grin, she executed a mock salute. "Yes, sir. I understand, sir." Before he could change his mind, she hurried from the room. Would she be able to focus as she claimed? *Lord, keep my feet steady and my voice clear.*

Two hours later, applause filled the auditorium and the houselights flooded the hall. The troop train was leaving in thirty short minutes, so the girls would forego changing into street clothes before heading to the canteen.

Geneva met Devon's gaze and tossed him a crisp nod. Her performance had been flawless, so he had no choice but to leave her in the show.

He formed his thumb and index finger in a circle, the other three fingers raised before turning to the orchestra with a smile. She couldn't hear over the noise, but knew he was praising the musicians as was his custom. It was no surprise all the performers gave him unswerving devotion. His gracious and supportive manner brought out the best in all of them.

She exited stage-right and threaded through the maze of hallways to the canteen. The sound of deep voices punctuated with high-pitched laughter filtered toward her. She entered the room searching for Ethel.

Her friend peered at the choices on the jukebox, punch glass in hand. Ethel never tired of dancing, even after a long performance. Wiggling her toes inside her shoes, Geneva sighed. As for herself, she could use a cool drink and some time in a chair. Perhaps, she'd get lucky and find a serviceman who wanted to sit and chat.

Drifting toward the counter, she waved at several local volunteers who were around her parents' age. These men and women always came to send off the boys no matter what time of day or night the train was scheduled to depart. Some had sons of their own in the armed forces, but others came for countless unknown reasons.

She climbed onto one of the metal stools, her feet searching for the foot rail. It was a wonder the government hadn't swapped out the stools for wooden ones or worse, nothing at all.

"Whatcha havin' tonight, Geneva?"

"A tall glass of water for now, and keep 'em coming. Temperature on the stage seemed extra warm this evening."

"Isn't any better outside. Weatherman says we're in for some scorchers over the next few days."

She groaned and propped her elbows on the glossy wooden countertop.

Denny placed her water on the bar then handed her a towel. "Let me know if you need another one."

Blotting the perspiration from her face with the cloth, she dropped it in her lap then brought the glass to her lips. She tried not to guzzle the cool liquid. Refreshed, she patted her hair and straightened her spine. Now to boost some morale.

Pivoting, she slid off the stool directly onto a pair of shoes, her heels grinding into the tops of the man's feet. Her face warmed. "I am so sorry." She raised her head and looked at the wincing Army officer. A nervous giggle escaped. So much for morale building. "I'm sorry," she repeated. "I didn't mean to be so clumsy."

"I'll be fine." The man's eyes widened. "Geneva Alexander? I hardly recognized you under all that makeup. I wondered what happened to you after high school. You were such a smart girl. And here you are."

"Milton Verost!" She poked at the bars on his shoulder. "Look at you. You're a second lieutenant. Congratulations."

He hugged her for a moment. "Thanks. I was fortunate to be accepted into Officer Candidate School. Poor Denny Hurst is in the infantry. He's a Private."

"Do you know where you're headed?"

"No, they wait until we're at the shipyard to give us our orders. I guess they're afraid some of the boys might put the information in a letter even though that sort of thing is forbidden." He crooked his arm. "How about if we find a nice quiet table and get caught up? You didn't look too comfortable dangling off that stool."

She tucked her hand inside his elbow. "Always the gentleman, Milt. That sounds wonderful." She grabbed her water then led him to the back of the room away from the jukebox and dance floor. They settled into the corner, and she dropped onto the chair and wrapped her hands around the glass. "What have you been up to since high school?"

"I went to Norwich University in New Hampshire. Boy, is it cold up there, but I got a swell education. I graduated with a mechanical engineering degree and had just found a job with the state of Pennsylvania when I was recruited, so here I am."

"Is there a Mrs. Verost?"

Blushing, he pulled out his wallet then slid a photo of a petite brunette across the table. "Only just last week. We were engaged, but when I got drafted we decided to tie the knot. I'm glad we did, because if anything happens to me, she'll get some benefits."

"How awful you have to think that way, but it's wonderful of you to take care of her like that. She's beautiful."

His color deepened, and he nodded. "The most beautiful girl in the world. I hope I can come home to her when this war is over." He waved his hand. "Enough about me. Looks like you landed on your feet. Do you like working for the USO? You must meet lots of guys. Anyone special in your life?"

"I love the USO. We make the guys feel good and hopefully a little less scared before they ship out. I've been here a few weeks, but something terrible has happened and Devon, that's the director and my...uh...boyfriend has been helping me with it."

"What happened? Is it your folks? Are they okay?"

"Father is in the hospital because he had a heart attack, but that's not the worst of it." She went on to tell him about being a suspect in Thurgood's murder and how Devon was helping her.

Milt's eyes widened. "You say this detective thinks you killed Thurgood? That's the craziest thing I ever heard. I hope this Devon character is a regular gumshoe."

Geneva giggled. "He's been incredibly supportive. I don't know what I'd have done without him." She sobered up. "But there's more. I'm beginning to wonder if my parents were involved in his death."

"What?" He reared back. "You're folks aren't exactly the warmest people, but murder, no way. How come you suspect them?"

"Maybe I'm grasping at straws, but Mother had a compact just like the one found in Thurgood's hotel room, and Father commented that he couldn't let him get away with ruining our family's reputation."

"Those are pretty thin theories, Geneva. I'm no expert on cosmetics, but there are thousands sold on any given day, and I'm struggling to see your father killing to protect the family honor. It sounds like you want this detective to give you the benefit of the doubt. You should do the same for your parents."

She squeezed his hand. "You make a good point. I appreciate you listening to my woes. Here you are getting ready to ship out to battle, and I'm bothering you with my petty problems."

"They're not trivial, and I'll be praying this all gets sorted out as it should." He snapped his fingers. "Hey, how would you like to be a pen pal with my wife? I bet she'd love getting to know you, and it might help to make her less lonely."

"Absolutely. What a great idea."

"You're the best, Geneva. Wish we hadn't lost contact, but I'm glad we reconnected."

One of the stagehands approached the table. "Sorry to interrupt you, Miss Alexander, but there's a Mr. Imhoff here to see you. Says it's important."

"Tell him I'll be right there." She hugged Milt. "This has been grand, but I've got to meet this man. It could be the break in the case I've hoped for. He's one of the investors who Thurgood defrauded. Stay safe.

She headed toward the foyer, scratching her head. "How did he know where to find me?"

Chapter Thirty-three

Geneva hurried out of the canteen and headed toward Devon's office. There was no way she would meet the man without him. Her heart skittered, and her breath came in gasps. She stopped in the hallway and pressed a hand to her heart. *Lord, keep me calm. Did You prompt the man to come to see me?*

One of the office girls appeared around the corner. Geneva's face warmed, and she clamped her lips together. Smoothing her skirt, she squared her shoulders and continued down the hallway. She nodded to the woman as they passed in the sterile corridor.

Geneva arrived at Devon's office and rapped on the doorframe. He looked up and smiled. "To what do I owe the pleasure of your visit?"

"I need your help. Mr. Imhoff has come to see me. I don't want to speak to him alone. Will you go with me?"

"Of course. The name rings a bell. This is one of the men who invested with Thurgood, correct?"

"Yes. How did he find me?"

"And why is he here? I assume he is aware of the investigation, but how would he know of your involvement?"

Geneva gulped. "Maybe Mr. Claymore referred him."

"That's a good possibility." He winked and held out his arm. "There's only one way to find out, Miss Alexander."

She sighed. Why had she allowed herself to get so emotional about Mr. Imoff's visit? Devon must think her a ninny. She tucked her hand into the crook of his elbow. "Excellent point, *Mr. Royal.*"

They left the office and made their way to the foyer where Mr. Imhoff stood, fedora in hand. Bushy, white eyebrows hovered over piercing hazel eyes set deep above his ruddy cheeks. He extended his hand which Devon clasped.

"My name is Devon Royal. I'm the director here, and Miss Alexander asked me to accompany her."

Mr. Imhoff bowed. "A pleasure to meet you both. I only wish it were under more pleasant circumstances. I understand you were Mr. Mayfield's fiancée, and you are attempting to prove yourself innocent of his murder. I've known your father for many years and find him to be an honorable man. I'm going to go out on a limb and assume you are not guilty. There are other people more suited to the deed, and I have information that may be of help in discovering the identity of the true culprit."

"That's wonderful, but how did you find me?"

"Mr. Claymore's secretary. Apparently you've been in somewhat regular contact with her."

Geneva dipped her head. "Mr. Claymore has been…uh…unavailable at times."

"And less than forthcoming at others?"

She exchanged a glance with Devon before shrugging. "You could put it like that."

"Very diplomatic of you, my dear. Herbert Claymore is typically of assistance only if there is something in it for himself. An unfortunate characteristic, but it makes him very good at his job."

Devon gestured to the vacant chairs in the corner. "Please be seated, Mr. Imhoff."

"Thank you."

The trio sat down, and Mr. Imhoff laid his hat on his knee. "Frankly, I was intrigued to discover you had joined the USO, Miss Alexander. Most young women of your stature are rolling bandages or holding soirees to sell war bonds. Your father explained your desire to support the war effort in a more direct way. I applaud your dedication."

"Thank you." Geneva folded her hands. "I'm sure you're a busy man, so don't feel the need to make small talk."

"Very good." He crossed his legs. "Your father explained that you are aware of Mr. Mayfield's dealings, shall we say, and that the firm had addressed his fraudulent schemes. Despite his promise to change his behaviors, most of us knew he didn't have it in him to do so. It was a matter of time before he tried another underhanded ploy, so a group of us created an opportunity he couldn't resist."

"You set him up to fail?"

"If he had truly changed, he would not have fallen."

Devon shook his head. "A bit like inviting an alcoholic to a bar for dinner, wouldn't you say? Doesn't seem fair."

"Fair or not, we had to know if he could be trusted with our money."

"Have you taken this information to the police?" Devon asked.

"No. We've been working with a private investigator through the Pinkerton Agency." He pulled a card from his wallet and handed it to Devon who glanced at the card before sliding it into his pocket. "Here is the contact information for the agent assigned to us. I have told him to expect your call. The agency has been investigating a significant number of investors and other individuals who were harmed by Thurgood's misdeeds. I don't know the specifics, but I'm sure the Pinkerton man can shed light on possible suspects."

Devon rubbed his jaw. "Forgive me for saying this, Mr. Imhoff, but you're awfully calm about the situation. You've lost buckets of money through a guy who did you wrong. He then looked you in the eye and promised not to commit fraud again, yet weeks later perpetrated another dastardly plot based on you men setting him up. Seems to me, you're chock-full of motives to kill the sucker. Why should we believe you're here to help Geneva?"

Mr. Imhoff frowned. "Do you really think I would waste my time and rations to drive all the way to Baltimore on a ruse? Besides, what do I have to gain from this so-called charade?"

"If you appear to be helpful, the police wouldn't have a reason to suspect you."

Geneva laid her hand on Devon's arm. "Please forgive my friend, Mr. Imhoff. No one seems to be who they say they are, so we're a bit suspicious."

"Understandable, but Mr. Royal has been reading too many dime novels. I'm totally above board. Yes, I lost a great deal of money, but not enough to be of concern. Not that it's any of your business, but I'm quite wealthy, and Mr. Mayfield's scheme, though troublesome, did not impact my finances as greatly as you believe." He rose. "Now, if you'll excuse me, I must be on my way. As I said, the Pinkerton man can explain the fraud case and give you the particulars. I've included the names of investors on the back of the card who are willing to speak with you."

Devon and Geneva climbed to their feet and shook Mr. Imhoff's hand. "Thank you for coming to see me. I'm sure you're a very important and busy man," Geneva said. "You could have called or telegrammed the message."

Mr. Imhoff donned his fedora. "Your father means a great deal to me, Miss Alexander. He handled a rather touchy situation for me with great tact and diplomacy. I would do anything for him or his family, and that includes a personal appointment to deliver the information." He cocked his head. "I also wanted to meet you and see what sort of woman you are. After our conversation, I believe you to be honest and trustworthy. I wish you the best in getting to the bottom of this unpleasant matter. If there is anything else I can do for you don't hesitate to contact me."

He bowed slightly and swaggered from the room.

Geneva closed her eyes and rubbed her forehead. The cadre of possible suspects continued to grow. How many men had Thurgood defrauded, and where was all the money he had skimmed?

Devon laid his hand on her shoulder, and her skin tingled at the warmth of his touch. Should she quit the USO and wade through the list of investors? Would they even speak with her? Men of her father's age and wealth had little use for young women tramping about in their world. They probably wouldn't give her the time of day. Should she rely on information the Pinkerton man garnered instead?

He leaned close. "It's going to be all right. I promise you. We'll find the scoundrel who did this, and you'll be in the clear."

Her lower lip trembled. "You keep saying that. On the one hand we have a new lead, and indications Father is above board, but I'm struggling to believe it. This is shades of *Murder on the Orient Express*. Everyone seems to have wanted Thurgood dead, and the men who could have done it aren't the type to discuss the case with me. You have a show to direct and don't have time to traipse up and down the Eastern Seaboard interviewing possible suspects." Tears ran down her cheeks, and she swiped at them in a fruitless effort to stop the torrent. "I can't do this anymore. I should just go home and wait for Detective Lazarus to arrest me."

"Nonsense!" Devon enveloped her in a fierce embrace and pulled her to her feet. He held her to his chest letting her cry. Moments passed, and her tears soaked the front of his shirt.

Embarrassed at her lack of composure, but unable to stop sobbing, Geneva gulped in an attempt to get control of her wayward emotions. She took several deep breaths. Her tears subsided, and she pulled away, fumbling in her pocket for a handkerchief.

A rainbow of colors from her stage make-up stained Devon's shirt. "Oh, Devon, look what I've done, and I must look frightful."

He tipped her chin up until she met his eyes. Winking, he said, "A tad messy, but never frightful. You're a beautiful woman, Geneva. Never forget that." He pulled out his handkerchief and dabbed her face. "You are innocent. The truth will come out. Let me pray for us, then we can devise a way to continue our investigation while keeping our commitments at the USO."

Mutely, she nodded.

Devon pulled her back into his arms and tucked her head under his chin. "Father, Geneva is very discouraged right now. She feels empty and afraid that her innocence will not be proven and the real killer will go free. We know You have a plan for her and for this case, but we're struggling to see how everything is going to turn out. Please give us peace about this situation. Give us and the authorities wisdom in tracking the murderer. We ask all these things in Your Son's name. Amen."

Light filled Geneva. Once again, God had covered her anxieties with His peace. When would she stop reacting with doubt and dread? She didn't deserve a man like Devon. Whatever did he see in her?

"Thank you, Devon." A tentative smile lifted her mouth. "Thank you for guiding me back to God. I keep wrenching my problems out of His hands, and then I wonder why I'm so miserable."

"You're not the only one who does that." He tucked a stray wisp of hair behind her ear. "Now, let's take a look at that card Mr. Imhoff left us. Once we've figured out how to manage the investigation in conjunction with the show, our first step should be to visit the Pinkerton detective." He withdrew the card from his pocket and handed it to Geneva.

She read the name Lowell Perazon then gaped at Devon. "What?"

"This man. He lives down the street from my parents. He came and went at such odd hours, I always wondered where he worked and what he did for a living. His left arm and leg were badly injured in the last war. How can he be a detective?"

"As you've discovered with our numerous trips to interview people, detecting is primarily an intellectual pursuit. I believe a telephone call to Mr. Perazon is in order, wouldn't you agree?"

Chapter Thirty-four

Five long days had passed since Mr. Imhoff had visited the USO. Finally, she and Devon had an appointment with the Pinkerton man. Fidgeting with her pocketbook strap as she stepped out of the Philadelphia train station, she breathed deeply of the warm air. Floral scents mingled with automobile and bus fumes to create a tangy, palpable odor.

As she and Devon approached the curb, he whistled for a taxi. The sleek sedan eased to a stop in front of them, and Devon opened the back door. She slid into the seat, and he climbed in after her. Closing the door, he gave Mr. Perazon's office address to the cabbie.

She peeked at Devon, and he caught her glance. Smiling, he slid his arm around her shoulders. "Comfy?"

"Yes." She crossed her legs and smoothed her skirt over her knees. For once, her heart wasn't racing in anxiety or her palms perspiring in nervousness. Devon took care of things, but didn't make it seem like a burden or a big deal. Instead, she sensed he liked handling details for her, not because it made him seem more important or that she was totally helpless, but out of sheer enjoyment.

Thurgood had lorded over her like some benevolent dictator deigning to give a loyal subject the benefit of his expertise and time. How could two men be so completely unlike each other?

To keep from dwelling on Thurgood's brutish behavior, she thought about the conversation she had with Devon about Mr. Perazon. Trying to reconcile the memory of the limping man with the empty left sleeve, to her notion of a gun-wielding, villain-chasing detective took some effort until Devon convinced her that she was the one who had been the one reading too many dime novels and her idea was out of kilter. He likened the Pinkerton men to Sherlock Holmes, reminding her that a keen, logical mind and attention to detail solved more cases than strong-arming a suspect, and performed correctly, an investigation rarely resulted in running after an escaping criminal.

The cab bumped and bounced over the macadam. Sirens sounded in the distance, and she cocked her head. "Do you hear that?"

"Hmm?"

"The sirens. My heart goes out to whomever is suffering right now. Whenever I hear that sound, I pray that God will comfort those in distress."

"That's my sweet girl, always thinking of others. If I'm not mistaken, it's a fire truck." He pointed to the sky. "Ah, see that column of smoke above the buildings? That must be where they're heading. Could be serious. These sky buildings hold thousands of people."

Lord, take care of the people and get them out safely.

The cabbie glanced into the back seat. "That's where we're going, too. Hope it ain't your destination."

Cold fingers of dread gripped Geneva's heart. Surely it wasn't the Pinkerton agency. Weren't they too clever to allow their building to catch fire?

The vehicle turned the corner and drove down the block. Before he could make the final turn, a uniformed policeman held up his hand to stop them.

Geneva gaped at Devon. "Could it be…?"

He squeezed her clenched hands. "It's too soon to tell. Let's not panic yet." He leaned forward. "Take us back one street and drop us off at the corner."

"Yes, sir."

Moments later, after paying the fare, Devon and Geneva climbed out of the taxi. Acrid smoke billowed above their heads. Their eyes teared. Shrouds of gray smog hid the sky. Shouts, screams and the sound of gushing water echoed between the structures. People raced past them, bumping and shoving as they ran.

Geneva coughed and blinked. "Now what?"

"We still don't know that the building in question belongs to the Pinkerton agency. I say we see how close we can get and at least figure out if we're going to be able to meet with this Perazon guy. Sometimes a fire department will evacuate adjacent structures, so even if Pinkerton's isn't burning, their employees may have been sent home."

"Will we be allowed nearby?"

Devon shrugged. "Only one way to find out." He handed her his handkerchief, then gripped her hand. "Hold the hanky over your nose and mouth and keep hold of my hand. I don't want to lose you in the confusion or the smoke."

She did as he instructed, and they set off, swimming upstream in a sea of pedestrians. They ducked into the alley behind the Pinkerton block and snaked their way toward the flaming structure. The black smoke thickened, and Geneva's eyes burned. Tears poured down her face. Her lungs fought against the acrid fumes. *Lord, please keep us safe.*

They arrived at their destination, and Devon pulled her so close to the building, the threads of her dress snagged on the rough bricks. She pressed herself against the structure. A paroxysm of coughing overtook her. She bent over trying to catch her breath. Would she die trying to prove her innocence? How ironic.

Devon wrapped his arm around her shoulder and spoke into her ear, "Maybe this wasn't such a good idea."

She shook her head. "We've come…" Her words sounded scratchy and deep. She swallowed heavily. "We've come this far. Let's see what we can find out."

Turning, they stumbled over a pile of metal gas canisters painted olive drab. She looked at Devon, her eyes wide. His mouth gaped as he returned her glance. He picked up one of the cans and twisted off the cap. He held the can to his nose and sniffed. His head jerked back. "Smells like kerosene."

Stuffing the handkerchief in her pocket, Geneva grabbed a can from the stack, the outside slick with petroleum. Sliding from her grasp, the container clattered to the ground and splattered noxious liquid onto her shoes. She jumped back. Palms up and her fingers splayed, she grimaced at Devon.

He squatted next to the jumble of tanks and methodically searched through them.

"What are you doing?"

"Trying to find any sort of clue as to who might have left these. It's hardly a coincidence they're here. They could have been used to start the fire."

"Do you really think someone would be foolish enough to leave a clue?"

"Most criminals aren't very smart. With any luck, he or she tossed…" He grinned and reached behind the remaining can. "Hello. What have we here?" He held up a pair of grimy leather gloves. "I believe our culprit forgot something."

"Oh, Devon, that's wonderful. How clever of you to look for something. We need to give those to Detective Lazarus and tell him about the kerosene."

"He won't have anything to do with this. His jurisdiction is Baltimore, not Philly." He stuffed the gloves into his jacket pocket. "Wipe your hands on my coat, then put the hanky back over your mouth. I want to find someone in charge to see if we can get into the Pinkerton building."

Pressing her lips together, she quickly rubbed her hands on his coat, then pulled out the handkerchief and covered the lower portion of her face. The smell of kerosene clung to her skin. Was it worse to inhale the smoke or the fuel fumes?

She followed Devon as he strode around the building.

He froze, and she bumped into his back. Peeking around his shoulder, she ogled the chaotic scene. Dozens of helmeted firefighters in long, rubber trench coats and rubber boots wrestled the cobra-like hoses, spraying gallons of water toward the sizzling structure. Wearing breathing tanks and masks, the men lumbered inside, dragging the bulging tubes.

One of the men separated from the mayhem and stomped toward them. Gesticulating wildly, he indicated they were to leave the area.

Devon shook his head and shouted, "We need to get into the Pinkerton building."

The fireman pushed him and bellowed through his face shield, "Go home. We've vacated every building on this block."

"When can we return?"

"Days, maybe longer. It's up to the fire inspector." The masked man drew himself up to his full height, and he towered over the pair. "Now, get away from here before I have you arrested."

Geneva tugged at Devon's arm. Her eyes swam and her singed throat throbbed. "Let's go. There's no one here. We can go to his home. I know where he lives."

Nodding once, Devon pivoted on his heel and led her away. The smoke lightened from black to gray and began to clear in the onslaught of water. Halfway to the corner, Geneva's eyes widened. Detective Lazarus and another man in a suit marched toward them, scowls darkening their faces.

Chapter Thirty-five

Geneva clutched Devon's arm, and her heart skipped a beat. Detective Lazarus's presence couldn't be a coincidence. Had he followed her or was he here because of the fire? Devon pulled her hand through the crook of his elbow and drew her close.

"For a woman who touts her innocence, you certainly have a knack for showing up at crime scenes, Miss Alexander."

"Crime scenes?" Her voice broke.

"Sure seems that way. The stench of kerosene clings to you like honey on a biscuit, and the pile of gas cans behind the burning building wasn't landscaping. I thought you were a smart girl. Why would you leave evidence behind?"

"Evidence?" She was beginning to sound like a parrot. *Buck up, Geneva!* She clenched her fists and stiffened her spine. "And I thought you were a smart man, Detective. First of all, how many containers were there? Five? Six? Do you think I can lug that number of *filled* cans down the street? Second, what's my motive?"

Detective Lazarus jerked his head toward Devon. "Maybe your boyfriend here helped you, and as far as your motive, obviously you wanted to cover up something."

Devon scowled. "That's a wild accusation, Detective. Just what do you think that *something* is?"

The suited man held up his hand. "Show some respect. You gotta admit you're being here seems mighty fishy."

"No, I don't *gotta.*" Devon turned to Lazarus. "Who is this guy?"

"Pardon my lack of introduction, *Mr. Royal.* This is Detective Mackel." Sarcasm dripped from the detective's words. "And in case you're wondering why I'm here, he called me after reading the police bulletin about the investigation. Seems the Pinkerton Agency was checking up on your Mr. Mayfield. I figure they uncovered a juicy tidbit that makes Miss Alexander the guilty party, and she decided to take care of it."

"With a fire? Isn't that a little much, Detective? Surely I could have simply sneaked into the office and stolen whatever you think they have on me."

"Maybe you couldn't find it."

"And maybe I would have only burned the office instead of an entire building. Do you really think I'm dumb enough to hang around and risk asphyxiation?" Geneva jutted out her chin. "Your comments are ridiculous, and I'm not going to let you bully me into saying anything you can misconstrue. I'm going to tell you what happened, and you can choose to believe me or not." She looked at Detective Mackel. "And that goes for you, too."

Mackel raised an eyebrow. "You weren't kidding about her, Lazarus. She is a feisty one."

Geneva swallowed and winced at the burn in her throat. "You want to know why I reek of gas fumes? I was stupid enough to pick up a can when I saw the stack. The blasted thing slipped from my hands and splashed all over me when it hit the ground. We're here because another one of Thurgood's investors told us about the Pinkerton investigation of Thurgood's misdealings. Mr. Perazon lives down the street from my parents, and we had a nodding acquaintance. I thought he might be willing to share his findings with me. When we arrived, the building was already in flames, but we didn't realize it was the Pinkerton place. We approached one of the firemen to see if we were allowed into the agency, and he shooed us away, indicating it was the Pinkerton structure that was one fire." She opened her purse and withdrew the card she received from Mr. Imhoff and handed it to Detective Lazarus. "This was our lead. There are names on the back of other investors. As I said, we were hoping Mr. Perazon could shed some light on the situation."

"So, you're still interfering in my case, eh?"

"Only because you're like a terrier with a bone about my guilt. I cannot trust you to perform an unbiased investigation."

Detective Lazarus shrugged. "You're entitled to your opinion."

"My opinion?" Geneva barked a harsh laugh. "It sure seems like a fact to me. Thurgood Mayfield created strife ever since he appeared in my life, and it seems like he's still causing trouble even though he's dead. Did I dislike the man? Absolutely. Did I kill him? Hardly. And I'm going to work to find the real killer with or without your help."

"Detective Mackel! Detective Lazarus!" A uniformed officer raced toward them, his face red and streaming with sweat. "The fire chief says you gotta come right away. We found a body, and he thinks it's that Pinkerton agent you were asking about. Perez?"

"Perazon?"

"Yeah, that's it. And it looks like he wasn't killed in the fire. His skull's been bashed in."

Geneva's head swam and her vision tunneled worse than usual. Swaying, she swallowed again the nausea that threatened to overtake her. Unsuccessful, she bent and threw up her breakfast. Mortified, she glanced at Detective Lazarus.

He narrowed his gaze at her, then tossed his handcuffs to the policeman. "Cuff these two on suspicion of murder and put them in the car. I'll be back as soon as I can." He frowned. "And clean this mess up."

Devon raised his fist. "You can't arrest us."

The cop yanked Devon's hands behind his back and locked his wrists together. "We can, and we did. And you just made it worse by threatening a detective."

Two hours later, Geneva and Devon sat in a small windowless room in the police station. The acrid odor of burnt coffee and stale sweat clung to the air. The dingy, gray walls were bare except for a small sign stating "Prisoners will remain seated at all times."

Still handcuffed, she pressed her lips together willing herself not to cry. She had to show Lazarus he couldn't intimidate her. Her chin trembled. Who was she kidding? She was terrified. *Lord, it seems like the only praying I do lately is calling to You for help. I keep getting into one bad circumstance after the next. Is this my fault? Should I stop what I'm doing or are You using me to find the truth?*

The door banged open, and Geneva jumped.

Detective Lazarus strode into the room, flipped the vacant chair around, and straddled the seat. "I've got a deal for you."

Devon frowned. "How about you uncuff us before we have this little chat."

"Fair enough." Lazarus stood and pulled a set of keys from his pocket. He sauntered around the table and unlocked their fetters before returning to his seat.

Geneva rubbed her reddened wrists and winced. Would she ever live down this humiliation?

Devon shoved his hands into his pockets and leaned back in the chair. "We're listening."

"You tell us everything you've discovered, and I do mean everything. Don't leave out one piece of information, no matter how significant." He leveled his gaze at them. "Or personal. Understood?"

"How is that a deal?" Devon asked.

"The deal is I don't charge either one of you with Mayfield's or Perazon's murder."

Grinning, Devon lifted his chin. "Let me guess. Our alibi about the fire checked out. You confirmed our train tickets were legit and we couldn't possibly have gone inside the agency to crack Perzon on the noggin or start the blaze. You also can't confirm Geneva's presence in the Mayfield's hotel room other than finding her hanky there, which means nothing. So you're not really offering a bargain. You need our help in solving this thing."

Detective Lazarus dropped his head and sighed. He scrubbed at his face, then ran his fingers through his hair. "You're right. This case has been one giant tangle of knots. There are so many people who Mayfield defrauded, deceived, or swindled there are not enough hours in the day to interview them all. We got a bit of a break when we discovered Perazon had done a bunch of work, but there are still too many suspects."

"And is Miss Alexander one?" Devon leaned forward.

The detective pursed his lips. "No."

Devon gave a curt nod and crossed his arms.

Geneva let out a huge sigh and pressed a hand again her throat. She closed her eyes. *Thank you, Father.* Opening her eyes, she stared at the detective. "What haven't you told us?"

His head jerked up, and he smirked. "I keep sayin' you're one smart cookie."

"And you want me to use my smarts to help you?"

"Yes, but it could be dangerous, and the higher-ups aren't too pleased with the idea. You don't have to do it if you don't want."

"I'm already in danger." Geneva's stomach fluttered. "I'm trying to find a killer who would like me to take the fall for his deed. I'll do whatever you want me to."

Detective Lazarus turned and rapped twice on the door. It swung open, and a towering, broad-shouldered man squeezed into a tan suit stood in the doorway. He ducked his head then sauntered into the room.

He poked a finger at Geneva but looked at the detective. "She's agreed then?"

"Yep, she's all yours. I'll be back after you've given her the skinny." He saluted at Geneva and Devon and ambled from the room, closing the door with a muted thud.

"I'm Agent Carley from the Pinkerton Agency. Detective Lazarus seems to think you're up for the assignment although I'm not crazy about using civilians." Carley perched on the wooden chair vacated by the detective, his girth making the seat look like a child's. "I won't lie to you. We're at the end of our rope. Perazon was working undercover, posing as one of Mayfield's victims. He finagled his way into the good graces of the firm and was making real progress, at least according to the cryptic reports we were getting. He owed us another report today, but we can't find his notes. Probably went up in the conflagration."

Devon laced his fingers with Geneva's. "You want her to step in somehow, don't you? It isn't' going to work. They already know who she is."

Geneva bolted upright. "What? Is this true?"

"In a way, yes. But you're already involved. Don't you want to see this through to the end?"

"What would I have to do?"

"Here's the thing. We think Perazon's cover may have been blown, and that's why he was murdered. We had another man involved, but he recently took quite ill." He cocked his head. "Had a heart attack, if you get my drift. You could take his place."

Her eyes widened. "My father? You're talking about my father, aren't you?"

Carley nodded. "He's been an agent for about year. He didn't really want to get involved because of Mayfield's relationship to the family, but we convinced him that's why he would never be suspected as being bait. I don't think he realized just how bad this Mayfield character was, or he'd never have agreed to the engagement."

"That was all part of the investigation? You had them set up the marriage as a way to bring down Thurgood? How dare you manipulate my life. Do you play God with other families' lives as well?"

A flush covered Carley's face. "We're not proud of our techniques, but they get the job done. And your father only agreed to come on board because he owed us. He has a rather unfortunate incident in his past that we…uh…made go away."

Geneva leapt up and began to pace. How naïve she was, a country bumpkin who thought people were honest and forthright in their dealings. First Thurgood, then her parents, and now law enforcement doing despicable deeds because they think the ends justify the means.

Listen, My child. I can use even this for your good.

She froze, tears clinging to her lashes. Warmth enveloped her, and peace descended over her like a cloak. Devon approached her, but she held up her hand. Pivoting on her heel, she faced Agent Carley. "Fine. I'll do it, but you have to promise me when this is over, you will leave me and my family alone. You will release my father from his agreement. Is that understood?"

Chapter Thirty-six

Agent Carley's lips twisted giving him the appearance of having eaten something bad. His brows met above his nose, and he shifted side to side as a bull might when considering how to charge the matador.

Silence pervaded the room, and Geneva glared at the man. She was done being pushed around. It was time the detectives played on her terms. It was bad enough they had separated her from Devon with some vague explanation about national security. She found that unlikely, but whatever persuaded them to agree with her terms was fine. Devon would fill her in later, so she'd bide her time.

"You drive a hard bargain, Miss Alexander."

"I think not." She crossed her arms. "My family has given of ourselves for long enough. It's time we got something back. Hmmm?"

He glowered at her, mute.

Her insides quivered, but she willed herself not to sink into the chair and wilt like a discarded rag doll. How quickly the situation had become adversarial. She straightened her shoulders. Her parents weren't always kind to her, and they had made decisions about her she would never understand, but they loved her, and she loved them. She would protect them with her last breath. Perhaps Father had come to Christ and would be a changed man, but none of that mattered now.

She set her jaw. "Well, Detective Carley?"

"All right. We'll release your father from his agreement."

Nearly fainting with relief, she forced a firm smile. "Excellent. Let's discuss how this will work."

He gestured to the vacant chair. "Please join me at the table."

With a curt nod, she seated herself and laced her fingers in her lap.

Detective Carley cracked his knuckles then propped his arms on the table. "Your father will notify Claymore that he's made arrangements for you to take over his investments. He'll claim he's been tutoring you all along and that you have a mind for this sort of thing. Some girls do, you know. That will get you close to these men, and you can probe them for information and motive. You're to report everything to Lazarus who will pass the dirt to me. Simple, right?"

Geneva shook her head. "Let me see if I have this correct. I'm supposed to sashay into Father's firm and convince the businessmen that I'm a financial expert and have his blessing to take over their accounts. Rather irregular and unbelievable, don't you think?"

"It's the best plan we've got at this point. You're an actress. Persuade them you are who you say. At any rate, can you think of something better?"

"I'm a singer and dancer, not an actress. What makes you think I can give a credible performance?"

He smirked. "Because you're giving one right now. I have no doubt you are anxious and more than a little afraid, but your body language says different. You stood tall and gave me what for, all while meeting my eyes. If I wasn't used to people lying to me, I'd think you were confident. Besides, do you have a better plan?"

Three days later, Geneva entered the conference room at her father's firm. The sound of her high-heeled shoes was muted as she crossed the navy-and-cream Persian rug. Smoothing the skirt of the camel-colored silk suit Devon had unearthed from the costume closet, she swallowed and grimaced. Her throat was beginning to recover from the smoke inhalation, but still pained her. Maybe her Bette Davis-like huskiness would add to her performance as the "tough cookie" Detective Carley wanted her to be.

A quartet of oil paintings framed in gilt hung above the stone fireplace, the stern-looking men glaring at her from their perch. She had no desire to be in charge, but it would be wonderful if some day women's portraits lined the walls of companies around the world.

Voices sounded in the hall, and she gulped. Could she do this? Was it too late to run? No matter how much she and the detective talked they couldn't contrive a plan that included Devon. Disappointed, she agreed with Carley. Her involvement was far-fetched enough. Adding Devon would only convolute matters.

Her stomach quivered as if a colony of bunnies was running amok. Breathe, Geneva. You can do this. *Give me strength, Lord. Am I doing the right thing? I'm getting ready to give the performance of my life, and it's all a lie. You don't condone deceit, but do You understand why I have to do this?*

The door opened, and three men in identical charcoal suits, white shirts, and blue neckties strode into the room. She suppressed a nervous giggle. Had they coordinated their outfits or were they wearing the uniform of their industry? Surely their matching scowls weren't standard.

That didn't bode well. Her success depended on being stronger than they were. *I need a miracle here, Lord.*

"Gentlemen, thank you for seeing me on such short notice, but I'm sure you understand the urgency of the matter. As my father may have told you, his health is not good, therefore he has named me as his successor in the firm. I reviewed your portfolios with him and have a keen grasp of the situation."

She walked to the head of the eight-foot long cherry table and sat in the cordovan-colored leather chair. She gestured to the vacant seats then folded her hands on the gleaming table surface. "Please join me."

The men stared at her for a long moment, then glanced at each other, uncertainty edging onto their features. Taking advantage of the obvious crack in their emotionless exterior, she shrugged and rose. "It appears you're unhappy with the circumstances." She gave them a firm smile and added steel to her voice. "Frankly, Father has more than enough clients for whom I can make money, so if you're not on board, let me know your intentions immediately." She glanced at the watch pinned to her bodice. "I'm a very busy woman."

A knock sounded at the doorway, and Miss Paxton held up a small piece of paper. "My apologies for interrupting, Miss Alexander, but I have a call for you." She looked at the men, then back at Geneva. "Of a confidential nature."

Geneva turned to the men. "Well, gentlemen? Will you be staying or should I take this call?"

The youngest, who appeared to be in his early 40s, tugged at his collar then blew out a loud breath. "I'm Brian Paul, and I'm in." He dropped into the closest chair. "At least I'm willing to hear what you have to say. You're awfully young, Miss Alexander, but someone gave me a break when I was about your age. I guess I owe you the same opportunity." He banged his hand on the table. "Come on, chaps. It seems like the firm might be redeemed after those debacles with Mayfield."

Portly, balding, and sneering, the oldest of the trio shook his head. "No girly is going to manage my finances. I'll be withdrawing all my funds. You can pass that along to your father."

"And that will be your loss, Mr....?"

"Gibbons. And I'll take that risk." He pushed passed the secretary, nearly knocking her into the doorframe. His footsteps receded as he hurried down the hall.

The expression on the last man's face danced between contempt and skepticism.

As planned, Miss Paxton played the part of the concerned assistant and waved the note. "The call, Miss Alexander. It seems urgent."

Geneva leaned toward the man still standing. "By process of elimination, you must be Mr. Washington, and it makes no never mind to me what you choose, but you need to decide." She took the paper from Miss Paxton and glanced at it. It read: *You're doing great.* Just the encouragement she needed. Folding the page, she tucked it into the pocket of her skirt. "That will be all, Miss Paxton. Let the caller know—"

"All right. I'll stay." Mr. Washington yanked out the nearest chair and sat. "Let's get on with this."

"I'll take a message, Miss Alexander."

"Thank you. Be quick about it. I'd like you to take notes of our meeting."

"Yes, ma'am." The secretary turned and disappeared.

Geneva returned to the table and cleared her throat. "Thank you for joining me. You will not be disappointed. Now that Mr. Mayfield and my father are out of the way, we can move forward with additional solid, intelligent investments." She distributed a sheaf of papers to each of the men. "Based on my perusal of your files, these are my recommendations. I believe you'll find them more than acceptable."

Mr. Paul and Mr. Washington flipped through the portfolio, pages rustling in the silence.

Geneva pretended to review her copy. Her lack of peripheral vision prevented her from eyeing the men surreptitiously, so she mentally rehearsed her next comments.

A few moments later, Miss Paxton entered the room with her notepad and pencil. She dragged one of the chairs away from the table and settled in the corner. Crossing her ankles, she winked at Geneva who frowned. The woman would give away their ploy.

Finally finished reading, the men looked at Geneva.

Mr. Washington raised an eyebrow. "Interesting selections. Unless I miss my guess, you seem to have a gift for this. I'm familiar with all of the opportunities, but would not have bundled them." He peered over the rim of his glasses, his face smug. "And neither would your father. His...uh...capabilities...seemed to rest more along the same lines as Mr. Mayfield."

"What exactly are you saying, Mr. Washington?"

"Thurgood Mayfield was a swindler and a cheat who looked out for no one but himself. Initially, he was smooth enough that none of us noticed, but in the last several months, his behavior became erratic and downright paranoid. He got what he deserved. I don't want to degrade a man to his own daughter, especially when he's down, but your father's actions mirrored Mr. Mayfield's. His decisions seemed more in his best interests than in his client's. Let's hope the apple falls far from the tree, Miss Alexander."

She frowned. "You're entitled to your opinion, but I would appreciate you keeping your comments about my father to yourself."

Mr. Paul scribbled his signature on the top page and slid the document toward Geneva. "I'm not inclined to agree with my colleague, but I am impressed with this proposal. Send the official paperwork to me, but my John Hancock here gives you permission to move forward."

Geneva's heart seemed to ricochet in her chest. For whatever reason, the men believed her charade. Did Mr. Washington's attempt to cast doubt on Father's character make him guilty of giving Thurgood *what he deserved* or was he simply arrogant and condescending?

She handed Mr. Washington a pen. "As Mr. Paul has done, please sign the top sheet, and I'll begin the transactions immediately."

He signed and tossed the pen onto the table. She stood and the men clambered to their feet. Apparently, they still had their manners.

Hand outstretched, Mr. Paul's gaze swept her from her stylish hat to her well-shod feet. "I look forward to our continued association."

Her toes curled, and she shook his hand. "As do I." The lie slipped out with ease.

Dipping his head toward Mr. Washington, he brushed unseen lint from his sleeves and strolled from the room.

Mr. Washington bowed from the waist. "I had my doubts when your father contacted me, but I'm impressed with how you handled Mr. Paul and me. You managed to be knowledgeable and confident without losing your femininity. You might just be the refreshing change this firm needs. I'd like to have a further discussion with you." He buttoned his suit jacket. "Alone."

Chapter Thirty-seven

The following evening, Geneva climbed out of the taxi in front of Mr. Washington's home. Shadowed by mammoth elm trees, the boxy Italianate home was painted a creamy yellow, with five Corinthian pillars supporting the wide portico leading to the arched entrance.

She glanced down at her dress. Although the fanciest outfit she owned, would it enable her to fit into this man's world of wealth and power? Would he continue to believe the charade? Ethel had done Geneva's hair and makeup, turning her into a sophisticated-looking woman of the world. She patted her chignon and smiled. If Mr. Washington didn't believe her, it wouldn't be for lack of trying on her part.

Taking courage from the two life-sized lions guarding the steps, she straightened her spine and resisted the urge to smooth her skirt as was her habit when she was nervous. With the beaded clutch Devon had pulled from the costume room tucked under her arm, she marched up the walkway. The carved oak door opened on silent hinges as she ascended the stairs.

A tall, skeletal woman with jet-black hair stood in the doorway, gray dress hanging on her frame. Thick glasses magnified her dark eyes that swept over Geneva. The woman stepped back. "Come in. Mr. Washington is expecting you."

Geneva entered the house, and she gaped at the opulence. Her parents' home was well-appointed, but it paled in comparison to this luxurious interior. A Tiffany chandelier hung from the ceiling of the two-story foyer, its crystals dotting the walls with rainbow reflections. The tiles on the mosaic floor shone in what seemed to be a coat of arms pattern. Dark woodwork contrasted with the platinum-colored walls covered with gilt-framed artwork.

Apparently the man wanted no confusion about his prosperity.

The housekeeper cleared her throat and cinched the crisp white apron around her gaunt figure. "Please follow me."

Geneva's face warmed. So much for acting like a self-assured businesswoman. "Of course. The beauty of Mr. Washington's home is overwhelming. You must enjoy being part of it."

Shrugging, the woman led her down a hall wide enough to accommodate a car, then entered an enormous dining room. Butternut paneling graced the walls below the chair rail, and more artwork clung to the floral-papered walls. Seating for a multitude surrounded the lustrous, cherry Queen Anne table. A matching sideboard held a glistening silver tea set flanked with a pair of eight-armed, silver candleholders.

Movement near the stone fireplace caught Geneva's eye, and she stifled a gasp. She had been so enamored with the room, she hadn't seen Mr. Washington leaning against the mantel. He walked toward her and lifted her hand to his lips. "Thank you for joining me, Miss Alexander. You look lovely." He waggled his eyebrows. "You belong in a ballroom, not a boardroom."

"You flatter me, Mr. Washington, but just because a woman is attractive doesn't mean she can't handle the workplace. Our successful replacement of men has proven that, wouldn't you say?"

A look of irritation passed across his face. "Let's hold our discussions of more serious matters until after dinner." He pulled her arm into the crook of his elbow and led her to the end of the table where two places had been set with crystal, china, and silver. A wine bottle was nestled in a silver cooler on a stand.

Mr. Washington released her arm and pulled out the chair for her. As she sat, she dipped her head and smiled. He seated himself, then picked up the bottle. "Wine, Miss Alexander? It's French. Fortunately, I filled my cellar before the war."

She shook her head. "No, but feel free to partake yourself."

"Don't mind if I do." The straw-yellow liquid gurgled as he poured it into the cut crystal glass. He raised the drink. "To a lucrative partnership."

She picked up her water glass and clinked it to his. Sipping, she let the cold water ease her parched throat still tender from the fire. Her eyes widened as he downed the wine and refilled his glass.

A young woman appeared on soundless feet, carrying two shallow soup bowls. She set them down and withdrew. Fragrant steam rose from the concoction.

"Tomato bisque is my favorite, but how did you secure milk? It's terribly difficult to get."

"You'll have to discuss the logistics with my cook, but I wouldn't trouble yourself with such trivialities."

Geneva bit her lip. She might look the part, but if she continued to act like a naïve schoolgirl, he'd never fall for her deception. "Forgive my ignorant question, Mr. Washington, but serving at the USO exposes me to the shortages and difficulties of obtaining food."

He slurped the soup, then waved his spoon. "Completely understandable, and quite valiant of you to do your bit, as they say. Your parents could have been none too happy to see you performing in a dance hall. Perhaps that's why your father chose you to take his place." He drank deeply from his glass and splashed more wine into the vessel.

"Father selected me because I'm the best person for the job, and he trusts me implicitly." Geneva exaggerated her best high-society voice. "The USO is not a dance hall, and I resent your intimations."

"You're a fiery one, eh? I can respect that. Please accept my apology." He held up the wine bottle. "Are you sure you don't want any?"

She shook her head. "No, thank you." How could she steer the conversation to Thurgood and Mr. Claymore?

"Suit yourself." He topped off the liquid and drank. "You are captivating, Geneva." His words slurred, and he reached for her hand. "Do you mind if I call you that? All this Miss and Mister seems so formal."

"We barely know each other *Mr.* Washington. We'll save first names for another time."

He straightened and thunked his glass on the table. Wine sloshed over the edge. "Do you realize how well-connected I am? I could make or break your career. Just like I did with Thurgood Mayfield."

Geneva froze. Should she respond or would the man continue his tirade and give her the much-needed information she sought without prompting?

The door between the kitchen and dining room swung open. The serving girl entered the room and tiptoed across the floor. She whisked away the soup bowls and returned moments later with two plates filled with a beef filet smothered in gravy, steaming mashed potatoes, and glazed carrots. She bobbed a curtsy and hastened out.

Mr. Washington cut a slice from the meat, popped it into his mouth, and chewed slowly. After swallowing, he washed down the bite with a swig of wine. "Enjoy your meal, Miss Alexander. It doesn't resemble anything you get at your USO club."

"You're right, and you are very generous to invite me. The girls were jealous when they heard I was going to be dining with you."

"Were they now?" He preened as he continued to eat.

Deciding to stoke the fire of his ego, she said, "Yes. I told them how important you are. They were impressed."

"Too bad your Mr. Mayfield wasn't as dazzled. Or Herbert Claymore."

"Thurgood's opinion of himself was too well-developed. That was his downfall."

"An astute observation." Mr. Washington gulped from his glass. "Claymore has the same problem, but his temper also gets the best of him. He should never have gone into Mayfield's place without me. We were supposed to confront him jointly, but that idiot let his anger get the best of him. Next thing you know, Mayfield is dead, and I'm getting money to keep quiet."

Nausea swept over Geneva. Was Mr. Washington saying Mr. Claymore killed Thurgood? It sounded as if he was blackmailing Mr. Claymore. She pressed her lips together to stem the bile forming in her stomach. Her hand trembled, and she dropped her fork with a clatter.

Mr. Washington's head shot up, and his face reddened. He thrust back his chair, its feet screeching against the wooden floor. Jumping up, he swayed then staggered to the sideboard. He wrenched open the top drawer then pulled out a revolver and pointed it at her, the weapon wavering.

Geneva's heart pounded, and perspiration broke out on her upper lip. Her breath came out in gasps, and her vision tunneled worse than usual. Lightheaded, she wrapped her arms around her middle. Don't faint. Don't faint. Don't…faint…

The door swung open and banged against the wall. Geneva and Mr. Washington recoiled and pivoted toward the noise. Devon rushed at the man, his arms outstretched. Mr. Washington snarled and gripped the gun in both hands.

Geneva gasped and shrank in the chair. "No!" Where had Devon come from? Had he been in the kitchen the whole time?

Devon lowered his shoulder and rammed into the man. The men fell to the floor, bumping into the buffet on the way down. One of the candelabras teetered then dropped to the ground with a metallic crash.

The pistol fired.

Geneva screamed and ducked. The shock wave of the weapon reverberated through her chest, and her ears rang. She leapt to her feet, but her trembling muscles almost refused to support her. Her desire to flee from danger fought the urge to jump into the fray to help Devon.

Locked in an angry embrace, the men rolled across the floor, first one direction, then the other. Devon grappled for the weapon still gripped in Mr. Washington's hand. Grunting and huffing, Devon said, "It's over, Washington. You're not going to win this. I'm younger and stronger than you."

Mr. Washington bellowed, his face dripping in sweat. He squirmed underneath Devon's wiry frame. "Ha! That's a laugh. You're 4F, obviously too pathetic to get into the military."

Eyes wide, Geneva gasped as a red stain began to spread on Devon's shirt sleeve. The shot must have found its mark.

Devon grabbed Mr. Washington's wrist with both hands and banged it on the floor. The man howled, but Devon continued until the revolver fell out of his limp hand.

"Geneva, quickly! Get the gun."

Speechless, she stared at the weapon.

"Geneva, now! Get...the...gun!"

She stumbled forward and dropped to her knees a short distance from the weapon. She crawled forward and wrapped her white-knuckled fingers around the pewter-gray tang. Dragging it toward herself, Geneva picked up the gun, then nearly dropped the unexpectedly heavy revolver. She climbed to her feet and turned.

Strength seemed to have deserted Mr. Washington. He lay listless and mute, his eyes closed.

"Point the pistol at him while I figure out how we can tie him up."

Nodding, Geneva stretched out her arm, and the gun wavered in her hand. She tightened her grip. Her shoulders bunched, and her spine cramped. How could such a small item weigh so much?

Devon moved off of Mr. Washington, then grabbed his arm and hefted him to his feet. Shoving him into the nearest chair, Devon took the gun from Geneva. "Go find some sort of rope, and we'll tie him up."

Geneva hurried into the vacant kitchen. The cook and her serving girl must have escaped after the fracas started. She yanked open drawer after drawer, searching the contents. Nothing. Behind her, the door to the pantry stood ajar, and she peeked inside. A large spool of string probably used to truss up turkeys sat on one of the shelves. Would it be strong enough?

She grabbed the cylinder and rushed back to the dining room. She held it out to Devon. "The women aren't in the kitchen."

He shrugged. "The gunfire probably scared them off. The string will have to do. I'll tie him up. You call the police and tell them we've got a package for Detective Lazarus of the Baltimore police department. Then watch for them. When the cops arrive, we'll skedaddle out the back and head to Baltimore. We'll give our side of the story on home turf. We probably have less than a day before Lazarus or his goons show up on our doorstep."

Chapter Thirty-eight

Geneva strode through the hallway in the hospital. After they'd fled Mr. Washington's home, she asked Devon to return to Baltimore, convincing him she needed time with Father before she resumed her work with the USO. With any luck, the lieutenant would look for her there.

She stopped before reaching the room, smoothed her skirts and hair, then licked her dry lips. It was time to hear Father's side of the story, and she wasn't leaving until she got it. Here goes nothing. She squared her shoulders, then entered the room.

Father sat in the chair next to the bed, the lamp forming a halo of light around him. Engrossed in reading, he didn't look up. Geneva squinted at the black leather book in his hands. Was it a *Bible*? He hadn't known she was coming, so perhaps the renewal of his relationship with God was real.

Her heart softened. She wanted to believe it and trust him. *Lord, I'm going to go on faith here, that Father is changed as he said. Please give me a sign. I want us to be like other families who love and cherish one another, and we can only do that through You.*

She sighed, and Father raised his head. A smile bloomed on his face, his eyes crinkling at the corners. She froze, years of criticism and condescension sowing hesitation in her steps.

His smile faltered, and he closed the Bible. He laid it on the end of the bed, then folded his hands and dropped his gaze for a moment. His lips moved silently.

Was he *praying*? Was this her sign from God? Of course, it was. She laughed softly. *Lord, thank You for giving me such obvious proof of Father's love for You, and for showing me immediately. Forgive my unbelief.*

Geneva rushed forward and dropped to her knees in front of Father. Grasping his hands, she gazed into his face and smiled. His eyes flew open. Confusion, then joy crossed his face.

"Father, you look so much better than the last time I was here."

He extricated one of his hands and stroked her hair. Her scalp tingled at the warmth of his touch.

"I told you I'd make a full recovery. God has plans for this reformed reprobate." His voice cracked. "It appears you may have decided to believe your old dad. That means more to me than I can express. I have a lot to make up for with regard to how I treated you. I hope you can stay a while, so you can share with me about your new life at the USO. I'm so proud you decided to serve in that way."

Laying her head in his lap, she closed her eyes, the last vestiges of doubt falling way. *Thank You, God.*

She hugged her father then rose and sat on the edge of the bed. "It means a lot to hear you say that. I'll stay until you tire or the nurses toss me out, whichever comes first. I do want to tell you all about what I'm doing, and about Devon." Her face warmed. "He's a special man, Father. I think you'll like him. But before we get to that, we need to have a different discussion."

"Sounds serious."

"It is." Geneva began to smooth her skirt, then stilled her hands. She needed to stop that ridiculous habit. Lacing her fingers, she took a deep breath. "I want to talk about the investigation into Thurgood's murder, and your role as a Pinkerton agent."

"The agency told me they were going to share that with you."

"Did they also tell you I've been asked to go undercover in your place?"

He frowned. "Yes, and I'm not happy about it. It's too dangerous. What are they thinking in tasking a young woman to act as an agent?"

"Father..."

He held up his hands in surrender. "Forgive me. Old habits die hard, but a father can still worry about his daughter. Do you truly want to take this assignment? I don't want you to do it, if you are the least bit hesitant."

"I won't lie to you, I'm nervous and at times even fearful, but it's the right thing to do. I want to prove to myself that I'm capable. When I felt that you and Mother treated me as someone who couldn't fend for herself, I was upset, but I was doing the same thing. I was timid and second-guessed my actions. Devon and I prayed about the mission, and we feel God is calling me to do my part in catching the killer."

Father studied her face for several seconds, then nodded. "I will pray for your safety and wisdom." He grinned. "And, that I will let go of my concern." Sobering up he said, "Can you tell me what you're doing?"

"Yes, in fact I'm surprised someone from the agency hasn't spoken to you already. If one of your clients contacts you, you'll need to act your part as well."

"Then it's a good thing you came."

"I'll start at the beginning, but I'll try to be brief because you may already know some of what I'm about to say." She finger-combed her hair, then took a deep breath. "Thurgood discovered my location and arrived with the intention of convincing me to return home. I told him I had no interest in marrying him, and that I planned to serve with the USO until they no longer needed me. We argued, quite vehemently. He told me things…things about you, about who you really are." She closed her eyes as the memory of that night swept over her. The night Thurgood claimed her father was a rapist.

Father blanched. He swallowed heavily, then reached for her hand. "I'm sorry you had to hear about my past from Thurgood, but I'm sure he twisted it to make me seem guilty." He stared into her eyes, pain etched on his face. "Please believe me when I tell you I'm not. I can tell you about the whole sordid incident."

Peace settled over her like a cloak. God was confirming his innocence. "I do want to hear your story, Father, but not yet." She gave him a gentle smile. "Let me finish explaining about the investigation."

His grip on her fingers relaxed, and he nodded.

"Thurgood insinuated that he would put me in an institution and make your death seem like an accident."

Father's eyes widened, and his face darkened. "I had no idea he was so fiendish."

"It's not your fault. He was a smooth operator when he wanted to be. Anyway, I told him I wouldn't let him get away with his plan, that I'd see him dead first. He was killed that night in his hotel room. Because there were so many witnesses to my claim, I was arrested. There wasn't proof that I murdered him other than one of my hankies found underneath his body, so the authorities let me go, but they seemed determined that I was guilty. Devon and I decided to solve the case ourselves."

"Honey, you could have been injured…or worse."

"I know, but I refused to go to jail for a crime I didn't commit."

"Justice would have won out."

"Not necessarily, Father. I wasn't willing to take that chance." Geneva squeezed his hand. "Anyway, I haven't gotten hurt." She swallowed. Father didn't need to know about Devon's injuries. "We dug into Thurgood's past and met with lots of people he wronged, from a young woman who is carrying his child to investors he defrauded. Last night, we discovered that one of them, a Mr. Washington, saw Mr. Claymore kill Thurgood then he blackmailed Mr. Claymore. We were able to…restrain Mr. Washington, and he's been arrested."

Father gasped. "Claymore, a killer? It can't be. He's ruthless and selfish and…"

"It must be true, otherwise why would he pay a blackmailer?"

"You make a good point, but I'm having trouble believing it."

"I understand. But there's more, and it's rather distressing. Did you know that our neighbor Mr. Perazon was a Pinkerton agent?"

"Yes, he and I were working together on the fraud investigation."

"Yet, you gave your blessing for Thurgood and I to marry?" Her eyes widened.

"Initially, yes. But I would never have let the wedding take place. The agency requested that I continue the ruse of your engagement, so he didn't get wind of our suspicions, and I agreed. Please forgive me. It was inexcusable for me to involve you."

"It's okay, Father. I realize now that you were making the best of a bad situation."

"Thank you, but I am ashamed of my actions."

She laid her hand on his arm. "Let's talk no more of it. It's over and done with. But I have to tell you that Mr. Perazon was killed in a fire at the agency. Devon and I were headed there to speak with him about his investigation because we thought it might provide leads for our case. When we arrived, the building was in flames, and he was inside."

"Poor John. He was a good man." A tear trickled down his face.

"We know when we sign with the agency that we are risking our lives, but it's still painful to lose a friend, even for justice. Do the police have a suspect?"

She grimaced. "Not yet. They tried to pin it on Devon and me, but there was only circumstantial evidence, and the detective finally admitted he didn't think I perpetrated the crime. We struck a deal that if I took your place in the investigation, you would be released from your agreement with the agency. That whatever they've been holding over your head would be dismissed. They gave me a primer on how to act the part of an investment counselor in your place in an effort to ferret out Thurgood's killer."

A nervous giggle escaped. "It worked, but not in the way we anticipated. The theory was that one of his clients murdered him. As far as I know, Mr. Claymore was never considered a possibility. Now, we'll have to come up with a plan to expose his guilt."

"We? You need to leave that to the police. Notify them and then step away."

"I can't do that. I'm in the same position you were, Father. If I back out now, Mr. Claymore might realize the authorities are on to him. I need to complete my assignment."

Chapter Thirty-nine

The muted clink of silverware on china mingled with the buzz of conversation. Geneva pushed around the crab cake on her plate, then poked a small bite into her mouth. She laid down her fork and sighed. Despite being one of Haussner's signature dishes, the tender morsels of blue crab tasted like sawdust on her tongue. Devon shouldn't have sprung for such a high-end meal. Her appetite wasn't doing justice to their visit to Baltimore's iconic restaurant.

He reached across the table and took her empty hands in his. "I know the stress of this situation is affecting you, but you need to keep up your strength. If the crab isn't to your liking, we can order something else."

"I'm not sure anything would appeal to me. Every time I try to take a bite, my stomach clenches. This meal is going to be a waste of your money."

"Don't worry about the money. Let's enjoy the experience. This is the only restaurant I've been to that features artwork." He gestured to a gilt-framed oil paintings on the walls, then jerked his head toward the one at their table. "That's Eugene de Blaas's *Venetian Flower Vendor* the first piece Mr. and Mrs. Haussner purchased just before the war. Pretty, isn't it?"

She glanced at the picture and smiled. "It is. The women seem very happy, and the little girl with her braids and boots is cute. The restaurant has several nice pieces, but that ball of string near the door is odd, don't you think?"

He shrugged. "I'll admit it's unusual, but did you hear the maître d say it's been created using the laundry twine from the packages of tablecloths and napkins? Seems like a testament to honest, hard work. I like it."

"With the Haussners being from Germany, I'm surprised they've done so well. They've been in America less than twenty years. Several businesses in Philly operated by German immigrants closed because many customers stopped frequenting the shops."

"Baltimoreans apparently favor their stomachs over politics." He squeezed her fingers then released them. "Try to eat a little bit more, and then we'll take a cab to the riverfront. We can savor the views while I explain the operation to take down Herbert Claymore."

"I still can't believe Detective Lazarus is willing for us to be part of the sting operation."

"He wasn't happy about it, but after grilling me for several hours yesterday, he realized it was the best possible plan. If we start making changes to the charade now, Claymore could get suspicious. Because of Washington's arrest, Lazarus feels our quarry may be getting skittish anyway, thinking the blackmailer could rat him out."

"Why haven't the police already arrested Claymore?"

"Washington isn't talking. He's lawyered up, so Lazarus only has our word we heard Washington say he saw Claymore kill Thurgood. It's called hearsay, and it's not enough for a judge to sign a warrant. But Lazarus does want to move quickly. That's why the sting is scheduled for tomorrow."

Geneva swallowed and pressed her hand against her stomach. "And that would be why I have no appetite." She forced a grin. "Humphrey Bogart or William Powell would have had this case tied up days ago. Why does Detective Lazarus move so slowly?"

Devon chuckled. "Movie directors don't bother with important legalities like due process. I know it's hard to wait, but this will all be over soon, and you will regain normalcy in your life." He raised his hand and gestured to the waiter.

She tilted her head. "I'm not sure what constitutes normal in my life anymore."

The man hurried to the table and bowed. He looked at Geneva's plate, and his brow furrowed. "Is there something wrong with you food, miss? I can bring you another selection."

"No, I'm not very hungry."

"We'll take the check, now." Devon pulled his wallet from the breast pocket of his coat.

"Yes, sir."

Geneva sat in silence while the man strode to the kitchen and returned a short time later with the bill lying on a small, silver salver. He bowed again and set the plate on the table. "Whenever you're ready, sir."

Glancing at the slip of paper, Devon withdrew money from his wallet and handed it to the server. "Keep the change."

The man picked up the plate, dipped his head, and murmured his thanks before threading through tables to the kitchen.

Devon rose, helped Geneva to her feet, and kissed her forehead. Affecting his best Jimmy Cagney, he said, "Stick with me, baby. I'll show you normal, see."

She giggled, and they made their way out of the restaurant. A three-quarter moon brightened the inky black sky and lit the sidewalk. Two couples exited a cab at the curb, and Devon pulled Geneva toward it. He peeked into the open door. "Boston and South Clinton, please. We'd like to visit the waterfront."

The cabbie nodded. "A beautiful night for sightseeing."

Geneva slid into the taxi, then Devon climbed in and closed the door. The vehicle accelerated, and she sank into the leather cushion. Closing her eyes, she pinched the bridge of her nose.

Devon wrapped his arm around her shoulders, and her eyes opened. His teeth flashed white in the darkness. "If we're going to be Nick and Nora Charles, we have to get you a hat," he said.

She jabbed him with her elbow, and the tension melted from her neck. *Thank You for Devon, Lord.* "But there will be no martinis for you."

"Understood." He hugged her close and nuzzled her ear. Shivers raised goose bumps on her arms. He chuckled. "I'm not kidding about the hat. We have the perfect little number in the costume department. We've done well so far with your outfits. There are a couple more silk suits you can use. Nora would never wear the same dress twice."

"Suddenly, you're a fashion guru?"

He snickered. "No, but *The Thin Man* series is my favorite."

The cab stopped, and Geneva peered out the window. Moonlight glittered on the Patapsco River's rippling waters. "This is lovely, Devon. How did you know about this place?"

"When I first arrived, I did quite a bit of exploring, getting to know my new city. Baltimore has lots of nooks and crannies that don't seem to be well known. This is one of them." He paid the cabbie, opened the door, and got out of the vehicle.

Geneva grabbed his hand and scrambled out after him. They walked a short distance then sat on a wooden bench tucked under a large maple tree. Devon pointed across the river. "Can you see the dark humps in the distance? That's Fort McHenry."

She squinted toward the water. "I'm not sure." Her face warmed. "My vision is poor enough during the day, but at night it's much worse. Blackout conditions certainly don't help."

"I'm sorry. I shouldn't have asked." He pulled her hand through the crook of his elbow. "Besides, I can barely see it either. But I've read a lot about the fort."

"That's fascinating. Could we visit the fort at some point?" She giggled. "You know, during that normal life you promised me."

"I don't know if we can. Even though it's a national park, the Coast Guard is based there for the duration of the war."

"We'll have to add it to our things-to-do-after-the-war list. You do have one of those, don't you? Ethel and I started ours shortly after we met and compared notes about what we missed the most."

He chucked her under the chin, his smile glistening in the moonlight. "We'll definitely put it on the list." Sobering up, he said, "There are many places I want to explore with you, Geneva Alexander. We can take a lifetime to do that, if you'll let me."

His breath was warm on her face, sending tingles down her neck. Her heart sped up, and she curled her toes. She stilled. Was he asking her to marry him? Her lack of experience with men was a detriment at times, and this was one of them. *Lord, I need help here. I don't want to jump to conclusions and embarrass him.* "Um…"

Laying his fingers on her lips, he shook his head. "Don't speak. I shouldn't have said anything, but I got caught up in my feelings. I care a great deal about you, Geneva. You are a special girl, like no one I've ever met before. But maybe you don't feel the same way. I understand. I should be grateful you're even willing to be seen with a 4F."

Her shoulders slumped, and she ducked her head. "I'm sorry if I offended by not responding as you hoped. It has nothing to do with your military status. I care about you. A lot. But Thurgood's murder, the investigation, my parents…it's all jumbled up, and I'm struggling to keep my head above water."

"I understand, and I didn't mean to add to the turmoil. Let's focus on tomorrow."

Geneva shuddered. "Yes, tomorrow." How could she feel so much excitement and dread at the same. Excitement that Devon loved her but dread that she might not live to see another day. Herbert Claymore had proven he could kill once, which meant he could be willing to kill again, and she might be the one in the crosshairs.

Chapter Forty

Music from the orchestra pulsed. Geneva stood on stage with Ethel and four other dancers waiting for the curtain to rise. She squinted against the glare from the overhead lights and shivered despite the stifling heat. Pressing a hand against her chest, she blew out a large breath in an attempt to slow her racing heart.

Why had she agreed to the sting operation? She wasn't a detective or a private investigator. She was a timid girl from Philadelphia trying to do her bit for God and country. Nibbling her lower lip, she rolled her shoulders and sighed again. Ethel shot a look in her direction, concern and confusion etched on her heavily made-up face.

Geneva shrugged and forced a smile. Devon and Detective Lazarus insisted that she not tell anyone what was going to happen, even her best friend. However, smart cookie that she was, Ethel had already pressed Geneva for details, saying she knew all was not right with her. Fortunately, Ethel presumed Devon was the topic of conversation and gave him the evil eye every chance she got.

Devon. His image filled her mind, and she smiled. What had she done to deserve such a fine man? On the one hand, he treated her like a porcelain doll, fragile and precious. On the other, he valued her opinions and seemed to enjoy discussing topics on which their philosophies differed. In addition, he accepted her failing vision without qualms, more than once saying she saw more with her heart and mind than most people did with their eyes.

His voice resonated from in front of the curtain as he gave announcements and praised the troops for their bravery and willingness to serve. How did he feel about making that declaration? She had never seen any of the soldiers or sailors who came through be anything but gracious to him, but did he wonder if they silently judged his lack of uniform? He regularly derided himself. There were many ways to serve, but the swell of patriotism and rush to enlist since Pearl Harbor had to make it difficult for men to remain civilians.

Lord, help me focus tonight. My feelings for Devon and fear about confronting Mr. Claymore are clouding my mind.

The percussionist played a snappy drum roll, and a cymbal crashed. That was the dancers' cue. Geneva straightened her spine and fisted her hands on her hips. She extended her right leg and pointed her toes. She nodded at Ethel as the other girls moved into position. The curtain swept open on silent pulleys sending a blast of fresh air across the platform.

Devon gestured toward the girls and ducked backstage. Geneva fought the desire to watch him go. Applause filled the auditorium. Frozen in place, the orchestra leader stood with his arms raised, baton in hand.

A side door opened, and the maestro frowned. He laid down the baton and folded his arms. Three dim figures entered and strode to the front row where they took the last remaining seats.

Geneva stifled a gasp. She may not be able to see clearly, but she recognized her father's frame and distinctive walk next to Mr. Claymore's hulking figure and a man she didn't recognize.

What was Father doing here? Was he part of the ploy? When had he been discharged from the hospital? Did the doctors know he planned to take an exhausting train ride from Philadelphia to Baltimore?

Silence descended once more, and the orchestra leader lifted his arms. The instrumentalists came to attention. Seconds later, the baton came down, and music swelled. Hours of rehearsal kicked in, allowing Geneva to instinctively execute her dance moves as she sang while trying not to stare at Father's party.

Perspiration formed along her hairline and trickled between her shoulder blades. As she twirled along the front of the stage, she stole a glance at the stranger seated next to Father. The man's arms were crossed, his face expressionless. He seemed unmoved by the merriment and entertainment. Who was he and why had he come to a show he didn't seem to enjoy?

Father smiled, and her step faltered. Her face heated. Forcing her attention back to the routine, she finished the number as loud clapping engulfed the room. Mr. Claymore wore a polite smile, but Father applauded with vigor. The stranger continued to look unimpressed.

The dancers clasped hands and bowed several times before the curtain swished closed. The lights came up onstage, and the performers headed to the dressing room. Ethel pulled Geneva aside in the hallway. "What is going on with you? Who are those men? Their presence obviously upset you."

Geneva pulled her hand free and laced her fingers together. "The man in the charcoal suit with graying hair is my father. The Orson Welles look-alike is his partner, Mr. Claymore. I have no idea who the other man is, but I can't imagine why he's here. He looked miserable."

Ethel's eyes widened. "Your father? Did you know he was coming? Is that why you were so agitated before the show?"

"The last I knew Father was in the hospital." Geneva shook her head. "I had no idea he'd been discharged, although perhaps he sought to surprise me."

"It appears he did, but you never told me your dad was ill. You should have taken a break from performing. I'm sure Devon would have understood the need to go home to be with him."

"Devon knew about Father, and he tried to get me to stay home after I went to the hospital, but it's a complicated situation, Ethel. You must remember that I joined the USO to escape the arrangements he made for me. Only since his heart attack has he made an effort to be loving toward me. Besides, as unfeeling as this may sound, the murder investigation and proving my innocence has been my priority."

Ethel drew her into a quick hug. "I guess, but don't you think it was more important to see to your dad and let the professionals solve the case?"

"First of all, you may have a *dad*, but I most definitely have a *father*. There is a difference, and the professionals, as you call them, seemed intent that I was the solution to their investigation. I couldn't wait to let them build a case against me with circumstantial evidence. Father was under expert care at the hospital. There was nothing I could have done for him."

"You said he's been more loving. You could have spent time with him and your mother who must have been worried to death."

Geneva's stomach tightened. Her friend deserved to know the truth, but there was no time for a full explanation. And the detective would be angrier than usual if she disobeyed his order of secrecy. "Look, I know you mean well, but you don't understand. Just accept that I'm doing what I should be doing, and when the time is right, I'll try to repair the relationship with my parents."

Ethel gripped her shoulders and stared into her eyes. "I'm praying for you, Geneva. There are things you are not telling me, and I'm afraid for you, but I'm going to trust that God will work this out for good."

Squirming, Geneva nodded. Tears threatened, but she blinked them away. She couldn't let Ethel see her fear, or she'd never let her meet Father and the other men. As it was, Devon continued expressing his own concerns about her safety, despite knowing the plan was their only choice. Earlier, Detective Lazarus had called and given her one last chance to drop out.

"I get the feeling I can't ask you not to do anything stupid or dangerous, so I'll just say that I will do *anything* for you." Ethel searched Geneva's face. "Understood?"

"Yes." Her voice cracked and came out in a whisper. She cleared her throat. "Yes. I thought when I left home I would never find a friend as good as those I left behind, but God sent you to me. Keep praying, and I'll tell you everything when this is over. I promise."

"You better."

The women continued to the dressing room and kept close to the wall to avoid the crowd of performers headed to the stage for the next number. They entered the room where a handful of girls prepared for the final act. Their chatter filled the space as Ethel headed to her locker, and Geneva sat in front of the mirror to clean her face. She studiously stared at her reflection to avoid the periodic glances her friend tossed her way. She rubbed cold cream onto her skin then wiped off the heavy, pancake makeup. Oh, to remove the stain of guilt from her life as easily.

She may not have committed murder, but she had been prideful and argumentative with her parents before leaving home, then deceitful and underhanded with Detective Lazarus when she disobeyed his order to stay out of the case. Now, she was getting ready to perform subterfuge in order to capture Thurgood's killer.

A good reason for the deception, but did God condone sinful acts for the right motivation? If only there was another way to see this through to the end.

Sighing, she removed the last vestiges of color then washed her face with soap and water before pulling the pins from her hair. Geneva massaged her scalp, then brushed the knots and sticky spray from her hair until it shone.

What special outfit had Devon selected from the costume department for the evening's charade? She rose and opened her locker to find a mercury-gray, watered silk cocktail dress waiting on a padded hanger. Geneva slipped out of her costume and poured the shimmering concoction over her body. Made before the war and subsequent material rationing, its voluminous skirt rustled with her movements. The neckline was low enough to show off her chunky, silver necklace she clasped around her throat and to be sophisticated without being indecent. Unused to the amount skin showing, she tugged at the bodice.

Ethel walked by and squeezed her shoulder. "Stop fidgeting. They won't believe whatever you're trying to sell, if you keep fussing with your clothes."

"How did you—"

"As lovely as you look, that's not your style. I assume you're still on the case." She winked, patted Geneva's arm, and waggled her fingers in farewell. "Remember, I'll be praying for you." She tucked her clutch purse under her arm and left the room, closing the door with a soft thud.

Geneva pressed her lips together and pulled the package of nylons from the shelf, then she smiled. Difficult to find, they were a tiny silver lining in the evening's dark cloud. The stockings were from Detective Lazarus who claimed a woman in her position would have the means to find and purchase them. She could only imagine how he had gotten his hands on them. Contraband from the evidence room or had he scoured the city for the last known pair? Fingering the silky softness, she sat down and pulled them over her legs.

A knock sounded, and her gaze shot toward the door. "Yes?"

"Miss Alexander, your father said he and the other gentlemen are in Mr. Royal's office whenever you're ready." The stagehand's deep voice was muffled.

"Tell him I'll be right there."

"Very good, miss."

Her heart pounded, and Geneva slipped her feet into the patent leather, peep-toe pumps, another pre-war luxury. She rose and inspected her appearance in the floor-length mirror. A bit of lipstick, and the character she played would be complete. She dug into her pocketbook, found the tube, then applied the mauve color to her lips.

"You look swell, Geneva. Knock 'em dead," said the girl standing at the costume rack, an emerald-green, sequined dress draped over her arm.

"Thanks, Colleen." Geneva opened the door. "Here goes nothing."

She hurried to Devon's office, her heels clacking on the wooden floor. Music from the stage filtered down the hallway. Feigning what she hoped was a credible Bette Davis-like sophistication, she entered the room.

Father stood at the window, arms crossed. Mr. Claymore sat in the vacant chair near the desk, and the stranger leaned against the wall, hands stuffed into his pockets. Detective Lazarus was nowhere to be seen. Had the plan changed? How would she know what to do?

"Geneva, darling, you look stunning. Give your old dad a kiss. I've missed you." He held out his arms.

Hesitating for a fraction of a second, she rushed forward in a swirl of silk and embraced Father. "I didn't know you'd been discharged. How are you feeling? Does Mother know you're here?"

He released her then waved his hand in a dismissive gesture. "I told the doctors I'd had enough, and yes, your mother knows." He shrugged. "But it did take some convincing. She does worry." He pulled her to his chest again and put his lips close to her ear. "Lazarus has been delayed. Follow my lead."

A chill swept over her, and her knees threatened to buckle. How long before he arrived? She closed her eyes and licked her dry lips. *Lord, help me. It seems like that's all I've been asking lately.*

Father patted her back then turned toward the stranger. "Forgive my lack of manners. Mr. Tully. May I present my daughter, Geneva. Geneva, this is Mr. Dolson Tully, a client of mine."

The man dipped his head, a smile finally lighting up his face. "A pleasure, Miss Alexander. Thank you for your service to our boys in uniform. My son is in the army, somewhere in Europe if I interpreted his last letter correctly."

"It's the least I can do for them. I hope you enjoyed the performance."

"I'm not much of a Gilbert and Sullivan fan, but you girls did a nice job." He pulled out a pocket watch and glanced at the jeweled face, then gestured to the vacant chair near Mr. Claymore. "I'm sorry to rush you, but I'd like to be able to catch the seven o'clock train back to Philly. I hope you understand."

"Of course. I didn't realize you were part of the discussion, Mr. Tully." Geneva walked to the seat in measured steps then lowered herself on the chair before crossing her ankles. Hopefully, the men couldn't hear her racing heart. She offered her hand to Mr. Claymore. "Nice to see you again, sir. Thank you for coming on short notice."

He nodded, his face void of expression. "This had better be good, Miss Alexander. I'm a very busy man. I'm here as a courtesy to your father."

"Yes, sir. I'll get straight to the point."

"That would be most appreciated."

Father frowned. "No need to be rude, Claymore. We're all busy, but finding Mayfield's killer and getting the firm back on track are crucial and worth a bit of your time, wouldn't you say?"

"Fair enough." He laced his fingers. "However, I told your daughter when she first began nosing about that it's best to leave sleuthing to the professionals. After all, they are paid to do this sort of thing."

"Yes, yes, but as with the war effort, sometimes civilians are asked to do their bit."

Mr. Claymore narrowed his eyes. "What is this all about? I came to discuss a proposition regarding the firm. Did you get me here under false pretenses, Alexander?"

"No, this is definitely about the company." Father nodded to Geneva.

She opened her pocketbook and pulled out a folded sheet of paper. "Are you aware that Mr. Washington was arrested for blackmail, Mr. Claymore?"

"Yes, but what does that have to do with me?"

She patted her hair and held up the paper. "Come now, Mr. Claymore, surely you realize the police know you were his victim. They have certain...documentation."

The color drained from Mr. Claymore's face. "Yes...well...yes, he was blackmailing me, but as you said I'm the victim. What is that?" He looked at Mr. Alexander. "Wayne, why is this girl questioning me? When are we going to discuss the firm?" He tried to rise, but at some point Mr. Tully had moved behind him and now pressed his hands on Mr. Claymore's shoulders, keeping him seated.

"Unhand me, you oaf. I don't have to stay and listen to this." Mr. Claymore's face darkened.

"I'm afraid you do, Mr. Claymore."

Claymore huffed and crossed his arms. "Fine. Say your piece, Miss Alexander, and then I'm leaving."

She smoothed the paper and laid it on the desk. "The firm is offering an agreement to ensure your wife is taken care of while you're in prison in exchange for certain actions on your part. The partners agreed it was best for me to tender the proposal, although I admit I'm surprised Father accompanied you. I was to be the lone intermediary."

"What are you talking about? I'm not going to prison. This is preposterous."

Geneva held up a pen. How dare the man continue to lie about his innocence. She grit her teeth. "You are to provide information regarding Thurgood Mayfield's activities of fraud and the role you played in assisting him to perpetrate such fraud, and the firm will set up a fund from which your wife may draw for living expenses. She'll be required to sell that mansion of yours that was paid for with ill-gotten gains. If you'll sign here at the bottom, indicating your willingness to cooperate with Detective Lazarus upon his arrival..."

He batted down the pen and shot to his feet. His chair knocked into Tully who stumbled and fell against the bookcase. Mr. Claymore raised his fist. "I'm the victim here. I don't know what sort of *documentation* you think you have, but I'm not going to prison. I didn't do anything wrong."

Her pulse hammered through her veins, and adrenaline surged through her body. She would make him confess. She was not going to jail for a crime she didn't commit. Slamming her hand on the document, she shouted, "Yes, you did, and you continue to try to pin your evil deeds on someone else. First, Thurgood and then me for his murder. Well, it's not going to work. I didn't kill him. You did, and if you're lucky you won't get the death penalty for it."

"Geneva!" Father gaped at her.

Mr. Claymore whipped out a black-handled object and pressed a button on the side. A knife blade appeared, and he slashed at Geneva. "I am not going to prison."

Searing pain shot up her arm as blood spattered on her dress. She cried out and pressed her free hand over the wound, but blood seeped through her fingers. Spots appeared before her eyes, and her head swam. Firm hands grasped her from behind.

Tully threw himself at Mr. Claymore, and the two men wrestled for control. Shouts and grunts filled the room as the men banged into furniture.

Geneva's breathing quickened, and she gasped for air. Mr. Claymore bested Mr. Tully and jumped to his feet. He wrenched her from Father's grasp and yanked her toward him. With one arm wrapped around her body, he held the knife to her throat. His ragged breath was hot on her cheek. "You people are going to do exactly as I say or this will be Miss Alexander's last day on earth."

Chapter Forty-one

Geneva trembled, and tears coursed down her face as Mr. Claymore gripped her to his chest. The tangy smell of perspiration mixed with pipe tobacco clung to his clothes. She swallowed against the waves of nausea.

"Claymore, unhand my daughter." Father's voice thundered.

"And give up my leverage over you? Bah! I thought you were smarter than that."

"Take me instead."

Mr. Claymore barked a harsh laugh, and spittle sprayed onto her cheek. Geneva gagged, and he nicked her with the knife. She gasped at the cut's sting and trickle of warm liquid under her chin.

Father lunged at them.

Mr. Claymore dragged her toward the door, alternately brandishing the knife at her and the men. "Don't do anything you'll regret, Alexander. I hear you got religion, and you'd have a lot of explaining to do to your God, if you made me kill your daughter."

"Claymore, if you give up now, I'll speak with the police so they don't charge you with assaulting Geneva."

"Not a chance." He waved the blade. "Now, all of you need to move away from the door so I can get out of here. I'm not staying to be arrested, and the sooner you let me go, the sooner you'll get your precious daughter back."

Geneva held up one hand. "Father, Mr. Tully, do as he says. I'll be fine." Would she? Her arm and neck where he had sliced her were on fire. How deep were the wounds? Would she bleed out?

Her knees buckled, and he grabbed her around the waist. "Stand up and show some of that backbone you brought into my office, girl." He put the knife to her skin again then turned toward the men. "Move! I won't tell you a second time. If you don't get out of the way, I will slit her throat, and she'll be dead before she hits the ground. Is that clear?"

Father blanched and held up both arms in surrender. He nudged Mr. Tully way from the door. "Don't hurt her, Claymore. I beg of you."

Mr. Claymore chuckled, a deep maniacal laugh that prickled the hairs on the back of Geneva's neck. "That's better. Keep moving. I want you in the far corner, so you're not close enough to try anything clever with me."

The men trudged toward the back of the room. Geneva pressed her lips together. *Lord, please save us. Save me!* Father's wide-eyed gaze ricocheted between her face and the doorway. *Was he trying to convey a message? Was he plotting a rescue? Oh, that they had a closer relationship, she might figure out what he was doing.*

Mr. Tully shifted, and the floor squealed under his feet. Mr. Claymore whirled toward the noise. Geneva winced as the blade nicked her cheek. His grip tightened around her waist, and she struggled to draw a breath. Her captor rasped, "Don't be a hero, Tully. Get your hands in the air."

The large man held his hands forward.

"I said to put them up. What are you trying to pull?"

"Nothing, Claymore."

"Then do as I say."

"Sure." Mr. Tully lifted his arms to shoulder height.

"Higher!"

His hands moved above his head, and his jacket opened to reveal a revolver tucked into a holster under his arm.

Geneva gasped, and Mr. Claymore roared. "Toss that pistol on the ground and kick it over to me. Do it slowly, or the girl gets it."

Mr. Tully exchanged a look with Father before using two fingers to slide the weapon from the leather pouch and drop it to the wooden floor with a clunk. With the side of his shoe he punted the gun toward Mr. Claymore. It came to rest halfway between the two men who both eyed the firearm.

"Don't even think about it." Mr. Claymore's voice rumbled. "This is what's going to happen. The girl and I will move as one to the gun, which I will pick up. Then we will back out of the room, and you will stay here. Once I am safely in my car, I will release her. Is that understood?"

"Claymore, please let her go and take me."

"Stop whining, Wayne. Do you think me a fool?" He loosened his grip on Geneva and grabbed a fistful of hair jerking her head back until her neck was fully exposed. Her scalp burned. She whimpered and closed her eyes.

"Okay," Father cried out. "We'll do as you say, just don't hurt her."

"You used to be a strong man. Is it your God who has turned you into a sniveling weasel, or was your appearance of strength just an act? You're pathetic." Mr. Claymore closed the knife and shoved it into his pocket then wrenched Geneva toward the gun. In one smooth motion he bent, snatched the firearm from the floor, and released its safety. With one hand still buried in her hair, he swung the gun at Father and Mr. Tully. Their hands shot higher, and he cackled.

"Let me hear you count, *gentleman.*"

"One...two...three...four—"

"Very good." He released Geneva's hair and gripped her uninjured arm. "Let's go, Miss Alexander. And like I told your father, don't try anything that would force me to kill you. Understood?"

She nodded, her lower lip trembling. *Would she live to see another day?*

"...twenty-one...twenty-two...twenty-three..."

As he hauled her toward the door, she risked a glance at Father and mouthed "I love you."

Before she could see Father's response, Mr. Claymore dragged her from the room. He continued to keep an iron grasp on her arm, and with the other hand pressed the barrel of the gun against her side, the metal's cold seeping through the silk. Her steps faltered, and she put a hand out to steady herself.

He growled and pulled her close enough for her to feel his heart beat against her back. "Keep walking."

She inched her way down the hallway, her eyes searching for escape. Mr. Claymore turned the corner and they made their way to the door that led to the foyer. He released her and slid out of his coat. He crammed it into her hands. "Put that on and button it. I don't want any blood showing. When we go through that door, you are going to smile and pretend everything is fine. Once we're outside, I'll get into my car and you can crawl back to your Father and his cronies."

With shaking hands, Geneva donned the coat and fastened it. He shoved her arm through the crook of his elbow, then poked the gun into her side. "Let's go."

He pushed open the door, and the pair shuffled into the vacant lobby. Geneva's shoulders slumped. Her hope for a rescue from someone in the vestibule evaporated. They hurried across the carpeted expanse and out of the building.

Mr. Claymore froze. "Where is that idiot driver of mine? The car is supposed to be waiting by the curb."

A man-shaped blur of movement shot out from behind the large bush by the door and clubbed her captor. With a grunt, he fell to the ground and the gun dropped from his hand. Geneva screamed, and her vision swirled before everything went black.

"Geneva, can you hear me?"

The words seemed to come from the end of a long tunnel, muffled and garbled.

"Geneva, wake up."

Soft fingers stroked her cheek, and the voice seemed closer. She opened her eyes, then slammed them shut when the glare from the overhead light sent shards of pain into her head. Where was she? Moaning, she shifted on the rough, hard cement of the sidewalk.

The memory of the recent events with Mr. Claymore crashed into her mind. Where was he? She struggled to sit up, and her muscles protested with throbs of pain. Gentle hands held her down.

"Don't try to move yet. Your arm and neck wounds have been bandaged. Does anything else hurt?" Devon's familiar rumble held concern.

"Mr. Claymore…what happened?" Geneva blinked several times before her eyes finally agreed to remain open, and she looked at his face, worry lines bracketing his mouth and wrinkling his forehead.

"He's been arrested." Devon's chest puffed out, and he grinned. "I ambushed him when the two of you came out of the building. Do you remember anything after that?"

"Not much. I felt rather than saw some sort of movement from behind. Then Mr. Claymore released me, and..." Her face warmed. "I think I fainted. You must think me a ninny."

"Not at all." He leaned down and kissed her forehead. "Being taken hostage must have been terribly frightening. You were a brave girl. Anyway, you have nothing more to worry about. Claymore is on his way to the police station. Once he realized the detective had evidence that he killed Thurgood after one of their schemes went south, he tried bargaining with Lazarus."

Geneva shuddered and drew in a deep breath. "I can't believe it's over."

He brushed a stray curl from her face. "Can you sit up? How do you feel?"

She closed her eyes and took a mental inventory of her wounds. "Other than a bit bruised, I'm okay." Her fingers went to the gauze taped to her arm, and she trembled. "My arm and neck are sore, but my injuries could be so much worse, couldn't they?"

He nodded and put his arm around her shoulders, supporting her as she sat upright. Her vision swam for a moment, then cleared. Father hovered behind Devon, his eyes dark with anxiety.

"Father?" Tears sprang to her eyes. "Are you okay?"

He knelt beside her and kissed her cheek. "Right as rain, honey. I've been worried about you. Devon's right. You were a brave girl. I'm so proud of you. We have so much to talk about, but first we're going to get you to the hospital. The medics did a good job on you, but I'd like you to see a doctor. Will you let them transport you in the ambulance?"

"I'm fine, Father. I'd like to go home if that's all right with you." She looked at Devon. "I won't be much good at the USO until this arm heals, and I want to spend time with you and Mother. But first, I'd like to get off this hard ground and sit on a soft chair. I have lots of questions."

His face brightened, and moisture gathered in his eyes. He chuckled and turned to Devon. "Can you help me get our girl into the lobby where she'll have her choice of seating?"

Devon grinned and nodded.

With tender hands and slow steps, Father and Devon each wrapped an arm around her waist and led her inside. They stopped in front of the nearest chair and helped her lower herself onto the overstuffed cushion. She sighed as the softness enveloped her and tension trickled from her muscles.

The men dropped into nearby chairs, seemingly ready to spring to her aid at a moment's notice.

"Can I get you a glass of water? Anything?" Devon asked.

She shook her head. "No, I'm eager to find out what happened, so I can put all of this behind me."

"I understand. Do you want us to give you the skinny or do you have specific questions?"

She giggled. "The skinny? You've been watching too many Jimmy Cagney movies." She sobered up. "If you could explain things, but start with who Mr. Tully is and why he carries a gun."

"Tully is a Pinkerton detective. He took Mr. Perazon's place after he was killed by a man Mr. Claymore paid to do the deed. Claymore had reason to believe Perazon was getting close to figuring out his part in Thurgood's fraudulent schemes, and he thought the detective might also find out he murdered Thurgood. Tully is not happy Claymore bested him and was able to get you out of the building."

"What about my handkerchief and the compact in the hotel room?"

"Apparently, Claymore intended to frame you from the beginning." Father frowned. "Last Christmas I asked him for a recommendation about where to get you a set of monogrammed hankies. He remembered that and contacted the shop for a duplicate order. The one Detective Lazarus found at the crime scene wasn't yours. It was from the set Claymore ordered."

Devon crossed his legs. "As far as the detective can tell, the compact was a coincidence and had nothing to do with the case. It just so happened to be the same brand your mother uses. He said the challenging part of searching a crime scene is determining what is evidence and what is not. And speaking of evidence…Lieutenant Lazarus tracked down a pawn shop where Thurgood used to sell stolen goods to fund his subterfuge. Apparently he seemed to be an accomplished pickpocket and managed to filch pieces during parties and society events. Unfortunately, your mother's bracelet won't be returned until after the trial."

Geneva rubbed her forehead. "This is so much to take in."

Father patted her arm. "The detective said he'd try to keep you out of the proceedings as best he can, but he may need to question you, and you'll need to testify. He's still tying up loose ends; however, it may take a while."

"I understand. Good thing I'll have time to rest." She clasped her hands in her lap. "I'm ready to go home, Father, but I need to pack a few items before we leave."

Devon rose. "Ethel will take care of that for you, and I'll bring them with me when I come visit. I can't let my best girl forget me."

Her stomach fluttered. "You still want to see me after all this?"

"I want to do more than that." He got down on one knee and cradled her hands in his. "Geneva Alexander, we've only known each other a few months, but that's enough time for me to realize that you fill my heart like no other woman I've ever met. You are as beautiful on the outside as you are on the inside. Your keen intelligence, sharp wit, and kindness are overshadowed only by your faith in God. You have made me a better man, and I can't imagine my life without you. Would you please do me the honor of marrying me?"

Her breath caught, and she looked at Father.

He chuckled. "Why are you looking at me? As you reminded me not too long ago, you're a grown woman and can make your own decisions." He winked. "But if I were you, I'd say yes. Your Devon here seems to be a fine young man."

Laughter bubbled up inside her, and happy tears spilled down her cheeks. Turning back to Devon, she nodded. "Nothing would make me happier than becoming your wife."

Whooping, he danced a jig then gingerly placed a kiss on her lips. "I'd pick you up and swing you around, but I don't want to hurt you."

She wrapped her arms around him and pulled him to his feet. She giggled as she nestled her head under his chin. "Always looking out for me, aren't you? I never thought I'd want that, and now I don't ever want you to stop." His heart beat strong and steady under her ear, and she closed her eyes, relishing the rhythm of his love.

Acknowledgments

Although writing a book is a solitary task, it is not a solitary journey. There have been many who have helped and encouraged me along the way.

My parents, Richard and Jean Shenton, who presented me with my first writing tablet and encouraged me to capture my imagination with words. Thanks, Mom and Dad!

Scribes212 – my ACFW on-line critique group: Valerie Goree, Marcia Lahti, and the late Loretta Boyett (passed on to Glory, but never forgotten). Without your input, my writing would not be nearly as effective. (Where did I put that clue?)

Eva Marie Everson – my mentor/instructor with Christian Writers' Guild. You took a timid, untrained student and turned her into a writer. Many thanks!

SincNE, and the folks who coordinate the Crimebake Writing Conference. I have attended many writing conferences, but without a doubt, Crimebake is one of the best. The workshops, seminars, panels, critiques, and every tiny aspect are well-executed, professional, and educational.

Special thanks to Hank Phillippi Ryan, Halle Ephron, and Roberta Isleib for your encouragement and spot-on critiques of my work.

Tiger Wiseman – Thanks for providing the perfect writing get-away weekend. Your home is gorgeous, and you are the perfect hostess! Give Murphy a hug for me.

Thanks to my Book Brigade who provide information, encouragement, and support.

A heartfelt thank you to my brothers, Jack Shenton and Douglas Shenton, and my sister, Susan Shenton Greger for being enthusiastic cheerleaders during my writing journey. Your support means more than you'll know.

My husband Wes deserves special kudos for understanding my need to write. Thank you for creating my writing room – it's perfect, and I'm thankful for it every day. Thank you for your willingness to accept a house that's a bit cluttered, laundry that's not always done, and meals on the go. I love you.

And finally, to God be the glory. I thank him for giving me the gift of writing and the inspiration to tell stories that shine the light on his goodness and mercy.

Dear Reader,

I hope you enjoyed reading *Murder of Convenience* as much as I enjoyed writing it. Whether you did or not, I'd appreciate it if you would post an honest review on the review site(s) of your choice such as Amazon, Goodreads, and Barnes & Noble.

Blessings,

Linda Shenton Matchett

Connect with me!

www.LindaShentonMatchett.com

www.facebook.com/authorlindamatchett

www.pinterest.com/lindasmatchett

www.twitter.com/lindasmatchett

www.linkedin.com/in/authorlindamatchett

www.bookbub.com/authors/linda-shenton-matchett

www.amazon.com/Linda-Shenton-Matchett/e/B01DNB54S0

Newsletter sign up: https://bit.ly/2DDLmI2

Other books by Linda Shenton Matchett

Love's Harvest

Noreen Hirsch loses everything, including her husband and two sons. Then her adopted country goes to war with her homeland. Has God abandoned her?

Rosa Hirsch barely adjusts to being a bride before she is widowed. She gives up her citizenship to accompany her mother-in-law to her home country. Can Rosa find acceptance among strangers who hate her belligerent nation?

Basil Quincey is rich beyond his wildest dreams, but loneliness stalks him. Can he find a woman who loves him and not his money?

Three people. One God who can raise hope from the ashes of despair.

www.amazon.com/dp/B01DMB3ZX2

On the Rails

Warren, OH, 1910: Katherine Newman loves being a teacher, but she loves Henry Jorgensen more, which is why she's willing to give up her job to marry him. But instead of proposing, Henry breaks up with her. Devastated, Katherine seeks to escape the probing eyes and wagging tongues of her small town. A former Harvey Girl, Katherine's mother arranges for Katherine to be hired at the Williams, Arizona Harvey House. Can she care out a new life in the stark desert land unlike anything she's ever known?

Henry Jorgensen loves Katherine with all his heart, but as the eldest son of a poor farmer can he provide for her as she deserves? The family's lien holder calls in the mortgage, and Henry must set aside his own desires in order to help his parents meet their financial obligation. But when Katherine leaves town after their break up, he realizes he's made the biggest mistake of his life. Can he find her and convince her to give their love a second chance?

www.amazon.com/dp/B01MUYAGU3

Love Found in Sherwood Forest

Award-winning Broadway actress Leighanne Webster has it all until an on-stage panic attack brings her career crashing to the ground. Returning to England to help produce the annual Robin Hood Festival play could be the diversion Leighanne needs. But with ex-fiance, Jamison Blake as the play's director, focusing on her new job won't be easy.

Breaking his engagement with Leighanne so she could pursue her dream of being a Broadway star was the hardest thing Jamison Blake ever did. When she returns to Nottingham, his heart insists he made a mistake. Can he convince her to give their relationship a second chance, or will he have to let her go again? This time forever.

www.amazon.com/dp/B01MU3JDR3

A Love Not Forgotten (part of the Let Love Spring collection)

Allison White should be thrilled about her upcoming wedding. The problem? She's still in love with her fiancé, Chaz, who was declared dead after being shot down over Germany in 1944. Can she put the past behind her and settle down to married life with the kindhearted man who loves her?

It's been two years since Charles "Chaz" Powell was shot down over enemy territory. The war is officially over, but not for him. He has amnesia as a result of injuries sustained in the crash, and the only clue to his identity is a love letter with no return address. Will he ever regain his memories and discover who he is, or will he have to forge a new life with no connections to the past?

www.amazon.com/dp/B06XVZB38Y

A Doctor in the House (part of The Hope of Christmas collection)

Within weeks of enlisting as one of the first female doctors allowed in the US Army and Navy Medical Corps, Emma O'Sullivan is assigned to set up a convalescent hospital in England. When the handsome widower of the requisitioned property claims she's incompetent and tries to get her transferred, she must prove to her superiors she's more than capable. But she's soon drawn to the handsome, grieving owner of the estate. Will she have to choose between her job and her heart?

Archibald "Archie" Heron lost brother, parents, and his wife to the war. So when the British government requisitions his estate, he can't help but feel like a modern-day Jo losing family and home to devastation. The final straw comes in the form of a ginger-haired American woman...*doctor!* Archie decides this is one battle he won't lose. Or will he?

www.amazon.com/dp/B077656725

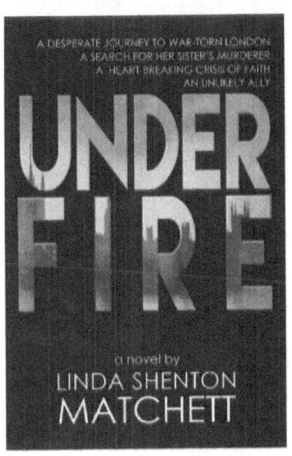

Under Fire

Set in April 1942, *Under Fire* tells the story of Ruth Brown whose missing sister Jane is declared dead. Convinced her sister is still alive, Ruth follows clues from their small New Hampshire town to war-torn London trying to find her. In the process, Ruth stumbles on Resistance members, smugglers, and the IRA-all of whom may want her dead for what she has seen.

www.amazon.com/dp/B0743MS95H

WWII Word Find, Vol. 1

Seventy-eight easy-to-read, World War II-themed puzzles. Fun and educational.

Solutions provided.

www.amazon.com/dp/0998526525